T0369461

COP
KILLER

Angelo Morelli

iUniverse, Inc.
Bloomington

Cop Killer

This is a work of fiction. All of the characters, names, incidents, organizations, and dialogue in this novel are either the products of the author's imagination or are used fictitiously.

iUniverse books may be ordered through booksellers or by contacting:

iUniverse
1663 Liberty Drive
Bloomington, IN 47403
www.iuniverse.com
1-800-Authors (1-800-288-4677)

Because of the dynamic nature of the Internet, any web addresses or links contained in this book may have changed since publication and may no longer be valid. The views expressed in this work are solely those of the author and do not necessarily reflect the views of the publisher, and the publisher hereby disclaims any responsibility for them.

Any people depicted in stock imagery provided by Thinkstock are models, and such images are being used for illustrative purposes only.

Certain stock imagery © Thinkstock.

ISBN: 978-1-4759-1419-1 (sc)
ISBN: 978-1-4759-1421-4 (hc)
ISBN: 978-1-4759-1420-7 (e)

Printed in the United States of America

iUniverse rev. date: 5/18/2012

CHAPTER ONE

AUGUST 1973

New York born and bred Frank Ardone knew better than to try to take on the Friday morning Midtown Manhattan streets in late summer. But today he had no choice. Using only his right hand because he had a gun in his left hand, he wheeled the beat-up Buick uptown through the choked streets all the while he spewed a steady stream of fuck this and fuck that, especially at the lousy air conditioner. But he did not rent the car for its amenities.

Frustrated, he slammed the AC off with the butt of his nine-millimeter automatic, sending the cheap plastic knob careening into the back seat. The novel use of the gun gave a moment of respite to Joseph Cutolo, Ardone's front seat passenger against whose ribcage the weapon had been pressed. Cutolo exhaled reflexively. He was used to gunplay. It was just that usually, it was he who was on the business end.

Cutolo was a tough man and looked it. A scar under his right eye traveled down across his cheekbone toward the center of his chin and made him look like the longshoreman that he was before becoming an enforcer in Ardone's crew. What made him attractive to Ardone

1

was his sheer physical presence; six feet-two inches tall, two hundred and thirty pounds, with huge hands that he could instantly turn into battering rams. Ardone employed such men to collect debts from those who were unwilling to pay.

Just short of reaching the Westchester county line, Ardone steered the Buick into a deserted construction site. He drove slowly down a rocky dirt road alongside the East River on the right and mounds of garbage on the left. He parked in a dark area hidden from the street. Loosening his imported Borelli necktie he turned to Cutolo, steadying the gun now aimed at this head.

"Why the fuck did ya try to set me up, JoJo? I mean after all I done for you. All the years we've been together, you ungrateful cocksucker!"

Cutolo swallowed; his usually fearsome face filled with terror. He tried desperately to ignore the nine-millimeter aimed at his head. Sweating profusely, the huge mobster finally managed to find his tongue. "Ya got it all wrong Cheech," he croaked. "I swear on my father's grave. It wasn't no set-up. Why would've I got in the car with ya if it was a set-up?"

Ardone's eyes bored into the frightened man's face. "Fuck you, JoJo. You tried to set me up and you know it. And what's more you got in the car because I didn't leave ya no fuckin choice. Now did I, JoJo," Ardone said.

"Please Cheech, listen. I…"

"No you listen, hard-on. I knew from the very beginning that something was up when you came to me with that fugazy fuckin deal; telling me you got a guy willin to sell three keys a shit for only forty large. And ninety percent pure, no less, then telling me to meet you on a street corner with the cash. I don't believe you, JoJo. Whadda take me for a fuckin idiot. Didn't you think I'd ask around? You dumb piece of shit."

"Please Frankie, ya gotta…'

"I don't gotta do nothin, JoJo," Ardone screamed. "And lemme tell you somethin, scumbag. It didn't take me long too find out about them two goons you brung along. They were ready to move when they seen my black Caddy turn the corner to meet ya. Me showing up in this beat-up red piece of shit fooled them real good. Didn't it JoJo?"

"Frankie, please. Ya gotta believe me. Whoever told ya this was a set-up got it all wrong." Cutolo was pleading now. "Ya gotta give me a chance to explain."

"Explain this, you shit head. My information was good and you know it. Now cocksucker, tell me who the sonofabitch is that gave ya the contract or I'll blow your fuckin brains out right here."

"Okay Frankie, okay," Cutolo whined now thinking he had a chance to survive this. "I'll level with ya. I went along with it, but it wasn't my idea. You gotta believe me. I'll tell ya anything ya wanna know. Anything!"

"Yeah, you'll tell me anything I wanna know. You mean anything that'll save your miserable fuckin ass."

"No, I'll tell ya the truth. I swear on my kids eyes."

Ardone smiled as he continued to press the weapon into Cutolo's skull. "On your kid's eyes, huh JoJo, what happened to your father's grave? Next time it'll be your sister's twat you lying piece a shit."

"Please Frankie, please. Lemme explain. For old times sake."

Ardone hesitated. "Okay hard-on. Explain. For old times sake."

Cutolo managed a faint smile. "It was Fat Tony who came to me. He made me go along with it. He sez you and him did a thing together a couple of months ago and you fucked him outta his end. He swore to me that no one would get hurt. He said he just wanted to get his."

"Bullshit! That fat cocksucker! And you, you miserable fuck. You believed him. Lemme tell ya something, JoJo, the minute them two goons that were waiting for me to show got their hands on the cash they thought I was carrying, they would a blown us both the fuck away... right on the spot. I guess they didn't tell ya about the other guy that was with them, the one that was waiting to get them outta there."

"Listen Frankie, I..."

"Speak up shit head," Ardone shouted over Cutolo's whimpering. "With all the fuckin noise around here, I can hardly hear myself think."

Ardone paused to watch as the boom swung on an immense construction crane, carrying a huge beam, a daring ironworker riding on it.

Then returning to the business at hand, he barked loudly. "Anyway, JoJo, I'm finished listenin to your explaining."

"Please Frankie! No! Listen! I'll make it up to you. Please. Gimme a break! We go back along way. It was only the cash they wanted. Ya gotta believe me. I didn't mean to let you down."

"Let me down? You fuckin idiot! What ya think the crew will think if I forget the whole thing? You made me look like a God-damn fool. And what'll the other capos think?"

"But I can..."

"I'll tell ya what they'll think." Ardone interrupted. "They'll think I'm weak. That I can't handle my own crew! That's what they'll think. Now get the fuck outta the car."

"Please, Frankie! Please! It don't gotta be this way" Cutolo pleaded, refusing to accept what was happening. "Ya gotta believe me,"

Ardone leaned across Cutolo's trembling body and pushed the front passenger's door open.

"I believe you, JoJo," he said calmly, "A hundred percent. I never doubted you for a minute. That's why I rented this banged up piece a shit with a phony driver's license. That's why I'm wearing these shit gloves. That's why I drove to this no fuckin no man's land where a fuckin bomb could go off and no one would hear it. Now get the fuck outta the car."

Cutolo continued to plead, refusing to leave the car.

Ardone's eyes went flat, emotionless as he raised his left knee and placed his foot against Cutolo's left side. He pushed violently and the big man's upper body fell to the ground leaving his legs behind, wedged between the car's floorboard and open door. Cutolo dug his elbows into the packed earth, trying frantically to free himself from the car.

Ardone scowling in disgust leaned across the passenger's seat and pulled the trigger twice. The bullets found their mark in the center of Cutolo's back. Ardone slid out of the car and calmly walked over to the mobster. He dragged his limp body along the ground and propped it against a pile of chipped rock. Then he fired a third shot between Cutolo's eyes, blowing away a portion of the back of his head. Blood and brains immediately colored the rock pile.

Ardone spit a vengeful good riddance. He smoothed out his slicked back hair and his impeccably tailored custom-made suit. Standing over the body he opened his fly and pissed on the man he just killed. Then he calmly walked back to the car. He eased the Buick over the hardened herringbone ruts in the earth and into the heavy stream of downtown traffic. Safely on his way, he exhaled certain he had meted out JoJo Cutolo's punishment unobserved.

CHAPTER TWO

Further South in midtown Manhattan Police Officer Terry McDermott putt-putted his beat-up Cushman motor scooter in and out of the Third Avenue traffic. The young cop was assigned to issue summonses to illegally parked cars and trucks that typically choked mid-town.

After ticketing an unoccupied double-parked box truck, he began to resume patrol when a car whizzed by narrowly missing him. The car stopped abruptly in front of a red and white "No Standing Anytime" traffic sign not more than fifty yards away from the startled cop.

"Sonofabitch," McDermott mumbled under his breath. "He almost runs my ass over and now he's parking right in front of me. What fucking balls."

McDermott made his way toward the beat-up Buick. He watched its well-dressed driver slide out of the front seat and walk towards the leather padded doors of the Blue Grotto Lounge. The young cop put down his scooter and walked to the lounge. When the driver pulled open the huge door to the vestibule of the lounge, McDermott was on his heels.

"Whoa mister, you're parked in a No Standing Zone."

Turning to the blue uniform behind him, the man quickly offered an apology. "I didn't notice the sign, officer."

"Yeah right," the cop shot back. "Then I guess you didn't notice me either when you almost ran me over a minute ago. Now lemme see your license and registration, please."

"But officer, I was only gonna take a peek inside to see if the help arrived yet."

"Well sir, that peek is going to cost you a twenty-five dollar summons, now the license and registration."

This simple command presented a problem for Ardone. His wallet was tucked in his jacket pocket a few inches from the gun he just used to kill Cutolo.

Managing a faint smile, he continued to try to talk his way out of the summons. "Listen officer, I'm Frank Ardone. I own a piece of this joint. Maybe you and your wife would like to stop by some evening and have some dinner on me. The food's excellent."

"I'm sure it is Mr. Ardone, but I ain't married."

"Hey, that's even better," Ardone said, now smiling broadly. "In that case come in with a couple of your friends some night. There are always a few ladies hanging around at the bar and if you see something you like I'll do the right thing by ya."

"McDermott stiffened; I think you better quit right there Mister. Now for the third time, lemme have your license and registration."

Ardone fought to remain calm. "Why sure thing officer, sure thing."

Ardone carefully opened the top button of his sports jacket keeping his eyes trained on the officer. But as he attempted to remove his wallet from deep within the jacket's inner left breast pocket the sport jacket opened just enough to reveal the butt of his weapon. McDermott spotted it triggering concern for his own safety. As training instructed, the cop took a step backwards, placing his hand firmly on the butt of his own weapon.

"Do you have a license for that gun you have under your jacket, Mr. Ardone?" the cop asked.

But Ardone's decision was immediate and irrevocable. He was a cornered rat. And the grim awareness that the weapon tucked away in his waistband had just been used to murder JoJo Cutolo left him no choice. With no more words Ardone yanked the gun from inside his trousers and fired at the cop. Two bullets were already tearing through the wall of his stomach when McDermott drew upon some primordial instinct to strike back. He managed to pull his own weapon. And as he fell mortally wounded he fired three rounds. One found the meaty part of Ardone's left shoulder.

Ignoring the pain, Ardone looked down at the dying cop. "To bad, kid, ya shoulda took the fuckin meal," he mumbled then dashed into the lounge and made his way out the rear fire exit.

Outside, the entire street was alive at the sound of the gunfire. People were running for cover. The killer was nowhere to be found.

Moments later, Ardone, was two blocks away. He breathed a sigh of relief knowing he had made good his escape.

What he didn't know was the crack homicide team of Samuels and Pirelli would soon be on his tail.

CHAPTER THREE

Samuels rarely flashed his gold detective's shield. Why bother? Every cop in Manhattan knew him by sight. The sixty-one-year-old first grader was an imposing figure. He stood about five-foot eight in his stocking feet and weighed-in at two hundred and forty pounds. But his girth was rock hard and worked to his advantage many times in the past. He was quick on his feet and even now given his advanced age for an on-the-street detective, he was still among the most active and productive members of the prestigious Manhattan South Homicide Division.

A devoted family man, his desk always sported the latest five by seven of Rae, his wife of forty years, surrounded by their two daughters and three grand children. He was a man of modest tastes. He never spent more than seventy-nine dollars for a suit in his life.

After his two daughters married and moved from the family home on Long Island, Samuels persuaded Rae to move back to the East Village neighborhood where he grew up. The eighty year-old apartment, on the third floor of a converted brownstone, had been completely gutted and renovated when he returned. The five-room apartment was thickly carpeted and filled with Danish modern furniture. The high ceilings, ornate moldings and the wood-burning fireplace gave the living room a rich and elegant ambience. A solid oak door opened onto a deck that overlooked a small but well-cared for garden below.

The only interest Solly had outside the family was competing in police sponsored pistol tournaments with his partner and best friend, Detective First Grade Anthony Pirelli.

CHAPTER FOUR

⌒⁄ℓ⌒

P irelli never aspired to become a New York City police officer. It
was not the realization of a lifelong dream. It just happened.

It all began in Brooklyn, the home of Coney Island and the
Brooklyn Dodgers. It was 1933 when Brooklyn was an intense
microcosm of the country. The working class struggled to survive
during a time when life consisted of impossible dreams and little
more. Aside from the ethnic and racial injustices, it was also an easier
time. How simple it all was then; three classes, the rich, the middle
class, and whatever was left included the poor. The entire city was
a labyrinth of complex ghettos formed by individual preferences,
all at a time when the black man was tucked away behind social
boundaries as effective as barbed razor wire.

1933 was a time when doors were left unlatched and when car
windows were cranked up only when it rained. Brooklyn, the city's
most populous borough was sprawled along the great waterways
that flowed into the mouth of the blue Atlantic Ocean. Brooklyn's
seventy-seven square miles housed a population that sought to work
for their sustenance; a time when exhausted breadwinners were
herded together on stifling subway cars and clanking electric trolleys;
a time of quiet respect for legitimate authority.

The city was pure and strictly democratic, with no other way it cared to go. Non-violent crime was on a gradual upswing, but assault and rape was still in check. Even the most cautious parent would think nothing of letting their teenager children take the subway to visit a grandparent or an aunt or uncle. And, while murder was hardly unknown, it was contained under the awesome shadow of "The Chair", a high voltage killer located in Ossining's Sing Sing prison.

With few exceptions, the men in blue were Irish. Some were cheerful. Some were sullen. All were big-footed, big-fisted and feared.

In the Pirelli neighborhood, the lusty Italian markets were rife with the pungent odor of provolone and parmegiano cheese. The trays were loaded with fresh ricotta, prosciutto and fruit-filled tomato-laden stalls spilled out to cover the sidewalks.

It was a time of cash or a promise to pay, a solid generation before the advent of the credit card. Automobiles were not yet a part of every household. Airlines were still in their infancy and travel beyond a hundred miles was reserved mainly for the affluent. The fur market in Manhattan was politically acceptable and flourishing with mink and silver fox, a prized gift for some woman. Most other women, less affluent, were chained to the home and kids and to a cloth coat from Klein's basement on Union Square.

Anthony Pirelli was born in 1933.

Like all children that grew up in Italian immigrant neighborhoods, Pirelli could tell stories of occasionally seeing victims of gangland killings lying in the streets while others were seen bent over the wheel of an abandoned automobile.

Delinquent debtors' fallen prey to unforgiving moneylenders could be seen hobbling around after bat-wielding hoods, delivering a message, blackened their knees.

Before he was twelve years of age, Pirelli had learned the ways of the street, mastering all ways of fraud and deceit. He found it easy to lie to the teaching Brothers and good Sisters of Our Lady of Peace Parochial School, without so much as batting an eye.

A born leader, at fifteen he masterminded the daily forays against rival street gangs. Only the most hopeful optimist would have imagined that the wiry youngster, clad in worn athletic shirts and hand-me-down trousers, would go on to become a detective in the prestigious Manhattan South Homicide Division.

If his older brother knew him like the cover of a well-read book, his parents knew him by its contents. And in the cramped Pirelli cold water flat in the southern part of Brooklyn, an unyielding discipline prevailed. It was absolute, there was no wavering and was occasionally augmented by a thick razor strop hanging in the kitchen. It was this constant, never bending authority that proved to be the counterweight against the street gangs, as it held in check and set the course for a boy who could have gone either way.

He grew strong, if temporarily unsettled and turned nineteen unscathed. He was old enough to be drafted, but did not wait to be called. He enlisted in the army. After a single tour of three long years, including a close call in Korea that led him to drink more than most he returned to the civilian world a prudent and wiser man.

The period immediately following his army days was a time of loose ends for Pirelli. Encouraged by his father, he decided to become a cop. He scored well on a difficult and competitive entrance exam and, in the fall of '57, at the age of twenty-four, Anthony Pirelli was proudly appointed a New York City police officer.

His transition from olive drab to the steel gray of the police recruit went well. During his nine months of training at the Police Academy, he worked hard, winning the coveted Police Commissioner's Trophy for excellence.

He developed a unique fondness for his Smith & Wesson, service revolver. The love of this firearm grew and matured during the passing years. They would be years of challenge and painstaking hard work as he literally spent hours and hours honing his marksmanship. Ultimately, he became one of the finest pistol shots in the law enforcement community, a skill that would later save his life.

There was no conflict between Pirelli's lifestyle and the police department. He'd been blessed with an unusual zest for life plus an easy disposition, genuine warmth, and a wily slyness, that were all significant factors in his ability to function very well as a police officer. He had a quick and ready wit. His presence, exploits and humor had spawned a compendium of hilarious anecdotes for his many friends and acquaintances.

A regular at a local health club, he remained remarkably trim and fit despite his regular, if not chronic, consumption of alcohol. Neatly coifed hair, professionally manicured nails and fashionable dress were part and parcel of his self-assured presence. He had a warm smile and eyes that were a piercing mixture of opalescent green and blue. Deeply tanned from frequent visits to West Palm Beach, he looked more like a corporate executive than a police officer.

With only himself to care for, he had leased a large one- bedroom apartment on Manhattan's fashionable East Side. It was a pre-war building with doorman service and had the added advantage of being located only a short distance from the precinct where he worked. Soon, a fine library of criminal justice writings sprung up and the purchase of quality stereo equipment had brought the world of semi-classical music into his life. To his surprise, he discovered he had an affinity for antiques. He had decorated his apartment with affordable pieces dating back to the Victorian era. He attributed this to his love of the past and warm bonds of family and country.

His preference for living alone had brought about some beneficial professional consequences. The absence of marital pressures to exacerbate other pressures faced by police officers, and the core person he was spawned an extraordinarily focused professional. Never in a rush to go home, he was free to attune his eye and ear to the smallest detail in the performance of his work. It was easy for him because there were no distractions unless one counted his love for competitive pistol shooting, and that really didn't count because it simply enhanced his mastery with the basic tool of his trade. And, until the desperation of lonely aging would finally catch up with him, he believed that he had made an excellent bargain with life.

Pirelli was unique in still another area. Fiercely independent, he set his own standard of conduct as a cop. Ever since his days as a uniform patrol officer he refused to accept even the most innocent gratuity from the public he served so well. Not that he believed one's true hospitality was improper, but he knew that often the hospitality was offered to the uniform and not the man who wore it.

He had few illusions about his curious ethics. He didn't take, because he didn't need. His wants were modest and whatever he earned was enough. All Anthony Pirelli chose to do was to give the public fair and impartial law enforcement and expected nothing more than his paycheck for doing so.

Yet, although free from avarice and corruption, he was always aware that he had no large mortgage to bear and no family to support. As such, he could view his colleagues who succumbed to temptation with simple compassion. But although he would never expose a fellow officer who may have broken a simple rule, he would never tolerate another's serious misconduct while in his presence.

After five years as a uniform patrol officer, the now much-decorated and street wise Pirelli was promoted to detective. As a detective there was no violence he had not witnessed and no grief he had not felt while traveling the streets of Manhattan.

Four years later he joined Solly at Manhattan South Homicide and soon a perfect marriage blossomed. Although each man's approach to an investigation often took a different path, their individual styles complimented each other. It was an unlikely, but ideal marriage. Always focused on the successful conclusion of a case, the team of Samuels and Pirelli was an investigative force with few equals in the NYPD.

CHAPTER FIVE

S olly Samuels sat restlessly at a hand-me-down, Board of Education desk like most found in detective squad rooms. He was fingering through several open homicide files, waiting for the frolicking Pirelli to join him. He puffed hungrily on a foul-smelling, three-for-a-dollar cigar, while silently cursing Pirelli who had spent the last half-hour chatting with a female police aid.

Finally, Solly barked, "Let's go Pirelli, we got things to do."

"What's the problem, Solly? We got all day to do what we gotta do. Be honest with me, you just wanna go to lunch.

"So what if I do?"

"So just say so and we'll go."

"Okay, then, lets go. On their way out of the precinct Solly stopped by the main desk to tell the desk officer he and Pirelli would be out for meal while Pirelli headed out the back door, made his way through a cluttered utility garage, and into the precinct parking lot that was reserved for a few select department autos.

Moments later, just as Solly began maneuvering his large frame into the squad car the dreaded call came over the car's police radio.

"10-13 cop down," the dispatcher cried. Vestibule of the Blue

Grotto Lounge, five-six-five 6th Avenue, between four-eight and four-nine Streets. Responding vehicles acknowledge."

Pirelli blasted away from the curb with tires screeching and siren wailing. Within seconds, no less than 10 units were on their way to the scene.

Hearing the number of units calling the dispatcher shouted: "No further assistance at the Blue Grotto. Break it off. Break it off," he shouted. "No further assistance needed."

More than a few police officers had been injured over the years while racing to the scene of a call for assistance where they were no longer needed.

Pirelli and Samuels continued and arrived at the Blue Grotto Lounge just as the wounded officer was being put into the rear of a patrol car for a quick ride to Bellevue hospital. Pirelli double-parked the squad car and sprinted to the lounge; Solly stopped by two uniformed police officers who were cordoning off the crime scene with bright yellow streamers.

A patrol sergeant was barking out instructions to several of his men. The officers nodded at the Sergeant and quickly disappeared into a crowd of bystanders.

When Pirelli approached the Sergeant, his trademark dry humor was conspicuously absent. "Whatta we got Sarge?" he asked grimly.

"Looks like the cop followed the perp into the vestibule of the lounge," the sergeant replied. "Then several minutes later I'm told five shots rang out. The only thing we know for sure is after the shooting the perp never came out of the vestibule. At least no one saw him come out."

"Did you get a chance to search the lounge yet?"

"Not yet. But we got the whole place secured. As soon as Emergency Service gets here we'll go through the place with a fine-tooth comb. If the cocksucker's still in there, we'll find him. But my guess is he beat it out the back door before we got here"

"How many people were in the bar at the time of the shooting?"

"Just a porter that was cleaning up the joint, the lounge don't open for business 'till six."

"Anyone talk to him?"

"Not yet. But I'll bet my paycheck he doesn't know a fuckin thing. He's one of your paisons, Pirelli, a greaseball straight off the boat. His name's Tranqualina. He's still inside if you want to take a crack at him."

"Not now, Sarge. When you get a chance have someone take him down to the precinct. We'll talk to him later."

"You got it."

"By the way, Sarge, did you come up with any witnesses yet?"

"Only one so far, but I got my men working the street. If there are any more witnesses out there, we'll find them."

"Great. And be sure they get everybody's name. Even the ones who say they didn't see anything. And make sure they get the plate numbers of all the cars parked in the immediate vicinity of the lounge."

"You got it,"

"By the way, Sarge, did the one witness you got give you anything?"

"Not too much! He sez he saw a well-dressed male white get outta that red Buick parked over there at the curb and walk into the vestibule of the lounge followed by the cop. But he can't identify the guy."

"Figures," Pirelli said.

Minutes later, Solly joined the pair, He smiled broadly at his colleague of thirty years.

"Well if it ain't my old buddy Sergeant Coltman, first on the scene again. How ya doin George?"

"Not as good as you Solly, I still work for a living."

"Very funny, George… very funny."

"And before you ask, nothing has been touched," the sergeant blurted out.

"Hey! It's about time you got it right," Samuels shot back. Then becoming serious, he asked solemnly, "How did the cop look?"

"Not too good, Solly, not too good. I had him taken to Bellevue in a radio car rather than wait for a bus (police lingo for an ambulance). That's how bad he looked. He caught one in the stomach and one right in the chest area. And I didn't see any exit wounds on the back of his shirt so it looks like the bullets are still in him"

"Do we know how many shots were fired?" Pirelli asked, reaching for his note pad.

"At least five that we can be sure of because we know the cop fired three and it looks like the perp fired at least two."

How do you know that, George," asked Solly.

Because I checked the cop's service revolver and there were three spent cases in the cylinder of the gun. That means he fired three. And there's two empty shells lying on the vestibule floor. That means the perp had an automatic and fired at least two rounds. So that's a total of at least five shots. Of course there may be other shells somewhere but right now it looks like five."

"I'm gonna take a quick look inside the vestibule, Solly," Pirelli said to his partner as he carefully entered the large enclosed vestibule of the Blue Grotto Lounge. After examining the crime scene, Pirelli walked out of the vestibule and turned to the patrol sergeant. "Looks like the cop may have shot the perp."

"What makes you think so?" Coltman asked curiously.

"Because there are only two bullets in the wall, add that to the two bullets in the cop and we got four so far. That leaves one bullet unaccounted for."

"And unless we find the other bullet somewhere," Solly added, "it means the perp walked away with it in him. You can follow that, can't you George?"

"Up yours, Solly, meanwhile, before you ask, I'll have an alarm transmitted to all the hospitals in the tri-state area,"

"Thanks Sarge," Pirelli said. "And when the crime scene technicians get here make sure they go over every square inch of the vestibule. Let's be sure there are no other bullets or shells anywhere. This way we'll know for sure the perp's got one in him. Meanwhile, me and Solly are going to run over to the hospital to talk to the cop."

When the detectives arrived at the emergency room, they saw the cop's grieving parents. The Police Department Chaplain was at their side offering his prayers for their slain son.

Pirelli bowed his head in silence and walked slowly over to the couple. "Mr. and Mrs. McCarthy," he said softly, "I'm detective Pirelli. I know there is nothing I can do or say right now to ease your pain, but I do want you to know that I'm truly sorry for the loss of your son. And if there is anything I can do for you, now or anytime in the future, please ask."

"Thank you, detective. And there is one thing that you can do for us, find our son's killer."

Pirelli looked directly into the shattered man's eyes. "I plan to do that, Mr. McCarthy. And you can be sure that no matter what, or how long it takes me, I'll find him. That's a promise."

Pirelli put his hand on Ms. McCarthy's shoulder then turned to his partner. "Let's go Solly, I think it's time we go talk to our porter friend."

CHAPTER SIX

When the detectives arrived at the precinct they found the Blue Grotto porter sitting alone in a small, austere, windowless interrogation room. Solly was first to greet the witness.

"How do you do Mr. Tranqualina?" he said with a friendly smile. "My name is Detective Samuels and this is my partner Detective Pirelli. We have a couple of questions we'd like to ask you if you don't mind."

The man nodded. "Ah sure," he said in a thick Italian accent.

The cops asked several preliminary questions before Solly got down to business.

"And exactly where were you standing when the officer walked into the vestibule," Solly asked."

"I was a behina da bar."

"That's fine! Now the bar is very close to the vestibule so that means you heard everything the officer and the guy that shot him were arguing about," Solly said, leaving the witness no room for denial. "So tell me everything you heard."

"I'm a hear nothing but the gunna shot noise, there was a no argument," Cosmo answered quickly.

"Is that right? Well then, after the gunfire, we know the shooter ran into the lounge so you hadda see him. What did he look like?"

"I'm a no see him. When I'm a hear the shots, I'm a jump on a the floor and I'm a no move until a the police a come."

"Is that right? You didn't hear nothin and you didn't see nothin. Is that what you're sayin?"

"That's a right."

"Well one thing we know for sure, the vestibule door was unlocked. So that means you were expecting someone," Solly said sternly. Now who were you expecting?"

"I'm a no expecta no one. The front a door she's a always open when I'm in a da lounge."

"The front door's always open, huh! And how about the back door, I suppose you leave that open too."

"No. Da backa door she's a always locked. But it's a for the fire. You justa push ana go out."

"Did the shooter run out that door?"

"I'm a no sure. I'm a…"

His patience worn thin, Pirelli interrupted the porter. "Listen goombah, lemme tell ya something. Right now you're only a witness as far as we're concerned. But I'm tellin you you're fast becoming an accessory to murder with your bullshit answers. Now if you wanna walk outta here today, you better start coming up with some answers real fast. Otherwise I'm locking up your grease ball ass up right now. Then tomorrow when you go before a Grand Jury, you'll be held in contempt and put in jail until your memory improves. Now what's it going to be? You wanna go home today, or do you wanna spend some time with us for a while?"

The porter paled. "I'm a wanna go home."

"Yeah! Then in that case stop with the bullshit and start givin us some straight answers."

"Okay. Okay. I'm a hear some a body runna thru the lounge and a pusha open the backa door. He runna out a the back a door."

"Good. Now we're getting somewhere. What did the person look like?"

"I'm a no see him. I'm a tella you da troot. I'm a on a da floor and I'm a no move. I'm a scared and I'm a hide a on a da floor."

"Okay then, tell us what the cop and the man arguing about before the shooting?"

"There's a no argument. You gotta believe a me. If a they argue, I'm a hear. But I'm a no hear nothing…"

"How about the shots?"

"Ima hear the shots. ma they no argue."

"Well then, how many shots were fired?"

"Five. I'm a hear five shots…That's a for sure"

After almost an hour of questioning, the detectives learned little more from the elusive Cosmo Tranqualina.

Finally, Pirelli was cordial, "Well, thank you for your time, Mr. Tranqualina. You've been very helpful. We probably won't need you again, but if we do we'll contact you at the lounge. And thanks again."

The porter thanked the two detectives and darted out of the squad room. After the porter left, Solly glared at his partner.

"I don't fuckin believe you Pirelli. Thank you Mr. Tranqualina, you've been very helpful Mr. Tranqualina. What the fuck was that all about?" Solly was on a roll. "Don't tell me you believe that lying ginzo."

"Give me a fucking break, will ya Solly? Of course I don't believe him. But we ain't got shit on him right now and we both know it. And for what I have in mind, I want him to think that he's done with us. Listen to me, Solly. Let's face it. In order to get him to tell us who ran through the lounge we'll need to get something to squeeze him with, and I mean squeeze."

"Schmuck what I am. I shoulda realized you had something up your sleeve."

"Right on. First we do a complete work-up on the cocksucker. You know criminal history, immigration status, family background, and whatever. Then we'll put together a surveillance team and take a hard look at him. With any luck at all we'll come up with something good enough to convince him to cooperate with us."

"Sounds good to me, kid?"

Pirelli and Samuels and a team of detectives spent the rest of the day interviewing all the people who were in the vicinity of the Blue Grotto Lounge at the time of the murder. None of the bystanders was able to identify the man the slain cop followed into vestibule of the lounge.

A warrant was gotten to search the illegally parked red Buick. Police lab technicians spent almost two hours carefully inspecting the car for fingerprints and for other trace evidence that might identify the suspect. Nothing!

A rental contract, found in the car's glove box, disclosed that it had been rented a day earlier to an individual named Benjamin Boffardi. But a search at the Bureau of Motor Vehicles disclosed that Boffardi was a fictitious character who rented the Buick with a phony driver's license.

Finally, the frustrated detectives decided it was time to call it quits for the day.

CHAPTER SEVEN

As usual, Solly headed directly home, wondering what kind of snack his wife would have waiting on the table.

Pirelli headed straight to his favorite watering hole. He walked briskly along Second Avenue as he made a beeline for O'Lunney's Alehouse. Upon entering the popular nightspot, he was greeted by the usual cloud of smoke that wafted over the bar area. The beautifully preserved turn-of-the-century interior of the pub included a vintage tile floor, etched glass, beveled mirrors, a nicotine-stained pressed-tin ceiling, and historic prints of the surrounding area as it was in the 1880's.

The waitresses that served patrons seated at the coveted high backed, wooden booths delivered burgers, salads, Shepherd's pie, meat loaf, chili and other typical pub food from the kitchen upstairs.

Pirelli's favorite stool at the far end of the long, U-shaped oak bar was waiting for him. He settled in and the familiar bartender walked over.

Joe Donnellan, fiftyish and balding, welcomed the sullen detective and, without asking, poured a double Chivas over ice. Pirelli downed the drink in two gulps.

Donnelan quickly refilled the glass. "I see you got a lot on your mind, Pirelli.

"Yeah. Sorta Joe."

"It's that poor cop!"

"He was only a kid, Joe. Went down fighting though! A tough cop!"

"And you and Solly are the lead detectives on the case?"

Pirelli nodded his head and took another swallow of his drink. "By the way, Joe, is Mary on tonight?" Pirelli asked.

"Yeah, here she is now."

The shapely waitress, spotting Pirelli sitting quietly at the bar, sensed he had something on his mind. She could feel his eyes following her as she hopped from table to table, delivering food and taking orders. Several minutes later, she joined the glum detective.

"Well, what do you know," she said smiling, "If it ain't God's gift to women. You gonna arrest me before or after I finish serving my customers?"

He looked at the tired body that was still attractive after forty-four years. "You got a good figure, Mary, and I felt like walking twenty blocks just to see it."

Several years ago, he had taken her home with him. And occasionally, they would meet to re-live the moment they both enjoyed. Yet somehow, during his frequent visits to O'Lunney's, they had always greeted each other as if nothing had ever happened.

"Okay," she smiled warmly. "So you walked twenty blocks. Now tell me what's really on your mind?"

"I'll tell you what's on my mind after you tell me what time are you getting off tonight."

She slowly shook her head. "Can't you ever get things right, Pirelli? I already have plans. But I'm free tomorrow night."

"Good, then I'll ask you tomorrow night."

She planted a warm kiss on his cheek, whispering in his ear. "I won't hold my breath."

Time slipped away quickly and so did an excessive amount of scotch that had been placed before the slender detective. Despite his easy humor and otherwise outgoing character, the melancholy of Pirelli's darker side often caused him pain; a side that only Solly knew, a side that caused him to drink often and more than anyone should. When this dark side overtook him, Pirelli anesthetized himself to forget the human misery, and his close encounter with death almost twenty years ago in a God forsaken place called Korea.

CHAPTER EIGHT

◦━◦

Shortly before the Panmumjon peace treaty, Anthony Pirelli, Private First Class, Infantry, squatted alone in a muddy listening post. Other than the sporadic exchanges of artillery and mortar fire, and the occasional air-bursts puffing in the sky, the listening post remained relatively quiet throughout the chilling cold night.

Across the mighty Papasan, the moon brightened the glare of the earlier snow. He scanned the barren hillside, rubbing his gloved hand against the grainy stock of his M-1. Squinting to read the faintly luminescent dial on his wristwatch, he muttered, "For Christ's sake, where the hell are they?" Half turned to avoid the sudden shifting of the wind he cursed the late return of his platoon's nightly patrol. They were fifteen minutes late. Something was wrong. Several minutes later, he heard feet crunching across the hard-packed snow. A frightening thought tightened his stomach. The sounds were coming from the wrong direction; from the northeast; from Red Chinese territory.

Instantly, Pirelli sank to a prone position and carefully eased the stock of his rifle under his cheek. He tried hard to control the sound of his heavy breathing. His eyes darted wildly across the sparsely wooded terrain. When the point man of the enemy patrol came into his view, Pirelli's lips formed a silent prayer. "Jesus, help me" he whispered, fearing the arrival of the enemy patrols main body.

The nineteen-year-old had survived thirteen months in the "police action" and prayed he would survive his remaining two.

"Jesus," he whispered again, lying motionless as he stared at the first Chinese soldier he had ever seen close up. 'How many are there?' he thought.

Controlling his breath, Pirelli tugged at his mitten until it fell to the ground. Then, he cautiously pulled the pin from a fragmentation grenade and awaited the confrontation that he believed was imminent. The wind and bitter cold brought stinging tears to his eyes as he watched the quilt-clad Chinese point man slowly approach.

With the point man now less than fifty yards from his position, Pirelli raised himself on one knee and prepared to hurl the grenade. Then, for no apparent reason, his foe suddenly turned and retraced his steps to the other side of the hill.

Pirelli released his breath in a deep sigh of relief, his fingers, frozen stiff, groped for the discarded grenade pin. He clawed at the ground in a circular motion, gradually widening its circumference, but the pin was gone.

The presence of the point man was replaced with an equally horrific problem. He started to panic as his fingers curled tightly around the spoon handle of the grenade.

"Christ," he muttered, staring down fearfully at the explosive in his now freezing hand.

As long as the spoon remained in place, the grenade posed no danger, but if the spring-loaded device managed to fly off, the miniature bomb would explode in less than five seconds, probably taking half of his body with it.

Now at a half crouch, he thought about throwing the grenade away from his immediate area. But considering the risk, he shook his head. That would surely alert the nearby enemy patrol.

Pirelli kicked his field phone unit over on its side. Forcing his knee down on its protective web case, he lifted the receiver with his left hand and tucked it between his neck and ear; leaned forward, and began cranking the handle. A voice finally crackled in Pirelli's ear.

"Command Post..., Over."

"Its Pirelli, he said, surprised at the firmness of his voice, "I'm alone here on the LP and there's an enemy patrol not more than five hundred yards in front of me."

"Enemy patrol?" the Command Post operator responded. "How many are there?"

"I don't know. I only saw the point man."

"If you only saw one man, how do you know it's a patrol?"

"It's gotta be a patrol," cried Pirelli. "What the hell would one man be doing out here alone... like I am."

There was a long pause until the Command Post operator said, "You're absolutely sure it's the enemy. Our own patrol is up in your area somewhere, too. You absolutely sure it's not our patrol?"

"I'm sure, Goddamn you. I saw the point man. He's a chink."

With his hand now aching, Pirelli, whispered into the phone. "Listen, I pulled the pin from a grenade and I'm holding the sonofabitch in my hand. I can't take a chance on throwing it. It will give my position away."

The operator's voice crackled past the static. "Stick the pin back in."

"I lost the pin, you fuckin idiot. Listen, you have the coordinates of where I am. Send in some mortar fire for cover so I can get the hell out of here."

"We can't throw in mortar fire," the operator said quickly. I'm telling you, we got our own patrol up there near you. Take it easy."

"Bullshit take it easy. Listen you dopey bastard, if you were up here instead of me I'd like to see how easy you'd take it."

Then the sudden whack-whack sounds from an incoming mortar round made Pirelli cringe and cradle his head into the ground. Still clutching the grenade, he managed to roll over on his stomach. He screamed into the field phone. But the unit had gone dead; the 120 millimeter round totally severed the communications wire.

Pirelli climbed to his knees. The dull ache in his hand served as a reminder of death's closeness. 'It's all over for me, ain't it?' he thought wildly. 'I'm gonna die all alone in this fucking no man's land."

Trying desperately to control his growing fear, a small smile began tugging at his lips as his thoughts turned from death to the memory of his childhood days.

CHAPTER NINE

For Pirelli, as for most other second-generation Italian-American children who grew up in Brooklyn during the 40's and 50's, his world was the neighborhood where he was raised. Everyone was Italian. His grandfather had migrated from Naples at the turn of the century. When he was able to save enough money, he bought a house that served as the family compound.

Pirelli vividly recalled how every Thursday evening and Sunday afternoon his family ate at Grandpa's house. Sitting in the mud in his listening post he could picture Grandma's kitchen and smell the garlic and onions, simmering in a pot of slow cooking gravy that awaited the freshly made macaroni. He could hear the hiss of meatballs frying in imported olive oil. Nothing tasted better than fried meatballs served with crisp Italian bread dipped into a pot of gravy.

He recalled the many Sunday afternoons when, before and after dinner, he'd play with his cousins in Grandpa's yard. He could see Grandpa's big and well-manicured garden. Not just a flower garden, but a garden in which he raised tomatoes, tomatoes, and more tomatoes. Of course he also grew peppers, radishes, basil, squash and anything else grandma wanted him to grow, all complemented by a grapevine and a fig tree nearby.

His thoughts turned to Thanksgiving and Christmas. Most grandmothers served turkey with stuffing and cranberry sauce. But in Grandma's house the turkey was served only after the antipasto, soup, lasagna, meatballs and salad was served first.

The three plus hour meal was always followed by an assortment of fruits, including figs from the tree in Grandpa's yard, cookies, pastries, freshly roasted chestnuts, and finally, all followed by stomach settling finocchio.

He pictured Grandpa, his pitcher of home made wine, flavored with freshly cut peach wedges floating on top, always by his side, smoking his stogie, his eyes twinkling, proud of the family he had worked so hard to raise. Grandpa would always remind his grandkids never to forget their Italian heritage. But he was also reminded them that they were Americans first, Americans of Italian descent.

The sweet memories of days past heightened his will to live, to enjoy being Italian with all its tradition. He didn't want to die. Not now! Not here! Not before he visited Grandpa's house again.

Pirelli returned from his reverie feeling oddly warmer than before; his numbed fingers kept telling him he would soon lose control of the deadly grenade. If only he could open his fingers for a few seconds.

Suddenly, the point man came back over the rise, this time followed by five members of his patrol. Feeling both relief and fear, he rose to his knees and watched the enemy's movements. They were moving closer to his burrow in the putrid ground. Dangerously close. 'Just a moment more,' he thought, 'just a little bit closer'.

When he to decided act, he hurled the grenade at the center of the unsuspecting Chinese soldiers. Then, falling to the prone position, he picked up his rifle and pumped a fusillade of bullets at the scurrying figures before they had the chance to return his fire.

His weapon no longer reigned out death and the quiet gloom of night once again settled over the glistening snow.

Minutes later he climbed to his feet and saw six Chinese soldiers, none older than himself, lying still on the snow-covered hillside. He stared at their lifeless bodies. He began to sob. Enemy or no enemy, all he could see were kids, kids like himself; kids that would never grow to be men, husbands or fathers; kids that would never visit their Grandpa's house again.

But he survived. He overcame a challenge few men ever face. He would never again feel fear. No man could bring him down.

CHAPTER TEN

I t was 3 a.m. when Pirelli left the bar. The night was clear and a bright moon hung over the city. He decided to walk home. He was thinking about the promise he made to the slain officer's parents and the man who had taken the young cops life. The man was here, somewhere within the City. With patience, perseverance and determination, he would be found and brought to justice. Pirelli would have it no other way.

Pirelli entered his apartment and headed to the kitchen to set the coffee pot for his morning eye-opener. Moments later he was in his king size bed, sound asleep.

By 6 a.m. he was answering the phone. He yanked the receiver from its cradle. "This better be you Solly and it better be fucking important."

"It's alive and it talks," Solly cried gleefully. "It's time to rise and shine, good buddy! I just got a call from the Greenwich, Connecticut police. A guy with a bullet was treated in their emergency room last night. That alarm Coltman transmitted paid off. You awake enough to listen?"

Pirelli slid from the bed jamming the phone between his neck and chin, listening intently, he lit a cigarette.

Hearing no response, Solly yelled, "Putz! Did you hear what I just told you?"

"I heard every word you said. We have a suspect in a Connecticut hospital."

"Yeah, about sixty miles from across the state line. About six hours after the shooting, this clown shows up at the emergency room with a gunshot wound to the left shoulder."

"Pedigree?"

"He's a male white about forty years old. That's all we're certain of right now."

"What the fuck are you talking about? That's all we're certain of. Didn't they get more information?"

"Oh, they got more information all right, but it's all bullshit. You ready for this? He identified himself as one Benjamin Boffardi, the same bullshit name that was used by the guy who rented the red Buick."

Solly paused, awaiting a response. He was rewarded by Pirelli's shrill whistle.

"This is our killer, kid."

"Sure looks like it, Solly. But we still gotta prove that this Boffardi guy, or whatever the fuck his name is, was in the vestibule at the time the cop was killed," Pirelli shot back.

"That's why they call us detectives, pal. Go finish getting dressed and get your ass in here. We got a lotta work to do."

Pirelli hurried into the kitchen, flipped on the coffee pot and waited. Minutes later, he poured a cup of black coffee and buttered the bread that had popped up in the near-by toaster. Pirelli gulped down a slice of toast and a cup of coffee then made his way to the bathroom. Twenty minutes later, showered and shaved, he was out the door and on his way to the precinct.

CHAPTER ELEVEN

A fter he killed the cop, Ardone scrambled through the lounge and out the rear fire exit. He had little pain and no bleeding from the bullet in his thick shoulder. He surmised the wound was not serious. Yet, he knew it had to be seen by a doctor.

Ardone had a critical decision to make. He knew he could find a doctor who would attend to his gunshot wound without reporting it to the police as required by law, but it would take time. And seeing such a doctor presented another problem. He was a high profile gangster known to frequent the Blue Grotto Lounge. Any mobbed up doctor that treated him would figure it was the murdered cop's bullet.

It was bad enough that the porter had seen him running through the lounge. Ardone was positive he would not identify him. And even if the porter did identify him, he was not an eyewitness to the actual shooting. The fact that he ran through the lounge after the shooting, absent more, would not prove he was the killer.

Ardone's mind was working overtime. If a physician were to testify that he treated him for an unexplained gunshot wound suffered shortly after the officer was killed, it would be dangerous. He would have no choice but to insure the doctor's silence. Permanently!

Such were his thoughts when Ardone decided to chance a visit to a small out-of-state, hospital. He knew the emergency room personnel would notify the local police of the gunshot wound. They were required to do so. But if he got there late in the evening, the uniformed officers that responded to the hospital wouldn't know about the shooting in New York. He would simply tell them that he was on his way up state to visit a friend and he stopped at a deserted rest area to relieve himself. On his way to the restroom, a mugger confronted him and demanded his car keys and wallet. Foolishly, he resisted and the mugger shot him and ran off.

Absent any reason to believe otherwise, the officers would simply take the report. The next morning the precinct detectives would learn of the New York alarm but it didn't matter. As soon as his wound was treated Ardone would scramble out of the hospital.

His decision made, he began his journey upstate stopping only long enough to drop the murder weapon into the Hudson River. The plan worked!

CHAPTER TWELVE

⌒*w*⌒

When Pirelli arrived at the Squad room Solly was sitting at his cluttered desk chewing on the second of two toasted onion bagels, smothered with lox flavored cream cheese.

"So what's the story?"

"The story is," Solly said, swallowing the last of the bagel, "This Boffardi guy is our man."

"By the way, did he say how he got shot?"

"Yeah, he did. He gave the Greenwich police some bullshit story that he was driving upstate to see some broad and stopped in a deserted rest area on the outskirts of Greenwich to take a leak and when he gets out of the car he gets mugged by a thin, dark-skinned guy that he can't ID of course, pointing a gun at him. He sez he was scarred shitless and started to holler. Then the guy panicked and shot him. Any questions before I go on?"

"Only one, Solly. At the time of this alleged mugging, did this Boffardi guy have his dick in his hand? It could be an important clue."

"You can fuck around all you want!" Solly snapped, "But this is our man. Also the X-Ray shows what appears to be a nine or a .38 slug in his left shoulder just below the collarbone.

"Why don't ya give the hospital a call, Solly. Let's get an up-date on his condition before we run up there and grab him."

Solly called the hospital and after having a conversation with the resident on duty turned to his partner.

"Looks like we ain't gonna be talking to him, kid."

"You mean he's DOA?" Pirelli said happily.

"No such luck. The doc sez he didn't even suffer a serious wound."

"So what the fuck do you mean we won't be talking to him?"

"I mean that the cocksucker walked outta the hospital."

"What! You gotta be fucking kidding."

"I wish I was."

"Jesus," Pirelli grunted. "When?"

"About four hours ago."

"What about the bullet?"

"The doc said that the bullet might have to be removed at some later point if it starts to move, but right now it don't present a problem for the guy. Anyway, it's all bull shit because he's gone."

"I don't fuckin believe it, Solly. How could they let him leave the hospital?"

"Hey, the guy had the right to sign himself out. Let's face it kid, I'll never tell, but we really fucked up this one big time. As soon as we learned the guy who rented the red Buick used the name Boffardi, we should have included it in our alarm."

"It wouldn't have mattered, Solly. Obviously, the uniform cops that responded to the hospital and took the report didn't know we had an alarm out. Anyway, what's done is done and we can't change that."

"Now what?"

A faint smile crossed Pirelli's face. "But you want to know something large one? Maybe his leaving the hospital without talking to us was a blessing in disguise."

"A blessing in disguise my ass, you know God damn well that the bullet in this Boffardi character--or whatever the fuck his name is--came from the cop's gun. That makes him our killer and we let him slip away."

"Yeah, but he won't be away for too long."

"What the fuck are you talking about?"

"Listen, we know for a fact that the cop shot our killer before he ran through the lounge, right?"

"So?"

"So even if our friend Cosmo is telling the truth that he was hiding behind the bar and didn't see the man who ran through, we both know fuckin well that he knows who it was. And I can promise you this much, large one, one way or the other the little bastard will tell us his name."

"And you call that a blessing in disguise?"

"Yeah, I do."

"Why's that?"

"Look at it this way, Solly. If we would've grabbed this Boffardi prick at the hospital, what makes you think we would have been able to prove that he killed the cop? All we got are several eye-witnesses who see a man get out of the red Buick and walk into the vestibule of the Grotto, but they can't identify him. Then we got the woman who rented the red Buick to a man named Boffardi, but she can't identify him either. And you wanna know something, even if anyone of them could identify him, it wouldn't prove that he's the one who shot the cop."

"Ain't you forgetting something Pirelli?"

"What's that?"

"The prick got the cop's bullet in him. For Christ Sake, what more do we need?"

"We need the bullet outta him. That's what we need."

"Can't we get a warrant to forcibly remove the bullet?"

"Maybe, but I don't think so. Remember Solly, the courts are more concerned about a defendant's rights than they are about a victim's rights. And if it turns out that we can't get a search warrant to forcibly remove the bullet, then what'll we have?"

Solly stared at his partner. He said nothing.

"I'll tell you what we'll have," Pirelli said. "We'll have a perp who knows that we're on to him. A perp who'll run on us the first chance he gets. At least now he thinks he's home free and he'll go about his business as usual. Then after we get his name from Cosmo, we'll see if we can get a search warrant to remove the bullet. If we can get the warrant, we go pick him up and our case is made. But if we can't get a warrant at least the bastard, whoever the fuck he is, won't know we're on to him. Then we can continue our investigation without alerting him."

"I never thought of it that way, kid but it makes sense. You know sometimes I think you have a Yiddisha Kup"

"Yiddisha Kup my ass. Remember Rome ruled the world for four hundred years." Anyway, we got our work cut out for us."

"That's for sure, kid. As soon as we can we'll get moving on our friend Cosmo."

"You got it, Solly. Meanwhile I'm going back to my apartment to catch up on some sleep."

"Buy the way, don't forget Rae's expecting you over for dinner tomorrow at the usual time."

"Tell your lovely wife I'm looking forward to it, Solly. See you at 3 p.m."

CHAPTER THIRTEEN

I t was a Sunday and as usual Pirelli spent most of the morning at his health club. After a three game match of racket ball and five laps in the Olympic size swimming pool he headed for the steam room where he would stay longer than recommended. Now he was ready for a relaxing afternoon and a mouth-watering dinner at Chez Samuels.

He walked the three miles to his partner's apartment. As he approached the East village, he took in the small groups gathered on the street corners, among the "crack vials" and discarded "zip locks." They drank beer for breakfast, blaming their shitty lives on everything and everybody but themselves.

Others were simply gathered to undermine the rule of law. They demanded unbridled freedom of expression. But the freedom of expression that they demanded for themselves they would deny to others.

"What are we becoming," Pirelli mumbled.

'Political correctness,' he thought. 'What a fuckin joke! So-called civil libertarians are busy spewing privacy rights while people in need of psychiatric confinement are free to roam the streets unsupervised.'

'Where children are slaughtered in the crossfire of ongoing

drug wars and each day 3 murdered souls find there way to an overcrowded city morgue.'

Pirelli just shook his head in despair as he reached for a cigarette and continued on his way.

It was precisely 3 p.m. when Pirelli knocked on his partner's apartment door. Solly's face opened to a wide grin when he saw Pirelli carrying a white box of assorted miniature Italian pastries.

After planting a kiss on Rae Samuel's cheek, Pirelli placed the box of pastries and two bottles of '60 Amarone on the kitchen table. Then turning back to his hostess he glanced inquisitively at the unfamiliar face standing next to her.

"Anthony," Rae said quickly, "This is my new neighbor, Mary Sorvino."

"Mary this is Detective Anthony Pirelli, he works with Solly, and he's his best friend too."

"Mary stopped by earlier, Anthony, and I insisted she stay for dinner. You two can get to know each other a little later, but right now me and Mary have to finish cooking. We won't be much longer."

Pirelli nodded and politely smiled at the two women before they disappeared into the kitchen. Then he turned to his partner with a "what's-this-all-about-look" on his face.

Undaunted, Solly rolled an unlighted cigar across his lips and slumped into his beloved worn out comfortable leather recliner.

Pirelli looked directly into his partner's eyes. "By the way, Solly," he whispered, "When you invited me for dinner, how come you didn't tell me about my blind date?"

"What blind date?"

"The woman that's helping Rae cook dinner, that's what blind date."

"Whatta ya crazy? Mary just happened to pop in on us earlier to say hello and Rae invited her to stay for dinner. She happens to live in the downstairs apartment. What were we supposed to do? Tell her to leave.

"Sure! She just popped in," Pirelli said, as he began to itemize on his fingers. "Let's see, Solly, a beautiful woman that's dressed like a mannequin in Sak's window just happened to drop by. Is that right, Solly?"

"That's absolutely right, pal. Mere coincidence! Listen kid, you're reading all the wrong things into this!"

"I am, huh?" Pirelli was relentless now. "Now we both know that you'd never lie to me, don't we, Solly?"

"More or less!"

"What's that supposed to mean, more or less."

"For Christ's sake, lay off will ya. It was Rae's idea, not mine."

"Oh, is that right? Well, you can tell your lovely wife to quit playing cupid. You know I'm not ready to settle down yet."

"And why the hell not," Solly demanded. "She's intelligent and a hell of a good-looking woman and Rae tells me she's a great cook. Settling down with a girl like this wouldn't be the worst thing that ever happened to you."

"Maybe so, Solly, but like I told you a thousand times, I just ain't ready to settle down."

"I just ain't ready to settle down," Solly repeated, mimicking his dinner guest. "And why the hell not," Solly grumped.

"Because when I tie the knot, I want to be ready to make a solid, one hundred percent commitment. I don't wanna be like half of the married guys in the squad. They all tell you how happy they are and how much they love their wives meanwhile they look to fuck anything that moves. And most of the other guys will grab it if it happens to come their way."

"All right, so you don't wanna get married. But it won't hurt you to go along with a friendly dinner for a couple of hours, will it?"

"Not at all, just as long we understand each other."

"Good. We understand each other."

Solly sniffed heavily at the aromas filling the air then he turned to the hushed voices coming from the kitchen. "Hey Rae," he yelled. "We're ready to eat."

"Pour the wine. We'll be ready in a few minutes."

Pirelli poured the wine into four long-stemmed wine glasses used for special occasions.

"Listen Solly," Pirelli said, "lemme run something by you while we're waiting for the girls."

"Shoot", Solly said.

"Why do you think the cop followed the perp into the vestibule?"

"C'mon kid, that's easy. Remember, he was on summons duty and the perp parked the red Buick illegally. He probably saw the perp park the car and followed him into the vestibule to give him a summons."

Pirelli shook his head and said softly, "But there's one big problem with your theory, Solly."

"And what's that?"

"Who kills a cop over a parking summons? All the sonofabitch had to do was take the fucking thing and that's that."

"Look kid, you asked me why the cop followed the perp into the vestibule, not why the perp shot him."

"Something happened in that vestibule, Solly, something that caused the death of a cop."

"Well, it looks like we got our work cut out for us, kid. Meanwhile the girls are comin so let's put the case aside for now and enjoy the dinner."

Rae walked into the dining room carrying a large pan of lasagna. Mary carried the meatballs in one hand and a pitcher of steaming hot gravy in the other.

After putting the food on the table, Rae, smiling looked to

Pirelli. "We apologize for taking so long in the kitchen. But I was fascinated by the way Mary prepared her very own recipe for lasagna. I really mean it, Anthony, she cooks so good she could open her own restaurant."

Rae paused, glanced at Solly and smiled. "Are you boys finished talking business? Mary and me won't mind listening if you're not."

"It's okay, honey, we're done," Solly said.

Everyone sat down at the dining room table. Rae immediately began talking while Mary sat silently, appraising the detective seated directly across from her.

'He's even better looking up close,' she thought. 'And talk about men dressed in the latest fashion. The last thing I'd ever take him for is a police officer.'

The dinner went exceptionally well. Mary had done an excellent job on the lasagna, though she complimented Rae on boiling the macaroni to just the right tenderness. Rae had put all her culinary talents into a creamy cheesecake that won everyone's approval.

Since sitting down at the dinner table, Pirelli had tried to avoid meaningful eye contact with his unexpected date, but with the day wearing on it was becoming more difficult. Peering at her with his pale green eyes, he judged her to be in her middle thirties. Her hair was chestnut in color and her soft waves framed a truly beautiful face. Her eyes were large, brown and bottomless; they sparkled with warmth and sensuality and her soft voice was calming. Adding to her classic Italian beauty was a turned up nose and a soft mouth tastefully coated with an appropriate shade of lipstick. She looked healthy and full of spirit. He liked this woman. He would see her again.

CHAPTER FOURTEEN

The next morning, Pirelli arrived at the precinct earlier than usual in order to tackle some overdue case reports. He wanted to clear his desk so he could focus on finding a cop-killer.

The violent death of Officer Terrance McCarthy weighed heavily on his mind. He couldn't stop thinking about the promise he had made to the slain officer's parents. He would not rest until he found their son's murderer.

Pirelli knew it was patience with the mundane that made for a successful homicide investigation. Each detail and the many leads had to be carefully evaluated. The reports, the paper work, the countless interviews and re-interviews that were so time consuming. Sometimes you got lucky, most times you didn't. He wondered why he did it, why he gave his life to this frustrating, often depressingly gruesome job. But deep inside, he knew. He didn't know where the feeling in him came from or how he got it, but he knew what it was; a belief that the victims had rights, too. And so did their friends and the families who loved them. Murder was a horror he couldn't let somebody get away with, especially when it was a fellow police officer that was the victim. He had the experience and the authority to do something about it.

Thirty minutes later Solly walked in carrying a grease-stained brown paper bag and two large containers of steaming coffee.

"Where the fuck you been," Pirelli chided him.

"I stopped for some coffee."

"Whatta ya got in the bag?"

"Hot toasted bagels," Solly said smiling, all schmeared with cream cheese."

At his cluttered desk, Solly emptied the bag and attacked the first of three bagels he would call his.

"So did ya solve the case yet?" Solly said.

Pirelli blurted back, "You know Solly, I still can't figure why the cop followed the perp into the vestibule."

"Look, kid, why we beating this thing to death for? What the fucks the difference why he went inta the vestibule? He went in."

"Yeah, you're right, Solly," Pirelli said as he reached for half of a salted bagel and scraped off some of the excess cream cheese.

"You know fuckin well I'm right."

After the bagel was gone, Pirelli clasped his hands behind his head and turned to his partner. "By the way, Solly, you see that lieutenant from Internal Affairs standing over there," he said leisurely, nodding his head to the other side of the room.

"Yeah, I see him, so what about him?"

"I was talking to him before you got in. His team collared that guy sitting in the interrogation room."

"What did they collar him for?"

"Bribery. They grabbed him cutting up stolen cars. It seems that they had his office bugged and his phone tapped too. Would you believe that they actually overheard him bribe two cops that walked into his chop shop and caught him red-handed?"

"And so?"

"And so now they want the guy to give up the cops who took the bribe."

"So let them turn him. What the fuck business is it of ours?"

"That's just it. They can't even get off the dime with the prick. In fact, he won't even talk to them, no less turn."

"Now ain't that too fucking bad" Samuels said sarcastically.

"C'mon Solly, the lieutenant's looking for help and he asked me if I'd give it a shot."

"Hey, fuck the lieutenant! We're in homicide. Remember?"

"Why you getting so hot, Solly? He don't seem like a bad guy."

"For your information my skinny friend, it just so happens that I know the lieutenant, his name's Henetty. We came on the job together."

"No shit."

"Yeah, in fact we worked in the same precinct for a couple of years. He was real active too. Didn't take shit from nobody."

"So what's the problem then, large one?"

"The problem is when he worked the street he would take a fuckin hot stove. Bribes, helping himself at burglaries, contracts, you name it, he did it. Now look at him. The phony bastard, lookin to wind up his career locking up cops for doin the same things he did his whole fuckin career."

"Come on Solly! A lotta guys did those things before the Knapp Commission investigation changed things. It's what you do now that counts."

"Ah, I know you're right, kid. But it still rubs me the wrong way to see a cop locking up another cop. That my friend just happens to be the way I feel."

I know what you mean, Solly. And personally, I wouldn't wanna do it either. But somebody has gotta do it. And as far as I'm concerned, those guys that refuse to change and still look to earn, I say shame on them."

Solly agreed with his partner.

"Let's face it Solly, without Internal Affairs keeping the lid on things it'll only be a matter of time before things got back to the way they were. Just look at the people that are being recruited today," Pirelli added. "Some of them shouldn't be on the job in the first place. We gotta have somebody to keep them in line."

"Okay, okay, you win. But I still think Henetty is a piece of shit. And as far as turning their guy, don't get too cocky. For your information some guys just don't talk, no less turn. Period!"

"Yeah, well I'll tell you what, I'll bet you lunch that I get him to turn."

"Bullshit! Like you just said, Henetty and his crowd have been trying for most of the morning."

"Then take my bet. After all, the way you eat, it'll be like me giving you three to one odds."

"Blow it out your ass wise guy."

"What's the matter Solly? Afraid I might win the bet?"

"I'll tell you what Pirelli, you're on. And you know why I'm taking your bet?"

"No! Why?"

"Because the way I see it I'm a winner either way. In fact it'll be worth it for me to lose."

"Why's that?"

"Because I'd love to see you turn him and show Henetty how a real detective works. Yeah Pirelli, the way I see it, I'm a winner either way."

CHAPTER FIFTEEN

Pirelli straightened his necktie, buttoned his jacket, and headed for the sparsely furnished, windowless, interrogation room. As he strolled across the large detective area, he hesitated for a minute, thinking about how he would approach the defendant.

Pirelli knew that some defendants were easy to "turn" while others would never "turn."

'My guess is this guy falls into the easy category,' Pirelli thought. 'After all, I won't be asking him to give up one of his own. It's two corrupt cops that I'll be asking him to give up. Cops who stole his money, money he had risked his freedom for.

Pirelli also knew that if he were to be successful in gaining the man's cooperation he would first have to establish some kind of rapport with him. He also had to convince the man that the evidence against him was overwhelming and that he was certain to be convicted and sent to prison if he did not cooperate.

Game plan in hand, Pirelli walked into the interrogation room and greeted the docile looking defendant. "How ya doin, Steve?" he said.

The man nodded a polite hello.

At forty-seven, the defendant, a petty thief who had spent a quarter of his adult life behind bars, appeared unconcerned about the prospect of having to spend a little more time behind bars.

"Listen, Steve," Pirelli began, "I'm from homicide. The lieutenant over there that collared ya tells me you don't wanna talk to him and he asked me to give it a try."

"Listen detective, like I told the lieutenant, I don't wanna be no wise ass, but I know my rights and I don't gotta talk to nobody."

"You're a hundred percent right, Steve, ya don't. By the way, the name's Pirelli."

"Okay Pirelli, but like I just told them other guys, I ain't got nothin to say. And since we both know I don't gotta talk to nobody, why waste your time askin?"

"Listen to me Steve. I know we never met, but at the risk a blowin my own horn, believe me, I ain't a bad guy to know, especially for a guy like you. Now I checked you out and I know you been around. And I also know that you never been collared for anything more than non-violent shit. That, my friend is one of the reasons I agreed to help out the lieutenant and ask you to talk to me."

"Yeah, and what's the other reason?" Steve asked.

"Ya see, Steve, I just bet my not so slim partner sitting over there a lunch that I could get ya to talk to me. And the way he eats…"

Steve glanced at Solly's waistline and smiled.

Pirelli was encouraged by the man's smile and continued to press on. "Listen, Steve, I would consider it a personal favor if you would at least listen to what I gotta say. And if you do, I'll return one in the future. So if ya wanna make an investment, here's your chance."

The man's smile broadened and Pirelli pressed on.

"C'mon, Steve, all ya gotta do is listen to what I gotta say? Then after you listen to me, you don't have to cooperate if ya don't wanna, but at least gimmie a chance so I can win my bet."

Steve looked curiously at Pirelli but still remained silent.

Pirelli continued, "What's more, by listening to me, you'll get a heads-up on what they got on ya. And like I said, for whatever it's worth, I'd appreciate it. So whadda ya say, Steve?"

The defendant looked at the smooth-talking detective. "By the way," he asked, "What did you say your name was?"

"Pirelli. Why?"

"Pirelli huh!. Lemme ask ya something, Pirelli, did you happen to lock up a guy named Johnny Dee about a year or so ago?"

"Could be, what was he collared for?"

"Manslaughter, got seven and a half to fifteen,"

"Oh! You must mean John DeSimone?"

"Yeah, that's him."

"Yeah, that was me. Why do ya ask?"

"You see, Johnny's a good friend of mine and it just so happens that when I seen him before he went away, he just happened to mention your name."

"Good or bad?"

"Good. He said ya treated him like a gentleman when you booked him. He was real surprised, too."

"Hey! That's nothing to be surprised about. If you act nice when you're collared, ya get treated nice. That's how it works around here. But if you're a smart-ass and break balls..." Pirelli purposely let his voice trail off.

"No!" Steve said emphatically, "Johnny said you went out of ya way for him."

"Is that right? And just what is it that I done for him?"

"He said ya got him some cigars before locking him up for the night."

"Shit, that ain't no big deal, Steve."

"Well for your information Pirelli, Johnny thought it was a big deal. And it just so happens that I do too. So as a pay-back for Johnny, I'm gonna listen to what ya gotta say."

"That's great Steve. That's just great."

"But I'm tellin ya now, Pirelli, after I hear you out I still ain't gonna cooperate."

"It's a deal, Steve. At least I got a shot," Pirelli said happily.

"Okay, now here's where it's at. The Internal Affairs people were tipped that you were cuttin up stolen cars in your yard and that you were paying off the auto squad for protection. They watched the yard for a couple of weeks and saw stolen cars goin in and being cut up. Then they got a court order to bug your office and tap your phone. And when those two detectives walked in your yard and caught you red-handed, they heard them shake you down for five big ones. They got it all on tape. And when you phoned your partner and told you to bring over the cash, they got that on tape too."

Steve just shook his head and smiled.

"What's so funny Steve," Pirelli asked curiously.

"What's so funny is the way I hadda bribe a cop so he could get inta my office and bug it."

"I don't follow you, Steve. Whadda ya mean?"

"You see Pirelli, one afternoon there's this telephone truck that parks up the street from my yard. A guy dressed like a repairman gets out, climbs up the pole and starts fuckin with the telephone wires. Next thing I know my phone's dead. So I run up to the corner and stopped the guy just as he was about to drive off. I actually had to beg the prick to look at my phone. Oh he played it real cool all right. Sez he couldn't help me. He gives me this shit about me needing a work order for him to come in my yard and look at the phone."

"So what'd ya say?"

"I sez I already got a work order."

"And?"

"He sez lemme see it. So I go inta my pocket and pull out a fifty. The next thing you know he's all fuckin smiles. He fixed the phone all right. He fixed it by putting a bug in it. I was wondering how anyone could get inta my office with all them fuckin wild dogs I got running loose at night."

"To be honest Steve, I don't know how they got the bug in there, but they did. Now I'll go get the tape and a set of headphones so you can hear for yourself so you'll know I ain't bull shittin ya."

"Forget the tape, Pirelli. You say you got it, I believe ya. So just keep talking. That's if you still wanna."

"Fine! Now listen Steve, if you're convicted, which believe me ya will be with the evidence they got, you can get up to seven years for bribing a cop. Now we both know ya ain't gonna get seven years, but I guarantee ya you'll get at least two."

"And so?"

"And so now you got an opportunity to help yourself. You see Steve the IAD lieutenant needs you to identify the cops that shook you down. Now I really can't speak for the DA's office, but ten will get you twenty that if you agree to give up the cops, they'll give you a walk. Well Steve, whatta ya gotta say now?"

"Like I told ya before Pirelli, don't get sore, but I still ain't interested in cooperating."

Pirelli was shocked. "Ya gotta be kiddin, Steve. You mean to tell me that you're willin to do two years in Attica rather than give up two fuckin corrupt cops. Cops that shook you down for five thousand! Cops that would have locked your fuckin ass up in a minute if you didn't come up with the cash! Come on Steve, they ain't askin ya to give up one of your own. These are dirty cops. You don't owe them a fuckin thing."

"Listen Pirelli, you seem like a regular guy. And to tell you the truth, you make a lotta sense. So don't take it personal. But it just so happens that right now I ain't interested in cuttin no deal. And that's that."

"Mind if I ask ya why, Steve?"

"No problem. First of all, it rubs me the wrong way to rat

anybody out. Even if they're scumbag cops who like to play both sides of the game. But to be honest with ya, that ain't my main reason. My main reason is that if they put me in the joint for a few years, they'll be doing me a favor."

"Doin ya a favor?" Pirelli blurted out. How's that, Steve?"

"Ya see, Pirelli, I'm forty-seven now and with the life I'm livin right now, I ain't gonna see fifty. And lemme tell ya why. I'm usually up all night chasing broads; I drink like a fuckin fish; I don't eat right; I don't sleep right and if that ain't enough, I got loan sharks chasing me all over the fuckin place. So like I just said, if they put me away for a few years they'll be doin me a favor."

"I still don't get it, Steve. How's that doing you a favor?"

"Because when I'm in the joint I'll be forced to dry out. I'll eat good, I'll work out in the gym, I'll read a few books, I could go on but I'm sure ya got the picture. Anyway, the bottom line is that if I do two years in Attica, the way I figure it, I'll be adding at least ten years to my life. And in my book, Pirelli, two-for-ten ain't so bad. So Pirelli, that's the reason why I ain't interested in no deal."

"So much for the jail system in New York State, huh Steve," Pirelli remarked dismally. "People looking to go in for forced physical rehabilitation."

"Ya got that right, Pirelli."

"I guess what we need here, Steve, is something like them jails they got down south. You know the ones where the inmates clean up the streets in chains during the day then afterwards get baloney on dry bread for dinner. And for dessert they get no smoking and no coffee. Then they're put to sleep in hot stuffy huts. Yeah Steve, I'll bet if this was down south you might reconsider cooperating," Pirelli said grimly.

"Maybe, but it ain't."

"Anyway, Steve, since ya ain't got a problem doing time, I guess we can't do business. And to tell ya the truth Steve, your reasons for not cooperating make a lotta sense, even if ya just cost me a lunch."

"Sorry about that, Pirelli."

"It's okay. Anyway, thanks for listenin. I'll see ya around. And when ya see DeSimone again tell him we're even."

"Wait. Before ya go, I could use that favor now."

"What is it, Steve?"

"How about getting me a couple of cigars?"

"You're a pisser Steve. What kind?"

Pirelli walked back to his desk and was greeted by his frowning partner.

"Too bad kid," Solly said sympathetically, "I was rooting for you. But like I said, some guys just don't turn. But just for trying so hard, I'm going to go easy on you."

"Gee thanks, Solly. Does that mean I only lost two lunches?"

"Fuck you Pirelli," Samuels said, "Let's go eat, I'm buying."

CHAPTER SIXTEEN

After a leisurely walk to a nearby restaurant, the detectives sat down at a table that afforded them more privacy than one would expect at a popular luncheon spot. Solly waved to a passing waitress, minutes later, he was sipping on a Dr. Brown's cream soda as he waited for his overstuffed pastrami on club while Pirelli was savoring a Vodka martini. Then Pirelli returned to the question that continued to nag at him.

"All right, Solly," he said, "We agree that the cop followed the perp into the vestibule to give him a summons. Now even if he did, we know one thing is for sure. He didn't get killed over a fuckin summons."

"Maybe the killer was carrying a bag of drugs and the cop saw it," Samuels opined.

"Possible, but the perp wouldn't kill a cop over a drug possession charge, either. And for that matter there's no way anybody would shoot a cop over some other bullshit thing," said Pirelli.

"The fuckin gun" Solly shouted. Maybe the cop saw the perp's gun."

"It's possible, Solly, but again the perp had to be concerned about something a lot more serious than a fuckin gun charge."

"Agreed. But ya wanna know something kid, I got a gut feeling that the perp's gun is involved in this somehow."

"Well if it's a gut feeling you got, it's gotta be a big feeling," Pirelli joked.

"I got your big feeling swinging, wise ass. I don't see you coming up with any ideas."

"That's because I didn't finish my martini yet."

After a moment of silence, Pirelli said, "But all kidding aside, Solly I think you're on to something. Maybe the gun connected him to a more serious crime? Like another murder? And that's why he couldn't take a collar and hadda shoot the cop"

"Hey, now that makes sense, kid. But do you really think the perp would be stupid enough to be carrying a murder weapon around with him?" Solly asked.

"I wouldn't think so, but then what if he just used it and didn't get a chance to dump it yet? Anyway, I think you're on to something, so let's pursue it."

Pirelli scrambled over to a pay phone that was mounted on the wall adjacent to the men's room and dialed the squad room. After two rings, the only female detective assigned to the homicide division answered the phone.

"Hey Davis, it's me, Pirelli," he said loudly.

"So? What am I supposed to do, clap for joy?"

"Listen Nancy, while you're sitting there manicuring your nails, me and Solly are squeezing in a little lunch while trying to solve a cop homicide."

"Really? I'll bet you're trying to solve your homicide with a dry one in front of you, straight up."

"Hey, that's good, Nancy, very good. I guess that's why you're a detective. Anyway, Solly was just telling me what a waste of taxpayer's money you are and I got something you can do for me to prove him wrong. If you wanna try that is."

"Fire away wise guy and we'll see who's a waste of taxpayer's money."

"Okay then. Call the Command Center and find out if we had a homicide with a gun that occurred around the time the cop was murdered. I'll be back to the squad in a few minutes. You can fill me in then."

"You mind telling me where you're going with this? I mean then maybe I can ask the right questions if I you gimme a little more info."

"Well, me and Solly are trying to figure out why the cop was killed and the only thing we came up with so far is the perp's gun."

"Whatta ya mean the perp's gun?"

"I mean maybe the cop saw the gun and the perp panicked because he had just used it in another homicide. It's the only thing that makes any sense."

"You got it," Davis replied, "I'll get on it right away. By the way, Pirelli, tell Solly that a Detective Scotto, from the two-three squad called. He wants to talk to him ASAP."

"Did he say what about?"

"No. All he said was that some guy he just locked up is throwing his name around. Sez he knows him and has something good for him. You want the number?"

"Yeah! Maybe it's got something to do with the cop killing. I'll have Solly call him right away."

After told of the Scotto's call Solly walked over to the wall phone and called the 23rd precinct. He spoke briefly with detective Scotto then returned to his pastrami sandwich.

"So what's the story, Solly?" Pirelli asked.

"The story is a stool of mine got busted and he's looking to talk to me."

"Anybody I know?"

"Yeah, it was 'Fat Mike'."

"Hey, he's given you solid info before. Maybe he's got something on the cop shooting."

"Wouldn't that be something? As soon as we get done with lunch, I'll run over to the two-three and see what's what. Then I'll meet you back at the squad room."

"You got it," Pirelli said. "Meanwhile I'll see if Davis came up with anything. I'll wait for you there."

CHAPTER SEVENTEEN

When Pirelli returned to the squad room he saw Davis sitting at her desk, scribbling on a yellow legal size pad.

"So whatta ya got for me good looking?" Pirelli asked.

Davis looked up from her desk and said happily, "You might be on to something, Pirelli. They got a fresh one with a gun in the four-five. The medical examiner fixed the time of death at around the same time that the cop was shot."

"No shit," Pirelli said with a big grin on his face. "What's the DOA's name?"

"JoJo Cutolo. The detective that caught the case sez he's a wannabe in the Grimaldi family. Sez he had a diamond ring on his pinky and cash in his pocket when they found him. So obviously, it was a 'hit'."

"Any witnesses?"

"Not that we know of. Cutolo caught it in a deserted construction site. No one even heard the shots."

"Did they find anything at the scene?"

"Yeah, three nine millimeter Winchester shells."

"Winchesters," Pirelli said excitedly. Hey, that's great. The shells we recovered in the vestibule were Winchesters. Thanks a lot, Davis. And just for being so helpful, you can take me to lunch tomorrow."

"I'll be my pleasure, so long as you pick up the tab."

Pirelli immediately called the 45th precinct. He left a message for the detective assigned to the Cutolo homicide to call him ASAP.

Pirelli no sooner hung up the phone than Solly walked into the squad wearing a big grin.

Pirelli eyes brightened when he saw his partner's shining face. "So lemme hear it, Solly," Pirelli said quickly. "I can see from that shit-eating grin on your face that your pigeon has something good for us."

Solly sat down in a not too sturdy wooden chair with a splintered armrest, I'll tell you this much kid, if he ain't bullshiting, he's got something very good."

"You mean he knows who shot the cop?" Pirelli said excitedly.

"Not that good, kid, but he claims he can give us 'Mad Dog' Nelson. Remember him?"

"Mad Dog Nelson! You mean the cocksucker that robbed the jewelry store on forty-eight and Madison a couple of years ago and blew away the owner for no reason."

"That's him, pal."

"Hey, that'd be terrific, but I don't know, Solly, Nelson's been in the wind since the murder."

"I know that, kid, but Joey tells me he'll be in town for a short visit real soon. He sez he'll gimme the details if we can cut him a good deal."

"What was he collared for?"

"Grand larceny, he got caught hijacking a trailer load of men's suits."

"That ain't too heavy. What's he looking for?"

"What else, a walk, or at least probation."

"What does his sheet look like?"

"Make that sheets kid. He's been collared so many times that a conviction here could put him away for more years than he's got left."

"No wonder why he wants to work something out. Whatta think you can do for him, Solly?"

"Well, he's never been convicted of a violent crime, so I'm sure the DA will cut him a good deal.

"So how'd ya leave off with him?"

"I told him I'd get back to him tomorrow, after I run it by the DA's office. I'll stop there first thing in the morning to see what I can do."

"Sounds good to me, Solly."

"By the way, kid, did Davis come up with anything for us?"

"As a matter of fact she did."

"Great, lemme hear it."

When Pirelli told Solly about the Winchester shells that were found at the scene of the Cutolo homicide, Solly held a clenched fist above his head and roared, "Yeah!"

Their guess paid off. Pirelli speculated that the cop-killer murdered Cutolo and headed straight back to the Blue Grotto still carrying the murder weapon. The cop saw Ardone carrying the gun and Ardone got the drop on him.

"We'll know for sure once ballistics compares the shells found at the scene of the Cutolo homicide with the shells found in the vestibule of the Blue Grotto Lounge," Pirelli said. "If the shells were fired from the same gun, bang, that's the motive for the murder."

"Poor cop." He goes to write a traffic summons and winds up buying the fuckin ranch. What a job this is."

"You're right, Solly. You never know what does gonna happen."

"Tell me about it," Solly said glumly. "It reminds me of the time when I was a young detective in the burglary squad. Me and my partner wanted to talk to some dick head about a bullshit larceny. The guy drove a cab at night so we decided to grab him in the morning when he turned in his cab. So, one morning we waited for him at the taxi garage. When he didn't show we left. Would you believe that later in the day we found out that during the night the prick stuck up the wrong bodega and got himself blown away."

"No shit."

"Yep. Now just imagine if it was the other way around and he'd done the killing. The sonofabitch probably would've turned in his cab in the morning like nothing happened. Meanwhile, me and my partner would've leisurely walked over to talk to him about the larceny. He probably woulda thought we wanted him for the homicide and would've blown us the fuck away before we knew what hit us."

"Unbelievable!"

"Yeah, and God forbid you're looking for a perp and you see a guy that fits the description. You go over to talk to him and he makes a move like he's reaching. What are you supposed to do then? If you shoot and it turns out the guy's clean the first thing that happens is that some of our 'upstanding citizens' look to crucify you."

Pirelli agreed with a nod of his head.

"They wanna know why you fired your gun," Solly was ranting. "He didn't have a gun, they'll say. Like you got some kinda fucking crystal ball that works in slow motion. Well kid, you wanna know what I say? I say if you have good reason to believe that your life, or anybody else's life for that matter, is in danger, I say empty your fuckin gun before it's too late."

"Your wrong Solly, You should never empty your gun at anyone, no mater how dangerous the situation appears to be. You should just fire one shot, stop, then look to see if the guy actually has a gun. Haven't you read the ACLU handbook?"

"Yeah sure," Solly said. "Meanwhile, you get blown the fuck

away. I'll tell you what pal. I'd rather take my chances with twenty three grand jurors than six pall bearers in blue uniforms."

It was a long and hectic day, but a productive one. The detectives were off to a fairly good start for a homicide investigation without a single witness. A ballistic technician confirmed the shells found at the scene of the Cutolo homicide and the shells found in the vestibule of the Blue Grotto Lounge were fired from the same gun. That fact did not help the detectives identify the killer, but they now knew that the man that killed JoJo Cutolo also killed the young cop in the vestibule of the lounge.

The detectives would follow the porter and observe his every move. As soon as they gathered enough information on the man to convince him to cooperate, Pirelli would confront him. Tranqualina knew the name of the man who ran through the lounge and the detectives were determined to get it.

The tedious and time-consuming task of following around the porter from the Blue Grotto Lounge began immediately.

CHAPTER EIGHTEEN

⁓𝓂⁓

The next morning Solly was up early. After a quick breakfast he headed directly downtown to meet with Deputy District Attorney Warren Buckner, Chief of the Homicide Bureau. Buckner was a tall and physically fit man in his late forties. His close cropped dark brown hair, square jaw and lean figure gave him an old-school military bearing, not surprising for a former Major in the Judge Advocates office and graduate of West Point, Class of '51. Solly and Buckner had worked many cases together over the years. Like most of the career prosecutors assigned to the Homicide Bureau, Buckner trusted Solly and valued his judgment.

After the customary how's everything Solly got down to business; a deal for Fat Mike in exchange for information leading to the capture of a cold-blooded killer named Nicholas "Mad Dog" Nelson. Solly reminded the ADA that Nelson had served twelve years for manslaughter, compliments of a younger Solly Samuels and a then newly minted prosecutor named Warren Buckner.

Shortly after Nelson's release from Attica three years earlier, he stuck up the owner of an exclusive Madison Avenue jewelry store. Nelson boasted that he would never return to prison and to make good his boasting put two bullets into the heart of the sole eyewitness to the crime.

Weeks after the murder, Nelson, felt the heat of Pirelli and Samuels closing in on him and fled the jurisdiction to places unknown, never to be heard from again. Samuels had put the word on the street that anyone willing to give up Nelson would be owed a favor, a very big favor. Now, Fat Mike needed that favor.

After he left the DA's office, Solly visited Fat Mike as promised. He told him that the DA had agreed to allow him to plead guilty to lesser charges and serve no more than two years in exchange for information leading to the capture of Nelson. Fat Mike took the offer. He told Solly that Nelson was planning a short stay at the Waldorf Astoria Hotel and would be flying in from California the very next day, traveling under the name of Robert Reed.

Solly returned to the precinct and immediately confirmed Fat Mike's information. A passenger named Robert Reed was ticketed to travel the next day from Los Angeles to New York on Pan Am flight 2438. The flight was scheduled to land at New York's LaGuardia Airport at 2 in the afternoon. Solly and Pirelli mapped out a plan to apprehend their prey. They would confront the unsuspecting Nelson as he entered the lobby of the Waldorf. Solly would move in from the side and Pirelli would challenge Nelson head on. Nelson was a small and slight man and the detectives knew they would have no problem over-powering him.

After going over their plan several times, Solly said soberly, "Oh by the way, kid, there's one thing more."

"What's that?"

"We don't tell anybody what we're up too."

"Not even the boss?"

"Especially the boss," Solly said emphatically.

"But won't he be pissed off? I mean if we don't tell him what we're doing?"

"Oh when he finds out he'll be pissed off all right, but who cares? If we tell him in advance he'll wanna send a sergeant and a fuckin army with us. And you know if that happens something's sure to get fucked up." No kid, we'll handle this alone."

"You sure about this, Solly, I mean…"

"Deadly sure, after we collar Nelson, we'll tell the boss we just happened to be in the hotel looking for somebody else when we spotted Nelson walking in. He'll know we're fulla shit, but so what. We'll have our man and everybody will be happy. We'll just have to move quickly and be careful, that's all," Solly said confidently.

"I know what you mean, Solly. This Nelson fuck is one dangerous sonofabitch."

CHAPTER NINETEEN

E arly the next afternoon Solly was sitting in a wide leather club chair just off to the side of the main entrance of the Waldorf Astoria, gazing at the hoards of people entering and leaving the hotel. It was a little before 1 p.m. and the lobby traffic was hectic.

Solly's call to La Quardia minutes earlier confirmed that Nelson's plane was on time and scheduled to touch down at 2 p.m.. Having more than an hour to wait, his apprehension continued to build. He was especially troubled by Pirelli's cavalier attitude with the entire affair. As soon as they arrived at the hotel Pirelli announced he had to relieve himself and whistled his way to a restroom.

Trying to relax, Solly leaned back in his chair and closed his eyes. His mind wandered to more pleasant thoughts. It was the fifteenth of September. The year had made its three-quarter cycle and the summer he loved so much was almost gone. And even though it wasn't official yet, fall had arrived and with it the promise of cool crisp days ahead. Solly could picture the parallel rivers of Manhattan sparkling, magically reflecting the mid-September sky above and the parks alive with early color. He could envision even more picturesque days to come.

Another season had arrived. The women looked grander and the children of fifty different cultures continued to play on the streets of the city. He smiled as he envisioned the street walking prostitutes that suffered minor strategic disadvantages, now having to use evening wraps to warm their wares.

Suddenly Solly's thoughts returned to the matter at hand. He was comfortable with the plan he and Pirelli had carefully plotted to apprehend Nelson, but now, as the time for Nelson's arrival grew closer, he wasn't too sure. He glanced at a huge wall clock and silently cursed his errant partner. Fifteen minutes had passed. 'Bathroom my ass,' he thought angrily. 'I bet the sonofabitch sitting at a bar somewhere.'

When he could wait no longer, Solly jumped to his feet and made a beeline for the hotel's cocktail lounge. The moment he entered the dimly lighted interior, he spied Pirelli seated precariously on a high backless stool. He was leaning forward engaged in jovial conversation with a well-endowed barmaid.

Solly climbed upon the stool next to his partner and whispered. "For Christ's sake Pirelli, Why the hell do you have to drink now for? Don't you know what time it is?"

"Relax Solly, we got plenty of time. You want a little taste? It'll help you calm down."

"Later. We can drink later for Christ sake," Solly shot back. "But not now, damn it!"

"Why not now?"

"Cause we gotta be sharp, that's why."

"That's your problem, Solly. You don't drink when you need it most. That's why every time we go to a pistol match you never shoot a perfect score," Pirelli said jovially. "C'mon, have a little taste. You look like you could use one."

Solly glared angrily at his partner, "C'mon kid," Solly pleaded, "I hope it won't come to it, but we may have to use our guns."

Pirelli shook his head and laughed. "More the reason to have a little taste."

Realizing that it was useless, Solly, slid from the stool and headed back to the hotel lobby. Preparing for the worst possible scenario he slipped his hand under his sport jacket and carefully slid the weapon from its holster and buried it into the waistband of his trousers for quicker access. Then he returned to his station in the opulently appointed hotel lobby wondering if Nelson would actually show.

A few minutes later, Pirelli placed an empty glass and a two dollar tip on the bar, blew a friendly kiss to the bar maid, then made his way to the men's room. He entered a stall and latched the door behind him. Unbuttoning his sport jacket, he removed his service revolver from its holster, opened the cylinder and carefully examined the gun's six shot load. Satisfied with his inspection, he closed the cylinder, listening to the re-assuring click of the mechanism locking in place. Then he returned the weapon back into its sheath and walked back to the hotel lobby.

"So here I am, Solly," he announced gleefully as he joined his visibly nervous partner. "How's about we play a game of liar's poker while we wait?"

Solly just shook his head in disbelief. "This ain't no time to fuck around, Pirelli. We gotta set up for Christ sake. He could be walking in the door any minute now."

"Relax Solly, I called the airport. The planes on time, he won't be getting here for at least another twenty minutes. That's if he comes at all."

Solly just sighed in frustration.

Pirelli took a position directly in front of the entrance way and waited.

Exactly twenty-two minutes later, Mad Dog Nelson calmly eased his way through the hotel's revolving door. The detectives were set to pounce on him.

"The best laid plans of mice and men…," suddenly became a reality. Nelson had no sooner entered the lobby when a small boy, standing not more than ten feet away, began fighting with his younger sister. At the sound of the little girl's shrill cry of rage, Nelson turned to see what was causing the commotion. His mouth went slack as he stared at the equally startled Solly Samuels. Nelson immediately recognized the rotund detective. Then he saw the other man he had run from three years earlier.

Pirelli's sport jacket was unbuttoned, exposing the bulge of his holstered gun just over his right hip.

"Well talk about a coincidence," Pirelli said to the man. "Here me and my partner are waiting for our ladies to arrive and who comes walking through the door but Nicky Nelson. Who'd ever believe that?"

Nelson was breathing rapidly, his brain now processing his dilemma. 'This can't be happening. It can't be over for me,' he thought wildly.

Nelson's right hand began inching towards his belt. His fingers now only inches from the revolver that was tucked into his waistband.

Some people were frozen in places while others kept coming and going from all directions.

A uniformed bellhop standing only a few feet from Nelson stared in open astonishment at the dark butt of a revolver now clearly visible in his waistband.

Just off to the side, an elderly woman had placed her hand to her throat, spellbound at the drama unfolding before her very eyes.

'It is now Pirelli's show', Solly thought. 'If only the kid hadn't screamed.'

Watching the way Nelson's hand inched lower, Pirelli shook his head and said calmly, "You really don't want to do what you're thinking, scum bag. Now be nice and put your hands over your head. I'm giving you this one chance to stay alive, so don't blow it. If you go for the gun, you're dead."

Although the unfolding drama had taken three years in the making, it now took but seconds for Nelson to find himself faced with the crisis of a lifetime. He swallowed thickly knowing that barely an inch separated his groping fingers and the gun in his waist band.

"Now it's just you and me," Pirelli said icily, watching the intense struggle in Nelson's eyes. "Listen my friend, I really don't wanna have to kill you, but I'm telling you, if you go for that gun, if your hand moves any lower, I will. You're a brutal bastard, killing a defenseless old man for no reason. And mister, I have no qualms about killing you. You go for that gun and you won't even get a shot off."

"Fuck you," Nelson cried hysterically. "You ain't taking me alive, you cocksucker." Suddenly Nelson's hand flashed down to the checkered butt and the weapon appeared in his hand.

Pirelli's years of firearms practice once again bore fruit. His movements were little more than a blur. His hand flipped up the tail of his sport jacket and his .38 caliber service revolver was already firing before Nelson could aim his weapon. Pirelli's gun boomed two times in the space of a second. The two shots found their mark. Mad Dog Nelson was dead before he hit the floor.

Horrified onlookers were screaming and people were fleeing in every direction.

Pirelli calmly stepped forward and looked down at the man who chose to die.

Solly held the crowd back as the detectives waited for the screaming sirens of the responding patrol cars grew louder.

By that evening the department review, the media and hotel chaos had all played down.

The partners were back on the trail of a cop killer.

CHAPTER TWENTY

The surveillance of the tight-lipped porter from the Blue Grotto Lounge paid off. He was easy to follow and after just three weeks the surveillance team knew more about Cosmo Tranqualina's past and present lifestyle than did the man's own wife. Pirelli was ready to pressure him into cooperating.

Pirelli and Samuels mapped out a plan. Pirelli would confront the man away from the lounge and convince him that no one would ever know he cooperated. Tranqualina did the weekly grocery shopping at a local supermarket. It was the perfect place for Pirelli to approach the unsuspecting porter.

On the day he planned to confront the porter, Pirelli was up before dawn. He decided to jog a few miles before meeting Solly. A morning jog, especially before a critical stage of an investigation, always helped to sharpen his thought process.

After his jog, he returned to his apartment, cleaned up and waited for Solly.

When they got to the supermarket they watched as hoards of morning shoppers began to enter the huge emporium. They saw their target enter the store. Several minutes later, Pirelli entered. Samuels remained in the squad car.

Pirelli found an empty shopping cart, placed several items into it, and began searching for his prey. A few minutes later he spotted the man at the rear of the third aisle, studying a long shopping list. He casually rolled his shopping cart along side of the unsuspecting porter and greeted him with a big smile.

"Hey Cosmo, how ya been?" he said cheerfully,

"Detective Pirelli, what a bigga surprise, I'm a no expecta ta see you. You shoppa here too?"

"Actually I don't," Pirelli replied.

"Then whadda you do here?"

"Actually, I've been lookin for you."

"You look a for me? In a da store?"

"That's right Cosmo. You see, I know you shop here every Thursday."

"Hey! How you know I shoppa here?"

"That was easy Cosmo. You see, I know a lot about you."

"Yeah but how…"

"I'll tell you how," Pirelli interrupted. "You see, me and a team of detectives have been living with you for the past three weeks."

"What! You mean a you follow me around?"

"That's right, Cosmo. And we've been asking a lot of questions too, discreetly of course. You see Cosmo, I need the name of the man that ran through the bar after the cop was shot and the way I figure you ain't giving it to me unless I make it worth your while."

"Listen, like I'm a tell a you before. I'm a know nothing, I'm a see nothing and I'm a hear nothing. Now why you no leave a me the fuck alone?'"

"I'll tell you what Cosmo, you hear me out a minute. Then if you still want me to, 'I'll leave you the fuck alone' as you so politely put it. Right now, I don't want you to say another word, just listen."

Tranqualina nodded his okay.

"You see Cosmo, I know you're a family man. I know you go to church with the wife and kids every Sunday and that you're into the honor and respect thing. You know all that good stuff. Now I bet your wife and kids would really be disappointed if they found out that you're visiting another man's wife," Pirelli said smiling. "Twice a week no less, like clockwork, every Tuesday and Friday afternoon if I recall my notes correctly. And I'll bet her husband would be disappointed too if I told him. I'm told Sicilians aren't too happy when someone's fuckin their wife, especially when it's a goombah of his," Pirelli said coarsely.

"What! You no gonna…" the man's voice trailed off in frightening disbelief.

"Hold on, Cosmo, I ain't finished yet. I got a lot more to say. Now screwing your friend's wife is bad enough but it ain't the worst of your problems. The way I see it, it's that bench warrant for that Florida thing you got involved in two years ago that you really gotta worry about. Oh I know it's a bullshit charge in the overall scheme of things, but it's enough to put you away for a year or so. And if I should happen to tell my friends at immigration about it, you'll have a big problem there, too. I mean after all, we both know that you're not a citizen yet. Now wouldn't that really fuck up your plans? Instead of moving your family out West like you're planning to do, you'll be moving them back to Sicily. You see Cosmo, I also know that you're getting ready to move to Arizona and out of that cesspool you're living in. Hey, not that I blame you. If I lived in your part of Brooklyn, I'd move out too. And I don't have a family to raise. Yeah Cosmo, I could hurt you real bad if you force me to, but I really don't think you want me to do that. Do you? Anyway, I said what I hadda say. Now that we got that out of the way do you still want me to 'leave you the fuck alone'?"

"Pirelli… I'm a swear. I'm a no see who shoot a da cop. You must a believe a me," Cosmo said trembling. "God, you must a believe a me," he repeated frantically, his voice crackling in despair.

.

"Hold on a minute, Cosmo. Relax. I believe you when you say you didn't see who shot the cop. But don't worry you can still get out from under this."

Tranqualina was visibly relieved by Pirelli's comforting remark. "Anything...anything," he said excitedly! "Just a so you keep a my name out. Just a tell a me what I gotta do."

"Good. Now all I need from you is the name of the man who ran through the lounge. Then when you give me the name, you'll be home free. I'll forget everything I just told you. It'll be like this conversation never happened."

"But Pirelli, I'm a no see the man who run a thru the lounge. I'm a swear. I'm a behind a the bar. On a the floor"

Pirelli's demeanor instantly changed. "Listen you lying piece of shit," Pirelli growled. "I'm through playing fucking games with you, so stop jerking me off. Now you take this fucking piece of paper and write the name of the cocksucker you no see run a through da lounge, otherwise I'm locking your miserable ass up right now. Then instead of going home with your pasta and provolone, you can call your wife from Rikers and listen to her bawl. And next week, after I send your ass back to Florida, I'll do you a big favor and drive your wife and kids to the welfare office so they can pay the rent. Now write the fucking name down before I change my mind. Then after I see the name you wrote, you can eat the fucking paper if you wanna. And don't try to be cute cocksucker, it better be the right name. It so happens somebody already gave me the name of the sonofabitch who shot the cop. So the name you give me better match."

"But what if I'm a give a you the right a name and it a no match the name like a you got?"

"If it don't match you're in deep shit. But don't worry, you gimme the right name and it'll match."

Pirelli stared menacingly as the terrified man reached for the paper and quickly scribbled a name on it.

Pirelli looked at the name on the paper and nodded his head. "Okay Cosmo, it matches. Now you can get the fuck outta here and forget we ever spoke. But if you tell anybody about our conversation the deal is off."

"Whatta you crazy? I'm a no tela nobody," the man said. "I'm a swear."

Pirelli pushed his cart to the front of the store and left the supermarket. He was smiling broadly as he slid into the passenger's seat of the squad car.

Samuels immediately congratulated him. "You did it, huh kid," Solly said happily. "He gave you the name, didn't he?"

"Hey, how'd you know?"

"By the shit eating grin on your face, that's how."

"You're right on, Solly."

"But how can we be sure he gave you the right name?"

Listen Solly, if you'd seen the look on his face when I told him about the broad, you'd know he was telling the truth. And then when I told him about the Florida thing, he went completely marshmallow. He didn't know whether to shit or go blind. No Solly, there's no doubt in my mine. He gave me the name of our man. I'd bet my life on it."

"Well let's have the name for Christ sake. Who is it?"

"Ardone, Frank Ardone."

"Ardone, Christ, he's a 'made man' in the Grimaldi family."

"I know, Solly. I know."

CHAPTER TWENTY-ONE

Ardone, 43, was raised by caring Italian-American, middle class parents who enrolled him in every conceivable sport and enrichment program. Yet to his parent's dismay, he was an unmanageable and disruptive child. He displayed a volcanic temper and early on acquired a formidable reputation among his peers as one to be feared.

Teachers noted that he seemed to be a born leader who apparently dominated a group of boys that gathered around him. They regarded his uncontrollable temper as unfortunate, for they saw a bright boy that, despite his innate intelligence, had little interest in a formal education. His lack of interest in school continued into his teenage years. He was convinced that his nimble wit and the visage he admired in his bathroom mirror were all that he would need to make it in life. But that teenage delusion was soon to disappear.

Shortly before his fourteenth birthday, his mother and father were killed in an auto accident and his world immediately began to crumble. After spending several days with a close family friend, the devastated youth went to live with an unmarried uncle. His two year-old sister having no other place to go was placed in foster care.

Ardone's uncle drank too much and parented too little. He lived in a low-income project in Brooklyn's notorious Red Hook section. Home for mostly Sicilian immigrants recruited for work on the Brooklyn waterfront, the "Hook" attracted people whom other Italian immigrants looked down upon. A life of back-wrenching work on the docks produced toughened men who walked around with cargo hooks hanging from their belts. Often, disputes were settled with the use of these hooks and the neighborhood had more scarred men than any other place in Brooklyn.

Ardone's new home was an unkempt apartment and the small room set aside for the youngster was sparsely furnished. It offered none of the comforts he had known before the death of his parents.

The first night at his new home was an experience the boy would never forget. Even the Saturday evening blasting of loud radios in and out of the building could not drown out the utter despair he felt. Burying his head in a pillow that needed laundering, he tried vainly to wipe out the recent traumatic events. Finally, after a restless and fitful night, he arose in his new surroundings and walked to the bedroom window for a breath of fresh air. Looking down at the huge courtyard below, he was surprised to see several homeless people, obviously in need of psychiatric care, roaming about unsupervised. Ardone's eyes traveled the entire courtyard. Soon he would learn that in his new environment, violence and criminality was an accepted way of life.

Later that morning, the youngster mustered the will to venture outside and into the huge courtyard. The denizens of the street turned suspiciously at the sight of an outsider on their turf. One strapping youth with hair slicked back into a prominent duck-tail, wearing a ribbed tee shirt and a spotted bandana tightly bound tightly around his forehead, was the first to challenge the bewildered youth.

"Hey!" he cried out, "You lookin for somebody?"

Although alarmed by the threatening sound of his inquisitor's voice, Ardone concealed his nervousness. "I just moved around here," he answered calmly. "And I'm checkin out the hood."

After explaining his presence in the area, Ardone was greeted, although coolly, by the group of teenagers that had gathered around to size him up. Unbeknownst to Ardone, this unscheduled turn in his life would prove to be the genesis of his descent into the world of organized crime.

It wasn't long before Ardone was accepted in the neighborhood gang. He started running with a bad crowd and before long he stopped attending school. His friends continually had minor scrapes with the law. The petty offenses that he and his newfound friends were arrested for resulted in little more than hollow rebukes from jaded judges and a quick release from an overcrowded court system. It was less than a year, however, before young Ardone had his first serious encounter with the criminal justice system. He and two of his friends were arrested for robbing a subway token booth clerk. After a relatively quick court proceeding and a plea of guilty, the now street-hardened youth was off to spend the remainder of his teenage years in a juvenile detention center in upstate New York. It was during his stay at the institution that he met Edward Grimaldi.

Grimaldi was a small youth, but fortunately the nephew of a reputed organized crime family "Don." Ardone was intrigued by his new roommate's tales about his uncle's glamorous way of life and plotted a course of action to ingratiate himself to him. Now close to sixteen, Ardone had grown considerably and his size alone soon had earned him the respect of the other boys. He would become Grimaldi's self-appointed protector in a world where only the fittest survived.

Ardone's plan worked well and before too long he and Grimaldi became close friends. Four years later, upon their release, Grimaldi spoke to his uncle about Ardone and soon both boys entered the world of organized crime.

Gaining acceptance in the Mafia is a slow process. A recruit puts in a period of apprenticeship as a made member's stooge; parking his car; running his errands; lighting his cigars, and more.

To accelerate his apprenticeship, Ardone sought assignments endemic to aspirants for higher family positions; assignments that included the collection of debts; strong-arming malefactors; matters involving prostitution; various other nefarious duties and, in some cases, killings. After ten years of performing the assorted jobs higher-ranking family members did not dirty their hands on, his loyalty and uncanny ability to get things done were noticed. He was regarded as an invaluable asset to the family.

Having had demonstrated a talent as an entrepreneur, with extraordinary organizational and business skills, Ardone steadily moved ahead in the family hierarchy. He demonstrated that he had the proper combination of qualities that deserve higher rank, most notably, a willingness to commit murder.

Five years later, he "made his bones" and was formally inducted into the family. He was given a crew of his own and was named to manage a number of sophisticated prostitution rings that operated out of several of Grimaldi's cocktail lounges and clubs throughout the city. Ardone made a great deal of money for the family and not much less for himself.

His one serious shortcoming, other than his foul mouth, explosive temper, and frequent violent outbursts, was his addiction to gambling. He traveled often to Atlantic City and Las Vegas and it was not unusual for him to lose hundreds of dollars on the turn of a card or on a single roll of the dice.

Gambling losses often prompted him to seek out other, although more risky, business ventures to supplement his income. It was this need for ready cash that proved to be his downfall.

He spent a lot of time at the Blue Grotto Lounge and whereas his visits hardly proved that he was involved in the murder of Police Officer McCarthy, the revelation further convinced the team of Samuels and Pirelli that Ardone was their man.

But did he have a bullet wound in his shoulder?

CHAPTER TWENTY-TWO

The detectives learned that Ardone was a health fanatic who had a standing appointment with a personal trainer every Tuesday and Friday morning.

Pirelli looked to his partner. "Well Solly, he said, it looks like it's time for you to lose some weight."

"What the fuck are you talking about for Christ sake? Lose some weight."

"Because you're gonna have to join Ardone's health club so you can take a peek at his shoulder to make sure he's got a bullet wound there. You can pretend you joined the club to lose weight. Nobody will ever suspect your wanting to lose weight is a ruse to eyeball Ardone's shoulder. Now would they Solly?" Pirelli said looking at his partner's huge waistline."

"Very funny, Pirelli. Very fuckin funny."

"I'm serious Solly. Before we can even think about applying for a search warrant to forcibly remove the bullet from the prick's shoulder, you're gonna have to swear that he's got a bullet wound there. Meanwhile while you're playing around at the gym, I'll get Buckner to subpoena the Greenwich hospital records. If the location of the bullet wound in Boffardi's shoulder matches the location of the wound in Ardone's shoulder, then with everything else we got, we should have the "probable cause" needed to get a search warrant."

"Hey, if it's 'PC' you're worried about, kid, there's an easier way to get it. All we gotta do is show the medical people in Greenwich a photo of Ardone. If they confirm that Boffardi and Ardone are one and the same, bingo, we got it."

"You're right about that, Solly. That'll give us the "PC" we need okay. But if we do it that way, there's always the chance that someone will tip Ardone that we're looking at him. After all, he's a cautious fuck. Who knows what he's done to cover his tracks. If he finds out we're on to him he'll be in the fucking wind before we can move. No Solly, I'd rather not talk to the people in Connecticut unless it becomes absolutely necessary. Doing it my way will be a little more work for us but I think under the circumstances, it's the safest way to go. Don't forget, as I told you, probable cause for a search warrant doesn't mean we're gonna get it"

"You're probably right, kid, whatever you say."

After several visits to Ardone's health club, Solly confirmed that Ardone indeed had a bullet wound in his left shoulder. Baring any constitutional constraints, the detectives were on their way to removing the incriminating bullet from Ardone's shoulder. They would have no problem showing that the bullet was of vital importance in their homicide investigation, thus establishing the need for a search warrant to forcibly remove it.

But they knew that before issuing a search warrant, the court would have to consider to what extent the health of Ardone would be impaired by its removal. The detectives were cautious. They did not want to apply for a warrant until they felt certain that the warrant would issue. If their application was denied, Ardone might somehow learn that he had been targeted as a murderer. A possibility they wanted to avoid until absolutely necessary to do so.

The detectives decided to seek a medical opinion from a police surgeon regarding the medical risk to Ardone.

Solly contacted the Police Surgeon's office and asked to speak to a doctor concerning the medical risk involved in removing a bullet from a suspect. They were fortunate. A Deputy Surgeon was available to meet with them the very next day. The surgeon had worked with the detectives in the past on other matters and when they arrived at her office, it was a warm reunion.

"Well if it isn't the dynamic duo from Manhattan South Homicide," she said. How's everything going with you gentlemen?"

"Fine, Dr. Ruiz, and thanks for seeing us on such short notice."

"Don't mention it, Solly. Now, what can I do for you two today?"

Pirelli looked at the shapely woman and grinned widely.

Responding to Pirelli's silent message, the surgeon added quickly: "I stand corrected Solly. What is it that I can do for YOU," she said emphatically. "I already know what I can do for lover boy here."

"Hey! That ain't fair, Ida," Pirelli said. "You put me in my place the last time I had the pleasure of being in your company."

"You're too much, Pirelli," the attractive woman said. "One of these days I may just surprise you and say yes."

"I should be so lucky."

"Okay. But let me warn you in advance that I always carry a scalpel with me on a first date."

"As far as I'm concerned pretty lady, it'll be well worth the risk," Pirelli said boldly.

After Pirelli was done flirting, the detectives got down to the business at hand. Solly handed the Boffardi x-rays and medical records to the surgeon and asked for her opinion on whether forcibly removing the bullet would present a serious medical risk to the patient.

"Give me a couple of days," she said. "I'll have something prepared for you by then. But I think you may have a legal problem here, too."

"Whatta ya mean, doc," Solly asked.

"Well I'm not a lawyer Solly, but in my opinion there's a right to privacy issue here, too. Have you spoken to anyone at the District Attorney's office?"

"Not yet," Solly replied. "We wanted to get a medical opinion from you before we asked for a legal one."

"Okay, I'll get back to you as soon as I can."

"Great. And thanks again, doc," Solly said, as the detectives got up to leave.

Pirelli just smiled and blew a kiss as he followed his partner out the door.

After they left the Surgeon's office Solly returned to the squad room determined to catch up on backlogged paper work.

Pirelli would visit the New York University Law Library to research the legal issue raised by the Police Surgeon. He had dated the school's law librarian several times and after setting the time and place for a future date, she was glad to help him with his research.

It was almost 6 p.m. before Pirelli had gotten all the information he had sought at the library. Exhausted, he called Solly and told him he was calling it quits for the day.

As he walked out into an unusually balmy fall evening, his thoughts suddenly turned to Mary Sorvino. Almost a month had passed since he first met the woman and, although he did not want to get involved with his best friend's neighbor, he just couldn't seem to put her out of his mind. He had made no effort to contact her since the Sunday dinner and decided it was time to pay her a call.

CHAPTER TWENTY-THREE

M ary Sorvino stepped out of the shower, reached for a towel and began toweling her hair. Then she slipped into an old terry cloth robe and walked barefooted to the kitchen. She poured herself a stem of white wine then returned to the living room to relax.

The sound of the door buzzer startled her. Since the buzzer had sounded from her apartment door and not from the tiny vestibule at the street entrance, she simply presumed the caller to be one of the neighbors. The downstairs heavy outer door of wrought iron and glass was always locked and could be opened only with a specially designed key. Mary felt safe in her apartment knowing that the building provided such security not to mention that a police detective lived in the apartment directly above her.

Quickly shoving her feet into tattered woolly mules, she padded to the door and called out softly.

"Yes? Who is it?"

"It's Mr. Lasagna," Pirelli's deep voice said from out side the door. "Who did you expect?"

"Whom did she expect? Indeed!" she thought, annoyed at the unexpected visit.

"Talk about nerve," she continued to simmer... "Does he really think all he has to do is come to the door and whistle?"

Mary shook her head, recalling in detail the abortive blind date of three Sundays past. He had dutifully escorted her to the door, but when he failed to ask her for her telephone number, she assumed that she would never see him again. Now, just like that, he had the gall to come uninvited.

"Hey lady," Pirelli sang out. "It ain't polite to keep a lasagna waiting in the hall all night!"

Mary smiled in spite of herself. Her hands flew mechanically to her hair, venting out the dampness as best she could. She took a deep breath, unlatched the security chain and opened the door.

Pirelli walked into a large living room. In one corner was an upright piano. Across from it, two five-foot couches sat at right angles to one another with a rosewood coffee table, in between. To the right of the doorway a narrow hallway led to a fair-sized bedroom and full bath. To the left of the doorway were the dining area, eat-in kitchen and a TV room.

"I wasn't expecting company."

"I'm not company," he said, stepping past her and entering the apartment as she shook her head in disbelief. She closed the door and leaned back against it, smiling wryly at what Rae had told her about his occasional quirky behavior. But now, increasingly irked by his insufferable chauvinism, she decided to show her disinterest with some polite conversation before inviting him to leave. A comeuppance for his arrogance was probably long overdue, she thought, slowly shaking her head. It wouldn't be the worst thing in the world to teach him some humility. But as she stared into his drawn, tired face, she found her consternation waning and was surprised at the sudden comfort she felt because of his presence. But why should she have feelings one way or the other, she wondered. Aside from the Sunday dinner, the man was still a total stranger to her. She would be the last one in the world to deny that since that day in the garden, it was his looks that had attracted her to him, but now, the only thing she should feel was indignation and annoyance. 'And will you just look at how he makes himself right at home," she thought, eyeing the way he threw his topcoat over a chair before casually settling into the sofa. Yet, she continued to be warmed by his presence.

"Would you like some coffee?"

Pirelli grinned at her. "Coffee is for breakfast," he told her. "I don't suppose you have any scotch lying around?"

Raising her brows at his presumptuous demand, she nonetheless headed for the kitchen, calling back to him, "As long as I'm getting the scotch, is there anything else you'd like; perhaps a sandwich or maybe even a steak? I mean, don't be bashful." Despite her annoyance she was in a playful mood.

Pirelli smiled and said, adopting a less abrasive style.

"Just the drink will be fine, thank you."

Placing the bottle and a glass filled with ice on the coffee table, she swept past him in a huff, heading for her bedroom. The door closed behind her with thud.

When Mary emerged ten minutes later, her chestnut hair had been brushed to form softly curling waves. She had applied some lipstick and now threw off the fragrance of expensive perfume. She had remained dressed in the old flannel robe letting him know that if she really were concerned about what he thought, she would have changed into something more appealing. She seated herself at the far end of the Victorian sofa and stared at him.

"I see that you managed to pour a drink all by yourself," she said bluntly.

Pirelli grinned at her. "Yeah, but to tell the truth, I'd enjoy it more if you joined me."

Mary ignored the overture and said matter of factly, "Before you knocked on my door," she said softly, "you were upstairs, visiting with Rae and Solly, weren't you?"

"Wrong," he said quickly, "I haven't seen Solly for three days."

"Really, suppose you tell me how you got in without ringing the outside bell?"

"Actually, I caught someone leaving and thought I'd surprise you."

She felt a strange bodily flash as she searched his face for signs of sincerity. "Are you saying that you came here just to see me?"

"That's what I'm saying."

"And you figured you could just come barging in without even a phone call? Do you think that your friendship with Solly and Rae gives you license to come and go as you please?"

"I'm not even sure myself, why I came, Mary, but I'm glad I did. This has been one helluva two weeks for me, not to mention the way today went. But if you want me to go, just say so."

He finished his drink keenly aware of how often she had crept into his thoughts since the day they met. Staring at her, he found those thoughts to be disquieting as he wondered why he should think of her at all. His lifestyle was structured to avoid permanent attachments; it was more than her body, he thought trying not to look at her. His was intimate with scores of beautiful women who would welcome his popping in unannounced.

He had given her the opportunity. All she had to do was suggest that now was the proper time for him to leave, but first she would clearly spell out the ground rules for any future involvement. 'There must be no room for any misunderstanding on his part,' she thought.

"Listen to me," Mary said, trying to pick her way through an interpersonal minefield. "I'll bet the thought of calling me up for a date never even entered your mind."

Pirelli nodded. "You're right," he said seemingly chastened. "But only because I've been so busy lately."

Not persuaded by either the poor excuse or its sincerity, Mary was about to point towards the door, when he turned to face her directly.

"The problem is that I'm so wrapped up in this case, that I can't do anything right," he said glumly. "And that includes after dinner that Sunday when I should have told you how beautiful you are."

He had said it so matter-of-factly, that Mary, still annoyed by his barging in uninvited, almost missed it. Then, realizing what he had said, she anxiously searched his eyes. Mulling over his almost incidental compliment, they sat stiffly at opposite ends of the sofa, quietly. Neither was willing to be the first to break the strained silence. It was getting late; the hour itself suggested a new intimacy, yet she remained unable to tell him to leave. She began to despair as she turned to him, trying vainly to say the words. But he stubbornly refused to help her. Other than their subliminal communication, there was silence. Mary's hands were becoming fidgety and she knew she had to move them, lest he notice how extreme her uneasiness had become. But when she reached for her drink, his hand closed over hers. It was a long time before she could find the will to pull her hand from the warm comfort of his. She knew being held in his arms would feel even better.

'Oh God, no!' she thought. 'Not like this, not if it's just going to be a one night stand for him...'

"No way," Mary told him, finally breaking the silence. "It's time for you to leave, Mr. Pirelli. I have no intention of being your flavor of the night."

"Come here," Pirelli said softly, still holding her hand.

Mary quickly shook her head. "No. You call me on the telephone, first. Call me. Ask me out to lunch or dinner. You can even call just to say you want to stop by for a cup of coffee or a drink. But whichever it is, you call me first."

He released her hand and climbed to his feet, staring intently at her. Then he tilted his head down and said softly: "You're right, Mary, I shouldn't have barged in on you like this. I'll leave now and I promise that I'll call you first next time. But you have to promise me that when I do call, you won't say no."

Mary smiled broadly. "I promise."

Pirelli stepped out of the apartment and heard the door close securely behind him. He darted down the stairs and out of the building and raced to a corner phone booth. Moments later, the phone rang in Mary's apartment.

"Hi Mary, it's me, Pirelli. I thought I'd drop by for a drink if you don't mind."

Mary laughed in spite of herself. But before she could respond, Pirelli added, "And don't forget the promise you made."

He quickly returned to the apartment. Mary opened the door and when he re-entered the apartment, she was still smiling.

"Rae was right, you are truly something else," she said.

"And so are you."

"You know Anthony, I might as well be candid with you. I was very disappointed when you didn't at least call and let me know you were all right after that terrible incident you and Solly had at the Waldorf. I had to read about it in the papers."

"You're right, Mary, I should have. And I'm very sorry I didn't."

"Rae told me that Solly said you could have been killed. That the man went for his gun. If I had been there watching, I think I would have died."

"It's over now, Mary. Why don't we just forget about it?"

"How do you forget something like that? Weren't you afraid that you might get hurt? Or maybe hit an innocent bystander when you fired your gun? Talk about taking a chance!"

"I really didn't' take a chance, Mary."

"How can you say that?"

"Because a long, long, time ago I made it my business to learn how to shoot. You see, Mary, I believe that when you carry a gun you should know how to use it. And I know how to use it."

"I hope I'm not annoying you, Anthony, it's just that I'm truly fascinated."

"That's all right."

"I still think it took a lot of courage to do what you did."

"I'm not denying that it took a little courage, but what it really took was years of training, practice and most importantly, self confidence."

Mary shook her head. "From what Solly told Rae, the man had a gun in his hand and he was pointing it straight at you!"

"First, it wasn't pointed at me and second he didn't have a chance."

"Did he know that?"

"Probably not, but I did."

"Have you ever had to shoot anyone before?" Mary said, continuing to press.

"Yes."

"Oh my God," Mary blurted out, fascinated at the simplicity of his reply.

"Isn't that a terribly hard thing to do?"

"It's a very hard thing to do, but sometimes there's no other way. Now that we got that out of the way, how about telling me what you've been up to since we last spoke?"

Two drinks and thirty minutes later, Pirelli planted a sound kiss on Mary's cheek and left for home, promising to call again.

CHAPTER TWENTY-FOUR

The police Surgeon's medical opinion arrived at Manhattan South Homicide via department mail. Pirelli was out of the squad room. Solly received it but decided he would wait until his partner got back before reading the opinion. When Pirelli returned to the squad room, Solly handed him the envelope.

"Here's the Surgeon's opinion, kid. Let's hope its good news."

Pirelli opened the envelope and began to read the report aloud:

> A metallic foreign body in the shape of a bullet is lodged beneath the rhomboid muscle in the posterior chest wall. In order to remove the foreign metallic body, an incision...

"Forget the medical procedure bullshit," Solly interrupted. "What's the bottom line?"

"I'm getting to it, Solly. Give me a fucking chance, will ya?" Pirelli looked for the Surgeon's conclusion at the end of the report and continued to read aloud:

> It is my professional opinion that the bullet could remain in the patient's body for an indefinite period without endangering his life or health. Therefore,

removal of the bullet at this time does not warrant the risk of possible complications brought about by its removal.

"Okay, so whatta think it all means, for Christ sake," Solly asked impatiently.

"Well, I hope I'm wrong, Solly, but it looks to me that we're fucked. Of course we'll run it by Buckner. Hopefully he'll disagree with me, but I don't think he will."

"Why do you say that, kid?"

"Because when I went to the law library the other day, my librarian friend found me a Court of Appeals opinion that hurts us."

"What was the case about," Solly asked curiously.

"A murder case, just like this one. Some dirt bag exchanged shots with a storeowner during a stick-up. The storeowner was killed and the dirt bag walked away with the store owner's bullet in him. Just like Ardone did after he shot the cop. The mutt was caught a few days later and the assigned detective got a judge to issue a search warrant to forcibly remove the bullet. The perp's lawyer appealed and the Appellate Division threw out the warrant. The Court of Appeals agreed. I got the case right here."

Pirelli pulled open the center drawer of his desk and pulled out the opinion. Then he turned to the section he had highlighted and began to read aloud:

> An operation to forcibly remove a bullet from the defendant's chest would violate the defendant's Fourth Amendment right to be free from unreasonable search and seizure, as well as his Fifth and Fourteenth Amendment rights to due process of Law.

And before you ask what it means, Solly, like I just said it looks to me that we're fucked."

"Shit!" Solly said, "So what do we do now, kid?"

"Well the first thing we do is keep our fingers crossed and hope Buckner can do some legal maneuvering. Maybe there's some other case or something. Anyway, I'm gonna run over to the DA's office and see Buckner right now."

"The question is where do we go from here if Buckner says we're out of luck?"

"That's a good question, Solly. But one thing's for sure, we'll come up with something. If he can't help us, we'll sit down and put our heads together. We'll come up with something to get that fucking bullet out of Ardone. We have to."

As Pirelli had suspected, Deputy District Attorney Warren Buckner advised him that the issuance of a search warrant to forcibly remove the bullet from Ardone's shoulder was out of the question.

Pirelli returned to the precinct to give his partner the disappointing news, but Solly was nowhere to be found. He had left a message for Pirelli to join him at the department pistol range.

"A little relaxation is the order of the day, kid," Solly had written. "Meet me at the range."

Pirelli agreed. He could use a little relaxation to clear his head.

CHAPTER TWENTY-FIVE

W hen he entered the Police Academy pistol range on 20TH Street, the familiar earsplitting bangs from the revolvers and automatic pistols greeted Pirelli. He cupped his ears with his palms and made his way up the main aisle. Rookies in gray uniforms or off-duty police officers in civilian clothes occupied all of the twenty shooting booths. Seated at the raised control desk, Oscar Hoffman, the Academy's range officer, was shaking his head. Making no effort to conceal his frustration with mediocre performances of some of the novice shooters, he shouted out instructions:

"Hey, number four." Hoffman yelled out to a young recruit. "You're jerking the trigger. Squeeze the trigger gently."

As Pirelli approached the control desk, Hoffman sung out, "Hey, Pirelli, how ya doin? I ain't seen you in a while."

Pirelli grinned up at the seasoned cop. "That's because a friend of mine built a range right in his warehouse. The putz even has a bar set up right next to the ammo locker. Oscar, I do my shooting in comfort now. So why the hell should I come down here?" The range officer shook his head. "You detectives are all the same, always living the good life."

"Talking about the good life, you don't seem to be doing so bad yourself, Oscar," Pirelli said smiling as he looked down at the man's waist. "I see you're putting on a few pounds. I hate to tell you this pal, but you're starting to look a little like Solly. When are you going to get off your fat ass and get back out on the street?"

Pirelli and Hoffman had been friends for years and never missed an opportunity to tease each other.

"Hey, give me a pair of muffs, for Christ's sake," Pirelli shouted while continuing to cup his ears.

The range officer handed him ear protectors and Pirelli, adjusting the headband, slipped the muffs over his head. The ear shattering noise was gone.

"Hey, Pirelli," Sergeant Coltman yelled out from a nearby booth. "C'mere and watch me shoot. Pretty soon I'll be good as you."

Coltman had gotten interested in bulls-eye competition several years earlier and worked hard at it. He had improved his skill considerably and wanted to impress the expert marksman.

Pirelli walked over to Coltman's booth. "Okay Sarge, let's see what you can do. Talk is cheap you know."

The sergeant replaced the bulls-eye target and proceeded to shoot a five-round string of rapid fire from a distance of twenty-five yards. When the smoke cleared, he pushed a control button and the paper target was automatically returned to the booth. Coltman had done well. Of the five shots he fired, three were tens, one was a nine, and the last shot had landed in the eight ring.

"Hey, that ain't bad Sarge," Pirelli said grinning. "In another ten years or so, you'll be able to compete against me."

"Ten years, huh? Bullshit! Maybe we should have a little match right now." Coltman said boldly. "With you giving me a ten point spot of course."

Pirelli laughed. "What chance would I have against a shooting great like you if I gave you a ten point spot? You'd end up by embarrassing me in front of the whole range. Besides," Pirelli added slyly, "I ain't got too much dough with me. We could only shoot for twenty bucks."

"No problem, Pirelli. But are you sure you can afford it?" Coltman said sarcastically.

"Not really. But I don't mind losing. It's no fun unless you're shooting for a few dollars. Makes it a little more challenging."

Coltman was delighted. 'There are a lot of people here today and he'll be under a hell of a lot of pressure,' he thought. 'He's got the reputation to live up to, not me. Who knows, maybe he'll choke. Me, I'm expected to lose.'

"Listen, Pirelli," Coltman said slowly. "We both know that I'm not in your league yet, so how about spotting me the ten points?"

Pirelli hesitated before replying. "I'll tell you what George, even though I think you're trying to hustle me, I'll give you five."

Samuels suddenly appeared from the far end of the range and joined in on the negotiations. "How many points is he giving you, George?"

Coltman turned quickly to see Solly Samuels grinning at him. "Hotshot here is looking to give me only five points. Would you believe that?"

"You ain't going to take less than ten, are you George?"

Most of the action had already ceased up and down the line and a crowd had suddenly appeared. Most of the onlookers had never seen Pirelli shoot and his prowess with the revolver was legendary.

"Hey Solly," Pirelli said slyly. "I come down here to look for you and look what you're getting me into. What's with this ten point spot horse shit?"

"So do I get the ten points, Pirelli?" Coltman said, continuing to press in a loud voice."

The crowd jeered, calling upon Pirelli to give the sergeant the ten point spot.

"You guys must think I'm crazy. If I give him the ten points, he'd win in a walk. Ten points," Pirelli repeated trying to show the crowd how ludicrous it was. "Listen! If I give the Sarge ten points and he shoots a two ninety, I'm dead. I'd have to shoot a perfect score just to tie him."

Shaking his head, Pirelli turned to look at the growing group of onlookers that was urging him to give the ten point spot.

"Okay," Pirelli said. "I know I'll be sorry, but the Sarge can have the ten points"

Word of the competition had spread. In minutes, some twenty cops were crammed together to watch the match.

The range officer agreed to judge the event. "Each shooter will fire a total of thirty rounds at a distance of twenty-five yards," he advised the contestants.

"Hey, Oscar. Let the Sarge shoot his match first," Pirelli

said. "I gotta go get my gun. It's in my locker and I'll be a minute." Pirelli was thinking of the flask he kept there just for match purposes. He always had a couple of nips of scotch before a match to take the edge off. It always worked for him.

"Is that okay with you, Sarge?" Hoffman asked. Coltman nodded and immediately marched up to the firing line.

"Okay, this will be slow fire," Oscar informed the shooter. "Ten rounds in four minutes. You will unload and reload at your own command. And remember, if you fire either before or after the sound of the whistle you get docked ten points."

Hoffman blew a shrill, short blast on his whistle signaling that Coltman had four minutes to complete his string of slow fire.

A high power spotting telescope had been placed on the rear control desk. Solly had been designated to view the target and signal the value of each shot as it passed through it, adding to the general excitement.

Coltman began shooting. He was nervous, perspiring freely, but clearly determined.

"Ten! Ten again!" Solly signaled. "Ten! Nine! Ten!"

Coltman finished his slow fire series some thirty seconds before the allotted time had expired. He had fired nine tens and one nine for a total of ninety-nine points. The audience began to buzz with excitement.

"Atta boy, Sarge," his supporters shouted out.

"Timed fire." Hoffman yelled out to silence the group. "This will be your first string of timed fired," he repeated, "Five shots in fifteen seconds."

Everyone was pressing forward to get a better view. Coltman swallowed nervously and steadied himself, preparing for the shrill scream of the starting whistle.

"Are you ready on the right?" the range officer boomed out.

Coltman gulped and pointed the Smith & Wesson .38 Caliber revolver at the target that was exactly twenty-five yards down range.

"And are you ready on the left?" he continued. Hearing no response from the shooter, the range officer declared: "All ready on the firing line."

At the blast of the whistle Coltman fired away.

"Ten!" Solly signaled. "Ten again! Eight! Ten! Ten!"

The whistle sounded just as Coltman fired his fifth shot. "Unload and reload for your second string of timed fire," the range officer commanded.

Coltman snapped open the cylinder, ejecting the five spent shells. He inserted five cartridges and carefully locked the cylinder in place.

The concluding string of timed fire was repeated with the same cadence as the previous five. When the score for the ten-shots was tallied, Coltman had scored a more than respectable ninety-seven points.

"All right," a Coltman rooter yelled out excitedly.

"Way to go, Sarge, just stay with it. Remember you got a ten point spot," another man exclaimed.

"Okay," the range officer cried out. "Here's where we separate the men from the boys.

"This will be your first string of rapid fire, five shots in eleven seconds."

To shoot a respectable rapid fire, absolute concentration had to be maintained by the shooter. Coltman was well aware of it. He had a ten point spot and knew that if he stayed cool and didn't panic, he could win the match.

Coltman held up under the pressure. When the smoke cleared, he had fired a remarkable ninety-three points for a match total of two hundred eight-nine out of a possible three hundred. Coltman flushed with pride hearing the shouts of praise and congratulations. A two ninety-nine with the ten point spot added.

Pirelli returned to the firing line just as Coltman's score was being tallied.

"You're in trouble now, Pirelli," said one young recruit. You should've seen his rapid fire. A ninety-three."

"Way to go Sarge. Its money in the bank," shouted a veteran police officer.

Pirelli knew he had to shoot a perfect score to win the

match. Not only was his money on the line, but, more importantly, his reputation.

Solly was still seated behind the spotting scope. He never figured that Coltman would have fired that well and he cursed himself for pushing the ten point spot. Coltman would have taken less and he knew it.

'This time it backfired on us,' Solly thought as his partner moved up to the firing line.

Pirelli loaded his target revolver and pointed its six-inch barrel down range, limiting its movement to within the perimeter of the five-inch diameter bulls-eye.

"Just watch the sights and squeeze," Pirelli reminded himself. He kept building a steady uniform pressure on the trigger until the gun roared and recoiled sharply to the left.

"A pinwheel," Solly signaled. The bullet had struck the bulls-eye dead center.

Pirelli's next twenty-nine shots were all tens. And twenty-one of those tens were in the center of the bulls-eye.

Pirelli had fired a perfect score. Thirty police officers had witnessed an unbelievable exhibition of marksmanship.

Those who had come to the range to practice now went back to the firing line determined to improving their skills. They had just witnessed an astonishing accuracy with a revolver that many had thought impossible. Some still couldn't quite believe what they had just seen.

Solly, his belly shaking from laughter, patted his partner on the back. "Did you get a look at George's face?"

"Yeah, I did. But next time don't cut it so close."

"Yeah I know what you mean. I was worried too. I figured you for a two ninety-eight, or maybe even a two ninety-nine. But a perfect score! Talk about sweating it out. But you're right, kid. I'll never cut it that close again."

CHAPTER TWENTY-SIX

A fter their frolic at the pistol range, the detectives were back to their investigation. On their way to the precinct Solly stopped at a corner deli and picked up some sandwiches and several cans of soda. Pirelli remained in the double-parked squad car thinking about the bullet in Ardone's shoulder.

Back at their desks, Solly poured some soda into a chipped glass in need of replacement and began to chew on an overstuffed potato and egg hero.

Pirelli set his sandwich aside momentarily and unlocked the top drawer of his cluttered desk. He removed the leather covered traveling friend that was always nearby. He removed the cap of a silver flask and slowly poured twenty-five year old single malt scotch into a matching cup, his manicured fingers lifting it to his lips in a regal gesture. He saluted Solly and swallowed its contents. He poured another and turned to his partner. "Okay Solly, now we can get some thinking done."

"Good," Solly said. "Where do you wanna begin?"

"At the beginning."

The detectives spent the rest of their day reviewing every shred of information twice over, including Frank Ardone's life history.

But they knew they had taken the investigation about as far as they could. They needed a plan to get the incriminating bullet out of Ardone's shoulder.

"Let's face it Solly, this is fucking crazy! Pirelli said. We know who did it and we can't prove it."

"Listen kid, sometimes you just gotta sit for a while and wait for something to break. Remember every stool we got on the street knows that solid information about the killing is worth a pass on just about anything. And there's the PBA reward, too. One of these days something will pop. Just you wait and see."

"Wait and see my ass, Solly. We gotta make something pop and we gotta do it soon. You know goddamned well that if too much more time passes we'll be on to other things and this case folder will be gathering dust."

"Yeah, I suppose you're right, kid. You got any ideas?"

"Not as we speak. But one thing's for sure. I'll come up with something to get that fuckin bullet outta the cocksucker. Even if I have to carve it out myself. That Solly, you can take to the bank."

CHAPTER TWENTY-SEVEN

A t the end of a long day Pirelli decided to walk home. It was a clear evening and as he strolled leisurely up Second Avenue, his mind began to wander. He stared at the filthy streets beneath him and shook his head angrily knowing that some of its inhabitants were constantly abusing the city he loved so much.

He looked up at the steep canyons of steel and glass that provided illusory barometers of prosperity and thought about all the kids who arrive here every day. From across the breadth of the land, they come, flocking to the great city by the thousands. Seeking the street paved with gold. They flood the east and west sides of Manhattan, gobbling-up apartments they can't afford, their refrigerators conspicuously empty. Their bare apartment floors furnished with odds and ends bought at flea markets.

Kids that try to, but can never, become New Yorkers. New Yorkers have special lines etched into their faces before they're even born. Even their search for the American dream is different. In fact, when a New Yorker is lucky enough to land a halfway decent job, most stick it out here for the rest of their working days. New Yorkers work until they can plunk down their life savings on a one or two-family house. Or else they end up renting a decent apartment in as safe a neighborhood as they can find.

Then shaking off his reverie, Pirelli hastened his pace. He was enjoying his brisk walk until his thoughts once again turned to the slain officer. His frustration grew with every step. He knew that without a plan to remove the bullet from Ardone's shoulder, he and Solly would be up against a brick wall and have to move on to other cases. He shook his head in despair. He had to come up with something and he had to come up with it soon.

He decided to pay a visit to the Blue Grotto Lounge. Cosmo had moved to Phoenix and he had not spoken to any other lounge employees. The people who run the establishment wouldn't even know who he was. No one would connect his visit to the murder of the young police officer. And even if they did, so what! His decision made, he headed straight for the Blue Grotto Lounge.

It was 8 p.m. when Pirelli arrived at the popular nightspot. He pushed open the thick leather-upholstered door and stepped across the vestibule where a young police officer had once lain mortally wounded. He grimaced and entered the dimly lit interior of the lounge, looked around and found a stool at the far end of the large U-shaped mahogany bar.

All around him people were laughing and drinking, many waiting for a table in the upstairs, four-star, restaurant.

A tapping on the window behind him caused him to turn his head. He looked and saw a young woman standing on the sidewalk, peering in, smiling. Pirelli thought she might be calling him until a young man two stools over jumped up, waved, and ran outside to meet her.

As he'd suspected, no one in the bar recognized him. He signaled for a drink. After the drink was in front of him, he sat among the smokey bustle of the fast growing crowd, staring into a double of Chivas Regal. Thinking!

Minutes later, he felt a female presence behind him. He swung around and was greeted by the hazel eyes of the beautiful woman who had tapped him on the shoulder.

"Hey! If it ain't the lovely Ms. Marlowe," Pirelli cried, grinning at the way she pointed the tip of her tongue at him.

The woman, slim and tall with soft brown hair stunningly styled, grinned back at him with genuine warmth. She wore a light green turtle neck sweater and tight fitting slacks, a shade darker. The greens went well with her light brown skin.

"Jesus, Iris, how the hell are ya?"

"I'm fine lover boy," she replied affectionately.

"I didn't know this was one of your places of employment, Iris."

"It ain't. I'm strictly socializing. Hey, even a working gal needs a little romance every now and then. If you know what I mean?"

Pirelli appraised the woman and shook his head in amazement. "Iris, you're as gorgeous as ever," he said sincerely.

"Really," she asked. Well if I'm so gorgeous how come you never once hit on me? You know when it comes to you there would never be a cover charge."

Pirelli turned his palms up and said softly, "It's got nothing to do with pay for play, young lady."

Iris rolled a moist tongue over scarlet lips glistening under the soft, indirect lighting that was placed above the bar.

"I bet it's because of those times when you stuck your neck out for me. You figure I'd just be paying you back for the favor. That's the real reason, ain't it?"

Pirelli emptied his glass with a single swallow. "That's not it at all, Iris. Listen, we both know that you helped me out plenty of times, too, and that no pay back is due."

The woman shrugged. "Then what is it?"

"It's just that I never mix business with pleasure, Iris. And that's that."

Iris half turned to him, pressing perfectly formed breasts against his shoulder.

"Okay," she whispered. You win. But I'm telling you now that I'm going to keep trying. And someday when I catch you in a weak moment, I'll proposition you just like Lauren Bacall did to Humphrey Bogart in that classic movie."

"What movie was that, Iris?"

"You know the one where she told him, 'If you need anything, just whistle and I'll be there.' Then she said, 'You know how to whistle, don't you? You just put your lips together and blow.'"

"That leaves me out, Iris. I never could whistle."

"No problem, lover boy, you don't have to know how to whistle. If you need anything, all you have to do is ask and I'll put my two lips together and do the blowing."

"You're too much Iris. Are you trying to make me an offer I can't refuse?"

But before Iris could reply, she felt a sudden pressure against her backside. She turned to the man who had deliberately rubbed against her.

"Hey, how about watching where you put your hands mister."

The stranger, a tall, heavy-set, man, who had too much to drink, grinned lewdly at her. But instead of backing off he continued to rub against her, his grin widening.

Cocking his head towards Pirelli, he chuckled, "I heard your friend here call you Iris. Baby, the last time you and I met your name sure as hell wasn't Iris. And don't tell me you don't remember me?"

"It just so happens that I don't remember you." Iris was angry. "Furthermore, even if I did, I happen to be with someone right now. So why don't you get lost."

The man was about to grope Iris again when Pirelli slid from his stool and stepped directly in front of him. Squarely facing the huge figure, he said sternly. "You're out of line friend. The lady said she doesn't remember you. And even if she did, she's with me. So why don't you just move along."

Loosing a string of obscenities, the stranger poked his middle finger into Pirelli's chest and cried, "Listen you little squirt, there's no way this bitch don't remember me. We spent time in bed together."

"Is that right," Pirelli said, sizing up the ass hole. "You spent time in bed together, huh? Well lemme tell ya something pal. You certainly are a big sonofabitch to look at, but maybe she doesn't remember you because you ain't big where it really counts.

The big man's face turned red.

Pirelli saw it coming and spoke quickly. "Now I don't want any trouble, pal. So like I just said, why don't you just move on like a nice fella and we'll forget the whole thing. Okay?"

"Why you little shit, one more word out of you and I'll tear ya fuckin head off."

Pirelli took the challenge. "Is that right? Well in that case pal, don't let anything but fear keep you from trying."

The man, infuriated by the challenge of a smaller man, pushed Pirelli backwards and cocked his meaty fist. But just as he was about to strike, Pirelli crouched nimbly to his right and ground the heel of his left shoe into the brute's instep, effectively pinning him against the bar. Then with his right fist held murderously low, he hit the man in the groin as hard as he could.

Overcome by an unexpected wave of pain and nausea, the huge body bent forward gasping as Pirelli stepped backwards and whipped his clenched left fist across the big man's sagging jaw. He immediately collapsed to the floor with a loud thud and Pirelli calmly returned to his place at the bar.

A frightened customer ran to the phone and dialed 911 just before two burly bouncers bulled their way through the gathering crowd.

As the bouncers approached him, Pirelli held up his hands sheepishly. "Its okay boys," Pirelli told them. "It's all over."

The bouncers cleared the area and turned to help the huge figure who was struggling to get up.

"That sonofabitch sucker-punched me," the man cried, clearly embarrassed at having been decked by a smaller man.

Glaring up at Pirelli's slender, five-foot ten-inch frame, the man growled, "He cold-cocked me for no goddamned reason. The sonofabitch hit me before I even had a chance to move."

"Let's not push this, pal," the taller of the two bouncers warned. "Why don't we just step outside for a minute and cool off."

The bouncers wanted to move everyone onto the street to avoid a problem in the lounge. But they were too late. As they were easing the man towards the door two uniformed cops arrived. After a brief conversation with the two bouncers, the younger cop walked over to Iris and questioned her about the incident. She immediately cocked her head toward Pirelli and said, "Listen, none of this was his fault, officer. He was just trying to protect me. That big sonofabitch over there had his filthy hands all over me."

The senior of the two cops turned to Pirelli whom he recognized from the precinct and asked: "What the fuck happened Pirelli?"

Pirelli shrugged. "I was just trying to keep the young lady from being hassled by that big fuck."

Then the officer turned to the man who had finally gained his composure, "You wanna go to the hospital, mister?" the officer asked solicitously.

"No. I'm all right," the man said. "It was one big misunderstanding. Let's forget the whole thing okay. Right now, I just wanna go home and get cleaned up."

The cop was relieved that the man wanted to forget an incident involving Pirelli. Then he turned to Iris and asked, "You wanna file charges, Ms. Marlowe?"

Iris looked to Pirelli.

Pirelli knew he should arrest the man, especially since he had to use force to keep him harassing Iris. But suddenly a thought raced through his mind. He hesitated for a minute reflecting on the thought. Then he whispered to Iris. "There's no point in you getting mixed up in this, Iris. The last thing you need is for everyone to know your business. Just give me a minute and I'll take care of everything."

Iris nodded in agreement.

Pirelli turned to the officers and said, "She don't wanna press charges. So let's forget the whole thing, okay."

The cops were surprised by Pirelli's decision. One took him by the arm and walked him behind the bar. "Listen Pirelli," he whispered, I don't wanna tell you your business, but don't you think you oughta lock this ass-hole up? I mean you gave him a pretty good working over. Not that I'm saying he didn't deserve it."

"Yeah, I know you're right. I guess I should lock his ass up. It's just that I'd rather not involve my lady friend here."

"Well it's up to you, but I'd give it some serious thought before we let the bum go?"

Pirelli nodded, "Okay I will."

The officer walked back to his partner who was busy admiring Iris's sultry evening ware, waiting for Pirelli's decision.

Pirelli continued to consider the idea that had crossed his mind. 'It's a long shot for sure,' he thought, 'but what the fuck, right now me and Solly ain't got any shot at all.'

After several more minutes, he signaled to the officers, indicating he'd made his decision. The senior officer walked back to Pirelli while his partner continued to make small talk with Iris.

"Thanks for your advice," Pirelli said calmly. "But all I wanna do right now is get outta here. Just make out a report if you wanna and indicate that you have no complainant."

"Okay Pirelli, whatever you say. But I just hope the guy don't change his mind later on and decide to file a complaint against you. If you don't lock him up and he does, it could be a problem for you, you know."

"Yeah, I thought about that, but I don't think he will," Pirelli said slyly. "But thanks for your concern."

Pirelli took Iris by the arm and eased her out of the lounge.

After Pirelli left the bar with Iris, the veteran cop thought about the opportunity that had just presented itself. He knew that a fight inside a bar was always a problem for its owner. No bar owner welcomed being called before the State Liquor Authority to answer charges of failing to maintain an orderly premise, especially a premise with a checkered past. He walked back to his partner and whispered into his ear. His partner nodded his approval and he quickly escorted the huge man out of the lounge. Then the cop motioned to the Grotto's manager. He wanted to speak with him in private. The manager, knowing why the officer wanted to talk with him, happily led him into a room behind the bar, cluttered with miscellaneous cases of wine and liquor.

After insuring they were alone, the cop turned to face the man. "Listen pal," he said slyly, "That detective out there is looking to lock up the trouble maker," he lied. "I sent everybody outside with my partner to cool things off, but I don't know what' gonna happen. Anyway, I thought I should give you a heads up."

"Ah shit!" the manager blurted out. "That's all I need, another SLA complaint. Is there anyway you can talk him out of it. I got enough problems around here and I don't need no more."

"Well, I don't know. You know with Internal Affairs all over the place it ain't easy to …" The officer's voice trailed off, waiting for the manger to speak."

"Listen officer, I don't want ya to take this the wrong way and I certainly don't wanna create more problems for myself than I already got, but is there anyway we can do something about this?"

"It's possible, I guess," the officer said, a friendly smile creasing his face. "Listen," the Officer said quickly, "Just say what's on your mind. If I don't like what I hear I'll tell ya and that'll be that."

"Good. Listen officer, my boss would really appreciative it if you can make this thing go away. If you know what I mean?"

"I know exactly what you mean, pal. But I ain't got time to wait around to speak to your boss,"

"You don't gotta. I speak for the boss."

"Really, in that case, talk to me."

"Listen," the manager whispered, "You keep that cop from making an arrest in here and you walk out with two hundred in your pocket."

"If it was just me that would sound fine, but there's another mouth to feed here, my partner."

"I'll tell you what then. I'll throw in another two for him. Just get the thing done."

"You got a deal, pal. Consider it done."

CHAPTER TWENTY-EIGHT

The next morning Pirelli got to the precinct early and was greeted by a fuming Solly Samuels.

"Are you out of your fucking mind?" Samuels roared.

"Good morning to you too, Solly. Now would you like to tell me what's up your ass?"

"I'll tell you what's up my ass. You cold cock a guy in a bar, over a fuckin whore no less and you don't lock him up. What the fuck is wrong with you?"

"Hey, how'd you hear about it, anyway?"

"I'll tell ya how I heard about it. The whole precinct is talking about it, that's how. I even heard that the uniform guys that responded told you to lock the guy up."

"Relax, will ya? For your information the sonofabitch was molesting a woman, a woman that just so happens to be a stool of mine. Right in front of me no less. What the fuck was I supposed to do? Watch? I tried to talk to the sonofabitch but he wouldn't listen. Then the prick tried to clock me."

"Putz, I'm not saying you shoulda watched. I'm not saying you shoulda done nothing. I'm saying you shouda locked the bum up after you slapped him around."

119

"Yeah Solly, maybe you're right. But don't worry, pal, if he makes a complaint against me everything will be just fine. I'm sure of it." Pirelli said, a faint smile creasing his lips.

Pirelli retreated to his desk, anxiously awaiting the call he hoped would come.

About three hours later, what Solly had feared most and what Pirelli had hoped for most came to pass. The big man filed a complaint with the Civilian Complaint Review Board.

When the Chief of Detectives learned of the complaint, he was furious and summoned Pirelli to his office.

Solly was furious too. "Ya see he filed a fuckin complaint. I hope the Chief buys your explanation."

"Don't worry Solly, he'll buy it. He has to."

An hour later, Pirelli was seated outside the Chief's office waiting for his "ass chewing".

CHAPTER TWENTY-NINE

J ohn Cochran was an impressive looking man. At fifty-nine he was exceedingly fit. His reddish blond hair was cut short and his clothes fit perfectly over a wiry, muscular, frame. He wore a dark blue suit, a white, button-down, shirt and a crested tie, befitting of a man who commanded a force of three thousand New York City detectives.

Cochran was credited for solving some of the city's most celebrated crimes like the shooting of a Mafia leader as he prepared to open the festivities of his self-proclaimed Italian-American unity day, to the assassination of a pair of police officers answering a call, by an ominous new group called the Black Liberation Army.

In a Detective Bureau known for men of independent thinking, Cochran stood out. He didn't say much, but when he did speak, people listened. Having been exposed to virtually all aspects of police work during his thirty-seven year police career, the street-wise Chief was known as a firm, but fair, man and had earned the respect of all those under his command.

Cochran hailed from a long line of police officers. On his right hand, he always wore a Shamrock pinky ring sprayed with tiny blue stones. The same ring his police officer grandfather wore when he patrolled the streets of "Hell's Kitchen," two generations ago.

At the turn of the twentieth century "Hell's Kitchen" was a virtual war zone where murder and mayhem was an all too common occurrence. Geographically, the area is located on the West Side of Manhattan, bordered by Twentieth Street to the South and Sixtieth Street to the North. In those days, few houses had central heating systems, and many had no bathing facilities. The only playgrounds kids knew were the streets and docks that lined the Hudson River. During the hot summer days, young boys could be seen skinny dipping in the polluted waters, swimming next to bloated dead animals.

The streets provided a variety of problems for the local police. Teen-aged gangs that lived in rat-infested tenement walkups, with a single toilet in the hallway for an entire floor, ruled the neighborhood. The older and bigger boys were a constant threat to the younger ones that were fortunate enough to have a few pennies in their pocket to spend.

Gang fights over turf often led to serious injuries…or death. From time to time, men like Joe Adonis, Lucky Luciano, and other major organized crime figures that controlled the gambling, shy locking, prostitution and a host of other illegal activities in the area, continually sought to buy the services of the cop on the beat. Usually, they succeeded.

Cochran was just seven years old when his grandfather walked into his favorite pub for a middle-of-the-tour taste of Jameson. Before he could taste the whiskey a robber panicked at the sight of the blue uniform and shot him. His grandfather was dead before he hit the ground. It was then that the Chief decided he would carry on the family tradition. At his grandfather's funeral, he'd made a promise to his slain grandfather that when he grew up he would help rid the streets of murderers, especially cop-killers. He always wore his grandfather's pinky ring to remind him of the promise he had made.

CHAPTER THIRTY

When Pirelli walked into his office a furious Chief of Detectives spared no words. "You know Pirelli," he said. "Of all the men who work for me, you're the last one in the world that I would've expected to see standing in front of me under these circumstances. I mean I just can't believe it. A week ago I'm giving you a medal for finishing off a cold-blooded murderer, now I gotta explain to the Commissioner that one of my most decorated and savvy detectives beat up a guy in a bar, over a pros no less."

"The guy was out of order Chief," Pirelli explained.

"That's just it. I'm told that you did nothing wrong, that you were cold sober. Jesus Christ, Pirelli, I just can't believe it. It just doesn't figure. You're too smart a cop to smack a guy around and not cover your ass with an arrest. You must have given some thought that the man might file a complaint against you."

Pirelli just nodded his head. I gave it a lotta thought, Chief.

"Well then just don't stand there for God sake," Cochran said angrily. "What were you thinking about?"

"Ardone," Pirelli blurted out. "Frank Ardone."

"Ardone," Cochran said quizzically. "What in hell does Ardone have to do with any of this?"

"Listen Chief, we both know that Ardone killed that young cop."

"So?"

And we both know that me and Solly are getting nowhere fast with proving it."

"I know, but I still don't see what Ardone's got to do with all this," Cochran said impatiently.

"I'll tell you what he has to do with it, Chief. You see, I was hoping that the sonofabitch would speak to some ambulance-chasing lawyer and file a complaint against me."

"What? Are you telling me that you're glad that he made a complaint against you? I don't get it."

"It's simple, Chief. Now you can suspend me. Listen Chief, you suspend me and I'll assume the role of a disgruntled cop who got screwed over a bullshit charge. Then I'll figure out a way to infiltrate the Blue Grotto. With a little luck, I'll be able to get next to the wise guys that frequent the joint, and then, hopefully, Ardone. Who knows where that'll take us? Let's face it Chief, the way it looks right now it's our only chance of nailing Ardone."

Cochran hesitated for a moment. He was inclined to summarily dismiss Pirelli's suggestion. Then he glanced down at his right hand and saw the glittering Shamrock pinky-ring that reminded him of the promise he had made at his grandfather's wake. The thought of another cop-killer going unpunished was too much to bear.

Pirelli pressed on. "I know it's a long shot, Chief. But it's the only shot we got. Right now me and Solly don't have much else to go on."

"Well, one thing's for sure, Pirelli. You wouldn't be the first suspended cop who got himself involved with the wrong crowd You know Pirelli, the more I think of it, with your line of bullshit, it just might work.

"Is that a yes, Chief?"

"Right now it's a maybe. I'll have to clear it with the Commissioner first. But if I push him a little, I think he'll give me the green light."

"That's great Chief," Pirelli said happily. "Push him a lot."

"You sure you want to do this Pirelli? It'll be a time consuming assignment, and it could be dangerous, too."

"No problem, Chief. As you know, I got no family to worry about and to be honest with you, I'm not exactly uncomfortable spending time around bars," Pirelli said smiling.

"So I'm told. Anyway, I'll speak to the Commissioner.

"Great, tell him I'll assume the posture of a bitter police officer that had been unfairly suspended. I"ll somehow convey this message to the wise guys at the Blue Grotto and, with a little luck, win their confidence. Then, I'll get close to Ardone and gather the evidence needed to charge him with the murders of JoJo Cutolo and the young police officer.

Cochran said little, he simply listened. The session ended with the Chief agreeing that Pirelli had a viable plan. Pirelli's only confidant would be Solly. No one else in the department, other than the Police Commissioner, was to know that Pirelli's suspension was part of a plan to further the investigation of the cop killer.

Pirelli was elated. After thanking the Chief several times, he left the office and immediately called Solly.

"Yeah, everything's fine," he said happily. "If you invite me over for dinner tonight, I'll tell you all about it."

…"Good, I'll see you at 6 p.m. and don't forget to invite Mary," he added, before he hung up the phone.

CHAPTER THIRTY-ONE

Pirelli arrived at Samuels's apartment promptly at 6 p.m. He was carrying his usual box of assorted Italian pastries and two bottles of Italian red.

Rae Samuels immediately greeted him. "What a nice surprise, Anthony," she said as Pirelli handed her the wine and pastries.

"I'm so glad to see you again so soon. And Mary is too," she added.

"Thanks, Rae. And I'm sorry to have invited myself for dinner on such short notice, but the way you cook."

"Oh stop it, Anthony. You always know how to flatter the ladies, even the old married ones."

Solly grinned and gave his partner a big hug.

"Come. Everything is on the table," Rae said. I made chicken soup and a pot roast, with lots of gravy and potatoes. Just the way you boys like it."

"And you should see the dessert," Solly quipped. "That's why I love when you come over for dinner, kid. Rae never makes me dessert when we eat alone."

"When you start looking like Anthony, then you'll get dessert every night. Until then dessert is for special occasions and people with waistlines."

Two hours and two pots of coffee later, Rae turned to the men. "I know you boys have a lot to talk about so me and Mary will go into the den until you're finished."

When the women were out of earshot Solly turned to his partner. "Okay, let's hear it," he said anxiously. "How'd it go?"

"Couldn't have gone better."

"Good, because to tell you the truth, kid, I was worried there for a while. I didn't know what the Chief would do. You know he can be a real hard ass at times, so when you called and said everything was okay, I was really relieved."

"Well, you're right about the Chief having a temper, Solly. He was roaring mad when I first got there. I mean he couldn't believe that I didn't lock up the guy."

"So how did you calm him down?"

"Easy, I told him to suspend me."

"Come on Pirelli. This is no time to putz around."

"I'm not kidding Solly, I told him to suspend me."

"And that's good news?"

"The good news is that my suspension is part of a plan to get that cocksucker, Ardone. I'll pretend to be a pissed-off cop that got suspended over a bullshit charge. Then I'll start hanging out at the Blue Grotto Lounge. With a little luck, I should be able to get next to the wise guys that frequent the joint. And with a little more luck, I'll be able to get next to Ardone. If I can pull this thing off who knows where it'll lead us."

"Holy shit," Solly cried, when no other words would do. "So that's why you didn't lock that prick in the bar up. You had this all planned out, didn't ya?"

"I'm told you I'd come up with something, didn't I? Listen Solly, one way or the other we're going to get that sonofabitch, Ardone.

No matter what or how long it takes. I'm telling you we're gonna get him."

"By the way, you'll be the only one besides the Chief and the Commissioner that'll know what's going on. You and me will meet at my place on a regular basis to plan our strategy."

"You sure ya wanna to do this, kid? I mean it could be dangerous."

"Yeah I know it could be dangerous, but then look at the fringe benefits. I get to eat and drink on the City. And what about the broads," Pirelli said happily. "From what I hear the Grotto is a jumpin joint."

"You're hopeless, Pirelli, anyway, when do we get started?"

"Tomorrow, as soon as the Chief announces my suspension."

Dinner ended on a happy note. Pirelli planted a kiss on Rae's cheek, bear-hugged his partner and escorted Mary to her apartment door. He asked if he could stop in for a minute. He had something very important to say to her. Without hesitating, she invited him in.

Mary showed Pirelli to the couch then disappeared into the kitchen. She poured a scotch over ice in a tall glass and a stem of chilled Chardonnay. She handed Pirelli the scotch and offered a toast, "To us" Finally, after twenty minutes of laid-back conversation, Pirelli got to the matter at hand.

"Listen Mary," he said softly, "I just want you to know that I enjoy your company very much and I'm growing fond of you."

Mary's face reddened slightly. "I enjoy your company too, Anthony," Mary responded. "So where do we go from here?"

"That's just it, Mary. We can't go anywhere, at least not for now. I got a little problem."

"A problem! What kind of problem?"

"I've been suspended from my job."

"Suspended? What did you do wrong?"

"That's just it. I didn't do anything wrong. It's all bullshit," he blurted out, followed by an apology for the coarse remark.

"Then why did you get suspended?"

"Ah, it was my own fault in a way. I tried to keep a guy from molesting a woman in a bar and I roughed him up a little. The sector car arrived and since the woman didn't want to press charges, I didn't arrest the guy. The next day, he turns around and files a complaint against me. I was suspended for not having taken the appropriate police action."

"That doesn't sound fair to me. I mean…"

"It's not fair and I'm real sore about it. Anyway, I won't be coming around to see Solly for a while, at least not until I straighten this thing out and get my life together. I don't want to jam him up. Unlike the shooting at the Waldorf, I didn't want you to read about it in the papers before I had a chance to tell you myself."

"I can imagine how you must feel, but that doesn't mean we can't see each other from time to time. Does it?"

"Maybe after the shock and the embarrassment of my being suspended wears off, we'll get together. But for now I need some time to figure out what I'm going to do."

Pirelli was not happy having to deceive this woman but he really liked had no other choice.

As Pirelli got up to leave, Mary said softly, "Please stay a little longer, Anthony, especially since we're not going to see each other for a while."

"I really don't think I should, Mary. I just told you that I'm growing fond of you. And I don't want this to lead to…"

"That's why I'm asking you to stay," Mary interrupted.

Pirelli looked into her eyes and held her tightly. "Are you sure, Mary?"

"I'm sure," she said, stroking back strands of hair that lay on his forehead. "Are you sure, Anthony?"

He cupped her face between his hands and looked into her eyes. He saw a need, a longing, and a desire as beautiful as his own. "I'm more than sure, Mary. But I'm not ready for a permanent relationship right now and I don't want to hurt you."

"I understand."

"Do you, Mary? It's important that I know."

"I don't want to get involved with anyone right now either, Anthony."

"No regrets later."

"No regrets." The words came out a plea as passionate as the way her body curved longingly against his.

His thumbs outlined her lips, detailing their shape before his mouth covered them. He kissed her passionately and at the feel of his lips, her body became limp and yielding. She opened her mouth to accept the probing of his tongue. Perfume and cologne blended pleasantly with their breaths of wine and fine Scotch.

She unfastened the buttons on her blouse allowing the garment to open. He breathed heavily when she slipped the blouse from her shoulders and he saw her scantily covered full marvelous breasts. Continuing to kiss, they quickly removed the remainder of the other's clothing then sank to the floor as if kneeling in prayer.

The room had grown very still and Pirelli became caught up with her fragrance and dampness in ways he had never felt before. Still on their knees, they melted together. They rocked back and forth, each stunned at how far it had gone so quickly.

Mary gasped and moaned, no longer wanting to wait. Hearing the way she cried out to him, he carried her to the bedroom and placed her gently on pale blue satin sheets. He stared down at the lovely face streaked with tears of passion. His eyes took in her nakedness as she lay submissive before him. She parted her thighs and he gently entered her. She sighed and called his name as he began to stroke her with shallow thrusts that gradually deepened. Her body bowed and bucked as he reached higher and higher inside her. Her legs curled tightly around him as she burrowed her face in his chest and called for all of him. He filled her completely and soon their world exploded around them.

CHAPTER THIRTY TWO

The next day two of the local dailies carried the story:

HERO DETECTIVE
SUSPENDED FOR BAR ROOM BRAWL

A highly decorated detective assigned to the prestigious Manhattan South Homicide Division was suspended without pay yesterday for his alleged involvement in...

HOMICIDE DETECTIVE
SUSPENDED FOR FIGHT IN BAR

A twenty-year veteran detective, who helped solve some of the City's highest profile homicides, was suspended today pending an investigation into an incident involving a woman that...

The news of Pirelli's suspension shocked his many friends and colleagues. Their votes of confidence and support for him was overwhelming and his answering machine was stacked with consoling messages every day.

Pirelli played the role of a disgruntled cop very well. His outrage at having been relieved of duty for what he and many of his supporters believed was an overreaction by the Chief of Detectives was carefully staged. He seized upon every opportunity to demonstrate his frustration with the department.

In the process of transferring his open investigations to his fellow detectives at Manhattan South, Pirelli expressed his indignation by continually mumbling obscenities directed toward the top brass.

Pirelli was busy sorting through his open case files when Detective Nancy Davis returned from a trip to the local deli carrying a large brown paper bag. She placed the contents of the bag neatly across Samuels's desk and nodded sympathetically to Pirelli who was standing nearby.

"I hope you got everything right this time," the fat man said sternly.

Davis grinned broadly. "Sure I got it right, Solly. You ordered two onion bagels with cream cheese and lox, two prune Danish and two teas with lemon, heavy on the sugar. Oh yeah, and you ordered a black coffee for Pirelli."

Pirelli smiled at Davis's vain attempt to cheer him up. "Thanks Nancy," he said. "I needed that more than I need the coffee."

Davis leaned over Samuels's desk, her voice falling to a soft whisper. "How's he dealing with the suspension, Solly," she asked.

Solly waited until Pirelli stepped from the small cubicle before replying, "He's pissed at the way the Chief treated him. And I don't blame him."

Pirelli stalked back into the cubicle and drew a deep breath. "Well, that's about it. I'm finished," he said as he headed for the door.

"I'll give you a call at home later," Solly called out after the swiftly retreating figure.

Pirelli just nodded and threw back a curt wave of his hand. His undercover role was officially underway.

CHAPTER THIRTY THREE

Relieved of his duties at Manhattan South homicide, Pirelli readied himself for the plan that he and Solly had thoughfully laid out. The first step toward visiting the Blue Grotto was for Pirelli to sever his relationship with O'Lunneys then begin to frequent the Blue Grotto Lounge. Not a pleasant task for Pirelli, but a necessary one. He went back to his apartment for an afternoon nap and braced himself for a visit to O'Lunneys later in the evening.

Despite the early hour, O'Lunneys was already doing a brisk business. Pirelli entered the well-stocked bar and grill and climbed onto his favorite corner barstool. Joe Donnellan, Pirelli's favorite bartender, greeted him with a faint smile and without saying a word, poured a double Chivas on the rocks.

"Did I ask for you for a double, Joe?"

"Wait a minute Pirelli, in all the years you've been coming here, the first one is always a double."

"Yeah well as you might have heard things have changed for me, so forget the double."

The bartender mopped his bald, perspiring brow with a bar towel. "Anything you say, Pirelli, I'm here to serve."

Pirelli downed the drink in one gulp then ordered another.

Donnellan quickly refilled his glass and asked: "Anything I can do for you, pal? I mean with your problem."

"Nah, there's nothing anybody can do right now. I'm just pissed off at the world and I'm taking it out on you. And you're the last guy I should be taking it out on. Maybe I just need a change of scenery for a while," Pirelli said lamely as he threw a ten-dollar bill on the bar, "I'll see you later Joe."

Pirelli slid from the high stool and walked out of his second home without another word. Although saddened by the rudeness he had just directed towards his friend, Pirelli knew that his erratic conduct would be blamed on his suspension and frustration with the job he so loved, a message that he wanted to send to all those who knew him.

Outside, Pirelli sighed heavily and continuing with his plan headed directly for the Blue Grotto Lounge. He was calm and focused as he pushed open the heavy padded door and made his way through the vestibule where a dying police officer once laid. The Grotto had just opened for business and bartenders were busy preparing for the evening crowd.

Pirelli found a vacant corner barstool the mainstay bartender filled his order for a double Chivas over ice.

He sipped his drink slowly, prepared to offer an explanation for his presence in the lounge. After he had drained his glass, the bartender walked over to his end of the bar and asked, "Can I get you another?"

Pirelli grinned tiredly. "Thanks pal, you musta read my mind. I'll have the same. Only this time make it a single."

As Pirelli had suspected, the bartender was curious as to why the suspended detective had visited the Grotto.

"Listen, pal, I usually don't pry into my customer's business, but you're detective Pirelli, ain't you?" he asked.

"That's right. How'd you know?"

"Because I was working that night you had the scrimmage with that big fuck at the bar."

"Really," Pirelli said softly.

"Listen, I read about your suspension in the papers and I just wanna tell ya that I think that you got fucked."

Pirelli was elated. The bartender had just opened the door for further conversation. "Listen friend," he said quickly, talking about that night how often does that cocksucker stop in here?"

"He don't. That night was the first time he was in the joint. And between you and me it was his last."

"You mean nobody in here knows him?"

"Nope," the bartender said.

"Ah shit," Pirelli grumbled.

"Listen pal, like I just said, I usually don't stick my nose into other people's business but do ya think it's wise for you to be looking for him?"

"What makes ya think I'm looking for him?"

"That's why you're here ain't it?"

Pirelli cracked a faint smile but said nothing. His first visit to the lounge couldn't have been going any better.

"Furthermore," the bartender continued, "If he caused me the problems that he caused you, I'd be looking for the sonofabitch too. But then I ain't no cop."

"Yeah, well I ain't one right now either," Pirelli said.

"Anyway Pirelli, the name's Mario."

"Hello Mario," Pirelli said.

"Look, Pirelli, like I just said I think ya got screwed, so if there's anything I can do for ya, lemme know."

"Hey, that's real nice of you, pal, but the only thing you can do for me right now besides keep filling my glass is to let me know if the prick that fucked me up ever happens to stop in here again. I'll stop by again in a week or so and you can let me know."

"You got it, Pirelli. But why not stop by sooner. You seem like my kind of guy. Besides, there are a lot of broads in here that you might wanna meet."

"Thanks, Mario, maybe I will."

CHAPTER THIRTY-FOUR

Pirelli's first visit to the Blue Grotto Lounge couldn't have gone better. But he knew he had to move slowly. The detectives agreed that Pirelli would wait at least a week before returning to the lounge. With time on his hands, Pirelli decided that a visit to Florida, relaxing in the sun, was just the place to wait.

The next morning he boarded the first plane he could get and landed in West Palm Beach airport before 10 a.m.

The early morning clouds had given way to a clear Florida sky and after checking in at the Ramada on the Beach, he settled into his suite. Soon he headed straight for some early afternoon sun.

The gentle rolling of the waves that settled quietly along the surf cast an aura of peaceful tranquility so comforting to a detective facing a difficult and possibly dangerous assignment.

Settling on a stretch of white sandy beach, Pirelli turned to a well-tanned woman that was lying nearby. "You know young lady," Pirelli said. "There's only one thing I find more relaxing than lying on a sunny beach."

"Really, and what's that?"

"It's lying on a sunny beach next to a beautiful woman," Pirelli said, presenting his most charming smile. "Do you mind?"

But before the woman had a chance to respond, he added: "My name's Pirelli. I'm from New York. I'm not married and I'm here for a few days to soak up some of this marvelous sunshine."

The woman smiled. "You know, I usually don't talk to strangers, but since you told me your life story, I guess it'll be all right. My name's Ava."

"Hi Ava, it's nice to meet you. Are you from Florida?

"Nobody's really from Florida. My parents moved here from Michigan when I was six. But I guess you might say I'm a Floridian now."

"Talk about a magnificent climate," Pirelli said. "The beaches are so clean and the women are so beautiful. Really, this would be an easy place to get used to."

The attractive blond, using her hand as a sunshade, peered curiously at the smooth-talking detective. "Are you planning to move down?" she said, arching her breasts to give him a better view of southern assets.

Pirelli grinned at her. "I wish I could, Ava. But I have a business back home."

"Really, what kind of business do you have?"

"Animal husbandry," Pirelli said without hesitation.

"Animal husbandry, you're kidding me," she said smiling, not believing a word of it.

"No! I'm serious, been doing it for years." Actually, it's a very sexy profession when you think about it," Pirelli said laughing.

Ava grinned. "Okay, so you don't want to tell me what you do. That's okay, I'm glad we met anyway."

"I am too, Ava. And if you really want to know what I do, I'll tell you. I happen to be a New York City detective."

Ava slowly shook her head. As an experienced barmaid she knew more policemen than she cared to admit and he certainly did not appear to be one of them.

"You're not really a detective," she said. "Are you?"

"I'll tell you what, Ava. After we get done here we'll go up to my room and have some champagne. I'll prove to you that I'm a New York City detective by the way I entertain."

Ava laughed. "You're something else, Pirelli. And to be honest with you, it sounds tempting. But I have to get to work in a few minutes."

Pirelli nodded. "Maybe it's just as well. I really should visit a few of my friends before I head home. I'm scheduled to leave tomorrow. That is unless somebody gives me a reason to stay a little longer."

"You just got one," she said, clearly intrigued with Pirelli's looks and his lean, well-proportioned body.

"Great," Pirelli said. How about we meet here tomorrow?"

"That'll work. It just so happens I'm off for the next several days."

"Great. I'll see you at about 11 a.m."

Ava climbed to her feet, shaking sand from her short shorts as Pirelli watched admiringly. Pirelli focused on the way the woman's rear swayed like a long-stroke pendulum as she finally disappeared from view. Then he turned over on his back and closed his eyes under the sun he loved so much. He would spend the next three days with the Florida beauty before heading home.

CHAPTER THIRTY-FIVE

Pirelli caught the late flight to Newark, ready to assume his undercover role.

The next morning he was up early. The first thing he did after brewing a pot of coffee was to call Solly to set a strategy meeting.

Thirty minutes of television, augmented by *The New York Times* kept him abreast of local and national news.

Pirelli found his new lifestyle quite comfortable. The one significant drawback was having been suspended from duty he couldn't practice at the department pistol range. Therefore, as a means of maintaining his skill with the firearm, he spent countless hours dry-firing his Smith & Wesson .38 caliber six-inch barrel target revolver.

After a late morning meeting at his apartment with Solly, Pirelli was prepared for his second visit to the Blue Grotto. He would again ask about the big man responsible for his suspension.

Pirelli got to the lounge early. He wanted to talk with Mario before the evening crowd flooded the bar area.

He entered the dimly lit lounge, headed for the same corner stool he occupied on his first visit, and was greeted by the mainstay bartender.

"Hey, good to see you again Pirelli, Mario said cheerfully. Where ya been?"

"I've been away for a few days and since I've been back I ain't had a free minute for myself. Anyway Mario, have you seen my friend?"

"No. And to tell you the truth, I don't expect to."

"That's what I figured," Pirelli grumbled.

"First of all if he did show up, the bouncers would throw his ass out. We got enough ball busters that we have to put up with in this joint without having a 'nobody' troublemaker hanging around."

"In that case, I guess I'll just have to relax for the evening. So set me up when ya get a chance, will ya."

"That was Chivas over ice, if I remember right."

"Make it a double and you got it."

The anticipated bar crowd hadn't arrived yet, so after serving Pirelli his drink Mario lingered for a while.

"So how are thing goin, Pirelli? With the job, I mean?"

"It'll be a while before I know anything. The cocksuckers on top ain't too worried about me. That's for sure."

"Well like I told you the first time you were in here, I think you got fucked. So if there's anything I can do for you, just let me know."

"Listen Mario, I don't want ya to take this the wrong way, but truthfully, I don't get it."

"What do you mean?

"I mean, why should you go out of your way for me?"

"Because the hump that got you jammed up was breaking balls all night and if the bouncers hadda done their job and got rid of him earlier, none of this would've happened and you wouldn't have got suspended."

"That's nice to hear, but what's the real reason?"

Mario smiled. "You're something else Pirelli. Okay, to tell ya the truth, when my boss read about your suspension in the papers, he got a little worried that your boys might get pissed off at the joint and start breaking balls. If you know what I mean?"

"Nah! What for? Everyone knows that I fucked myself up by not locking the prick up. So you can tell your boss that nobody is blaming the joint for my problem," Pirelli said shrewdly.

"In that case, do you mind if I ask you something, Pirelli?"

"Go ahead."

"Listen, the guy was definitely out of order, right?"

"Keep going."

"So how come ya didn't lock him up? You musta known that it coulda been a problem for you?"

"Yeah, I knew it could be a problem, but to be honest, I didn't think the cocksucker would file a complaint against me."

"Any other reason," Mario asked.

Pirelli hesitated for a moment. The conversation with the bartender was going smoothly. He moved cautiously. "Listen, Mario, no offense," he said politely, "But that's really my business."

"Just as well, but I bet I know what it is."

"Really, okay then you tell me!"

"You didn't want to involve the whore in the arrest."

"Pirelli smiled broadly. "Hey, that's very perceptive of you, Mario."

"What I can't figure out is why."

"Well, since we've gone this far, Mario, I might as well tell you everything. You see Mario in my business it's important to have friends on the street and the whore, as you so bluntly put it, happens to be a friend of mine. If you know what I mean."

"I know exactly what you mean. And in my business it's important to have friends in the police department. If ya know what I mean. So like I said, if you need me to do anything, lemme know."

"Thanks again, Mario. And just for the record, I just might take you up on that when I have my department trial."

"By the way, Pirelli, my boss said your money is no good in here tonight."

"Be careful Mario, the way I drink you may regret having made that offer."

"Not a chance, Pirelli, this joint can well afford it. He thinks you got fucked too. What's more he likes to have friends in the department too."

Mario cracked the seal of a fresh bottle of twenty-five year old Chivas and backed up Pirelli's drink.

"Good luck," Mario said as he moved up the bar to serve several waiting customers.

Throughout the remainder of the evening, Pirelli and Mario engaged in small talk. Pirelli's phenomenal ability to consume alcohol and still keep his wits about him served him well in his undercover role.

Several hours later, a bleary eyed Pirelli was puffing away on a Cuban cigar and talking to a young woman who was seated next to him when Mario poured him yet another drink.

"Ya wanna know something Mario," "I'm glad I stopped by this joint last week. It's got a lotta class and the ladies in here are gorgeous," he said nodding to the young beauty sitting next to him. "And what's more the drinks are certainly a lot cheaper than my usual watering hole," he said laughing.

"Listen, I'm glad you dropped by, too. And don't be a stranger."

"Anyway, with that being said, I'm outta here."

He turned to the young beauty sitting next to him and planted a good night peck on her cheek. "Catch ya next time, honey," he said, purposely slurring his words.

His second visit to the lounge was as fruitful as the first.

CHAPTER THIRTY-SIX

When visiting the lounge, Pirelli arrived early and stayed late, always sitting at the same end of the bar. Before long, he knew most of the Grotto regulars by face, and a few by name. He would spend the evening sitting at the bar smoking expensive cigars and buying drinks for unescorted ladies sitting nearby, compliments of New York City.

Pirelli was amused by the many wise guys that seemed to be everywhere in the lounge. They came in every shape, size and age. Many were associates seeking to rise in the hierarchy of the Grimaldi organized crime family. Always dressed in the finest suits, the wise guys projected an image of confidence and power. These were men who did not have conventional jobs. They spent their days just hanging out at certain social clubs and lounges. They were men with wads of cash in their pockets that thought nothing of putting a five dollar bill into the pocket of a shoe-shine boy, men that for some unknown reason never received tickets on their shiny black cars that were always in front of the lounge either blatantly double-parked or pulled up in a bus stop, the kind of ticket that led to the death of a young cop. They were men who were courteous and respectful to all, yet, they were men who were ready to kill, and would, if the need arose.

One evening, as usual, Pirelli arrived at the lounge early and sat on his favorite corner barstool. The crowd had not yet arrived and Mario spent a few moments chatting with his newfound friend.

"So what's knew with the job, Pirelli?" he asked

"Nothin! Like I told ya, my bosses couldn't give two shits about my welfare. They're dragging this thing out. It's a good thing I ain't got a family to support."

Then Mario shocked him. "Listen Pirelli," he said, "You seem to be my kinda guy. So if things get too rough for ya, lemme know. I can't promise ya, but maybe I can speak to somebody and get you a job here tending bar 'til ya get straightened out, that is."

Pirelli was elated by Mario's job offer. He was tempted to jump on the opportunity but decided against it. 'Wiser to move slowly.' he thought. 'Don't be too anxious.'

"Hey, that's real nice of you Mario. But right now I'm okay. However if my suspension takes too long, I may just take you up on the offer."

"Just let me know when you're ready," Mario said as he moved to the other end to satisfy a thirsty group that had just arrived.

Pirelli was sipping his drink when he felt a tap his shoulder followed by a sexy whisper in his ear. He turned to appraise the striking woman. She wore a tight-fitting, knee-length, black silk dress. Small pearl earrings that clung to the base of each ear, and a simple pearl necklace, accentuated the narrowness of her face. Her long shapely legs were covered with black stockings and a pair of black high heels with matching purse, rounded off her ensemble. Her eyes were painted with just enough mascara and eye shadow to highlight her light brown skin. She was dressed to please the man that purchased her company for the evening.

"Well if it ain't the gorgeous Ms. Marlowe again," Pirelli said smiling.

Catching Mario's eye, Pirelli signaled for service.

"What'll you have, Iris?" Pirelli asked.

The woman shook her head and grinned. "No time detective. The lady is on her way to work. In fact I'm already late for my appointment. But before I run, tell me how you've been."

"Actually Iris, things couldn't be better. Now young lady, why don't you tell me what's really on your mind?"

"To be honest, I'm worried about you. I saw Solly the other day and he said he hasn't seen you for weeks."

"There's nothing to worry about, Iris. Everything is just fine."

"Come on, Pirelli," Iris said. "Solly's especially upset that you haven't been calling him. He's been looking all around town for you."

"Solly's a good friend, I'll call him first thing in the morning."

"Hey," Iris blurted out, "Speaking of your buddy, you might not have to wait until the morning. Here he is now."

Pirelli half-swiveled on his stool and saw Solly working his large frame through the crowd of people that were waiting to be seated in the lounge's upstairs restaurant. Pirelli turned back to grin at Iris, but she was already on her way out the door.

CHAPTER THIRTY-SEVEN

arlier in the day, Pirelli planned Solly's visit to the Blue Grotto, rehearsing the conversation they would have at the bar. A conversation cleverly designed to lead Mario to believe that the suspended detective could be an asset not only to the management of lounge, but to the many wise guys that frequented it.

"Hey, Solly, where the hell you been?" Pirelli shouted as the fat man approached.

Solly opened his ancient lightweight sport jacket and removed a handkerchief from an inside pocket. The jacket was so old that it had come full cycle and almost fit perfectly with the style of the day. Carefully mopping the creases between his jowls and neck, he shook his head and growled at his partner.

"Don't pull that 'where-have-you-been' shit with me, Pirelli. Where the hell have you been? Rae's boiling mad that you haven't been by for dinner lately."

"Talking about your lovely wife, Solly, how's the best cook in town doing?"

"Never mind askin me how she's doing. Come over and see for yourself if you're so concerned."

Out of the corner of his eye, Pirelli could see Mario standing nearby, eyeing the strange face that had joined Pirelli at the bar. So far, everything was falling into place, just as the two detectives hoped for.

"You know, Pirelli, you're getting to be a real pain in the ass," Solly said.

"Hey Mario," Pirelli cried out, "ya got a minute? I gotta ask ya somethin."

Mario moved to Pirelli's end of the bar.

"I want you to meet my partner, Solly Samuels. He just accused me of being a pain in the ass. Now be honest, Mario, I've been stopping by here for a while now. Do you think I'm a pain in the ass?"

Mario laughed dutifully. "How ya doin Solly? Nice to meet ya. Can I get you somethin to drink?"

"If you don't have chocolate milk, he ain't drinking. Ain't that right, Solly?"

"Very funny, Pirelli, at least you didn't lose your sense of humor."

Turning to the bartender, Samuels said, "I'll have a Jack over ice. And make it a double.

"Whoa! What's the occasion Solly? You hit the number or something?"

"The occasion is that this is the first time I had a chance to sit down with you since your bullshit suspension, that's what the occasion is. Now what the fuck is wrong with you Pirelli?"

"You're a detective Solly, you figure it out."

"So the Chief threw you to the wolves. Come on, he was under a lot of pressure to take some sorta action and you fuckin well know it."

"Yeah, some action he took," Pirelli said angrily.

Solly took a sip of the Bourbon Mario placed before him. "Just take it easy, kid. After you get reinstated things will be back to normal."

Pirelli shook his head. "I know how it looks to you Solly," he said quietly. "But I'll tell it to you straight out. The way I feel right now, I ain't sure if I even wanna go back. And I'll tell you something else, Solly," Pirelli continued. "If I do go back on the job, I'm gonna start putting fuckin IAD to work."

"C'mon kid, don't talk like that. Did you hear what I just said? Everything is gonna be just the way it was."

Pirelli sipped his drink slowly and glanced at Mario.

"Listen Solly," he mumbled, "Nobody on top gives a fuck about guys in my situation."

Solly cut him off with a quick shake of his head.

"Bullshit," he cried. "Listen kid, I'm telling you. When you beat the complaint and come back to work everything will be fine."

"Solly, you know I love ya, but please, don't keep pushing it. Ya gotta gimme some time to think this thing out."

"I gotta keep pushing it. And ya wanna know why I gotta keep pushin? I keep pushin because of all the times you made sure that this fat, old, ready to retire putz didn't buy his wife a widow's pension. Always putting yourself on the line for me without thinking twice."

Pirelli intentionally began to sway back and forth on his stool, pretending to feel the effect of the alcohol he had consumed. He rubbed his eyes and mumbled, "That's because you always did the same for me, Solly. But those phony humps on top," he roared. "I've given the department the best part of my adult life and look where it got me. And speaking of humps, you remember that mutt that we were forced to blow away. You know the prick that killed the security guard in that Harlem bank and got away with over forty grand in cash. Remember Solly?"

"Yeah, I remember."

"What a fucking joke," Pirelli said, shaking his head. "We grab him three hours after the stick-up and recovered over thirty thousand that he had on him. Remember? Did anyone say what a good job we did? No! The first thing those scumbags from IAD wanted to know was what happened to the missing ten thousand, like we took it!"

"You wanna know something Solly, if I knew then what I know now about these phony bastards, that money would have gone down south, all of it."

"Don't talk like that, kid."

"Don't talk like that, huh? Listen, Solly, I'm telling you right now. If I had to do it over, I would've taken the money, all of it. What the fuck, they thought we glommed part of it anyway. You hear what I'm saying, Solly? Sure, I had a couple of drinks. And if that's what it takes to see things as they really are, then so be it."

Solly clamped a thick meaty hand on his partner's shoulder and said grimly, "Relax, kid. We'll talk about it another time."

Solly slid off his stool and turned to step away from the bar. Then, half turning back to Pirelli, he said sharply, "I'll call you tomorrow."

Wheeling about with surprising agility for a man his size, Samuels made his way through the crowd and was gone.

Mario overheard the entire conversation and now believed Pirelli would involve himself in illegal activities.

CHAPTER THIRTY-EIGHT

The days quickly turned into weeks. Pirelli established himself as a regular in the lounge. He was now an integral part of the bar crowd. He played his undercover role exceptionally well. But the investigation was not moving forward.

The time he spent at the Grotto finally paid off. It was early one Wednesday evening. Pirelli was sitting alone at the bar when an elderly man climbed onto the adjoining stool. He was a tall, thin man, with a great beak of a nose protruding from a mischievous face, thinning gray hair and slightly bent over shoulders. But the expensive stylish clothes, gold Rolex with diamond bezel and large diamond ring he wore on his right pinky counterbalanced these physical impediments.

Pirelli recognized the man immediately. He had spent countless hours studying the names and photographs of the more than two hundred made members and associates of the Grimaldi family, including the many wannabes striving to be inducted into the family.

Several minutes later, the tall man turned and glanced at the slender detective. Pirelli immediately nodded a friendly hello. The thought of talking to a capo in the Grimaldi family in a social setting was more than Pirelli could have hoped for this early in the investigation. He waited patiently for the right moment to make his move. Fortuitously, the courtly man was the first to speak.

"You're Pirelli, ain't you?"

"That's me," Pirelli replied with a smile.

"Do you know who I am?"

"Sure, you're Sal Rizzo. I'm told you're a good fella to know."

"What else were you told about me?"

"Well, I ain't one for repeating rumors, Sal, but since you asked, I hear that you're a capo in the Grimaldi family."

The man's face split into a pleasant smile. "I like people that don't go around repeating rumors. Especially ones that ain't true. Anyway Pirelli, I heard some nice things about you."

"Really? What did you hear?"

"For one, I'm told that you're a knock around guy with a lotta class."

Pirelli laughed. "I like that, Sal...a lotta class."

"Anyway, now that we got that outta the way, lemme buy you a drink."

"Mario," the elderly man called out. "Back up my friends drink and bring me a little cognac."

The bartender excused himself from a patron he was chatting with and immediately responded to the powerful man's call for service.

"You know Pirelli, my doctor tells me that a little cognac now and then is good for the heart," the old man said, sipping from the snifter that Mario placed before him.

"A little cognac is good for other things, too, Sal."

Rizzo smiled. "Anyway, tell me, how are things goin for you?"

"I've had better days."

"So I've been told."

"Where did you hear that, Sal?"

"Mario told me. For some reason he's a big fan of yours."

"That Mario has got a big mouth. How I'm doin is my business, ain't it?"

"Of course it is," Rizzo said smoothly. It's just that I got a reason for askin, that's all."

Rizzo paused, waiting for Pirelli's reply.

"You mind telling me the reason, Sal?"

"Not at all, Mario tells me he could use some help behind the bar and he thought you might wanna work here. He tells me that since your suspension you've become a regular around here. Not that you shouldn't be. After all, the Grotto is a completely legit joint, for the most part, that is."

"Listen Sal, the way my department has been treating me lately, I couldn't give a fuck what goes on in this joint so long as it don't involve drugs."

The old man laughed as he lifted the delicate snifter again, his diamond cufflink twinkling under the soft light. "I know what you mean, Pirelli. Anyway, do you need a job to carry you over 'til you get straightened out?"

"I guess I'll be reaching that point soon."

Pirelli turned to face the old man squarely, carefully studying the pocked, sallow face. He tried to conceal his excitement about the job offer. Speaking directly with an organized crime family capo at this stage of the investigation was no small achievement. He was tempted to immediately accept Rizzo's offer, but thought it unwise to appear overly anxious.

"I appreciate the job offer Sal, but to be honest with ya, I don't understand why you're concerned about my well being."

"I'm not," he said. "I just told you, Mario tells me he needs help behind the bar and that you need something to carry you over until you get straightened out. So give it some thought and let Mario know your answer. You won't be asked again," Rizzo said abruptly.

Pirelli followed up quickly, not wanting to end the conversation with the hoodlum. "What exactly will I be doing, Sal? After all, I gotta be a little careful while I'm still a cop,"

Rizzo smiled at Pirelli's caution. "I just told you, you'll work behind the bar."

Pirelli gulped down his drink. He stared at his prospective employer. "I work strictly behind the bar? That's all I gotta do?"

"Yeah," Rizzo said. "I'm also told that you're good with your hands too, so if the need arises, I would expect you to handle anybody that gets out of order. Is that a problem for you?"

"No problem there," Pirelli replied. But with all due respect Sal, I get the feeling there's another reason for your offer. So why don't you tell me what's really on your mind?"

Rizzo laughed. "You're a pisser, Pirelli. Okay, I'll level with ya. We both know that it don't hurt for me to know people that have friends in the department, if you know what I mean. Not that I'd ever ask you to do anything wrong you understand."

"I know exactly what you mean, Sal. Not that I would ever do anything wrong, either," Pirelli said coyly. "Anyway, if I take the job who do I report to?"

Rizzo lifted his hand and drained the last of the cognac. "Mario. He'll tell you what ya gotta do. As far as the job goes, he speaks for me. You'll be well paid and on the nights when you ain't working, if ya wanna sit on the customer's side of the bar, there'll be no tab."

"Hey, I don't know if you realize it Sal, but you just doubled my salary."

Pirelli turned and looked to Mario. He reached for the head bartender's hand and began to pump it up and down. "You just got yourself a helper, Mario. But I'm sure as hell going to miss my little corner perch on the customer's side of the bar," Pirelli said sadly.

He turned back to Rizzo and asked, "When do I start, Sal?"

"Work it out with Mario," the old man answered as he carefully slid off his stool and made his way to the upstairs restaurant.

'What a fucking break,' Pirelli thought. 'Wait till Solly hears about this.'

CHAPTER THIRTY-NINE

T wo days later, Pirelli started his job at the Blue Grotto Lounge. Mario spent several days introducing him to the operation behind the bar. He learned quickly. In a relatively short period of time, he was able to fill the multi-phased orders. His fingers squeezing limes and lemons and handling the vermouths and creams like a pro.

Pirelli's wit and personality proved to be a tremendous asset for the lounge. He quickly drew a clientele of his own, especially the women, and his presence behind the bar engendered additional business to the already booming nightspot. He was having fun.

Fortuitously for Pirelli, most of the Grimaldi family members that frequented the Grotto were involved in victimless crimes. Although Pirelli could legally refrain from acting on observed criminal activity in furtherance of a murder investigation, it would have been difficult for him to ignore potential serious crimes, especially those that involved violence or drugs.

Pirelli found himself to be increasingly humored by the shady clientele that frequented the lounge. His infectious grin and gregarious nature impressed most of them. They laughed at his seemingly unending anecdotes about the criminal justice system and cringed at his unbridled sarcasm about New York's organized crime families. As the days passed, they became more and more comfortable with him, especially since he effectively portrayed himself as not giving a shit about illegal activities.

On the hours he was not behind the bar, he began mingling with a group of "wannabes" that frequented the lounge on a regular basis. On occasion he was invited to dine with them at the expensive four-star restaurant on the second floor of the lounge; a restaurant that required advance reservations but always seemed available to a select few.

The suspended detective waited patiently for the day he knew would come; a request from one of the wise guys for help with a money making deal. Finally it happened. One evening, a Grotto regular came to him with a cleverly disguised proposition. Pirelli stared at the grossly overweight, up-and-coming, Grimaldi family associate. He couldn't help but smile at the imported silk tie that had been loosened at least two full inches from the man's tiered neck folds. The man rambled on but was vague about the actual purpose of his conversation with Pirelli.

"Listen Rocky," Pirelli finally said. "Why are we playing fuckin games here? If ya got something ya wanna say, just come out and say it for Christ sake. If I don't like what I hear, I'll tell ya and that'll be that. Okay?"

"What makes you think I got something to say," Rocky fumbled.

Pirelli just shook his head in disgust and walked away. Then he searched for Mario. Finding him in the store room behind the bar, Pirelli pressed the issue. He had correctly surmised that Mario, having received his orders from Rizzo, was behind the fat man's effort to determine if Pirelli would involve himself in illegal activities.

"Mario," Pirelli said indignantly. "We gotta talk."

"Why, what's wrong?"

"What's wrong is the way you sent Rocky around to feel me out. Listen, I told you several times before, but lemme tell you again. If you have something you wanna run by me just come out and ask me yourself. Don't worry, okay. Like I just told Rocky, if I don't like what I hear, I'll tell you and that'll be that. End of story."

"Okay Pirelli, Mario said. "The truth is I've been meaning to talk to you about something."

"So talk for Christ sake."

"Okay, I will. You see, Pirelli, there's this guy that would like to sit down with you. If ya know what I mean."

"I know exactly what you mean. And I don't mind sitting down with anybody so long as it don't involve violence or drugs."

"C'mon Pirelli, you know better than that. It's gotta do with gambling."

"Good. Then set something up. I'll be glad to listen to what he's gotta say."

"Great. I'll set something up as soon as I can."

CHAPTER FORTY

I t didn't take long. The next day, Mario arranged a meeting between Pirelli and a mid-level wise guy named James Malone. Malone controlled gambling along the East Side of Manhattan. Pirelli had Solly do a quick background check on the man. He was happy to learn that Malone limited his illegal conduct to gambling and loan sharking and had no involvement in more serious crimes. It made things easier for Pirelli to deal with the hoodlum.

The following evening, Malone showed at the Blue Grotto. Mario escorted him to a private office on the second floor. Twenty minutes later the bar phone rang and Pirelli was summoned to the office. When he entered the room he saw Malone sitting at a small table toying with a freshly poured Manhattan. Mario nodded to Pirelli and left the room.

"So you're Pirelli," Malone said as the detective joined him at the table.

"That's me," Pirelli answered.

"Hi ya doing, the name's James Malone. But my friends call me Jamie."

"And what do I call you?"

"Let's put it this way, Pirelli. If our little conversation goes the way I'd like it to go, you'll be calling me Jamie. If it don't, it don't matter because we won't be talking again."

"Fair enough," Pirelli said.

"But before we talk, Pirelli, what did Mario tell you about me?"

"He told me you're looking for a little help with your business."

"Did he tell you what kinda business I'm in?"

"Yeah! Gambling."

"Good. And what else did Mario tell you?"

"He told me that you stay away from drugs. That's the reason I here talking to you.'"

"I'll take that as a compliment, Pirelli."

"It was meant as a complement, Jamie" Pirelli said.

"Good. Anyway, Mario told me that gambling don't offend you too much right now. Is that right?"

"Let's put it this way, Jamie, even before I was suspended gambling didn't offend me too much."

Malone smiled at Pirelli's response and took the gesture as an invitation to get down to business.

"Okay," Malone said. "Lemme be blunt with ya. I got three banks where I run my business outta, strictly sports, horses and numbers. And it's one big pain in the ass every time one of them gets hit. Now I don't mind the arrest, but it fucks me up real good when they take my work."

"I know what you mean," Pirelli said, nodding his head.

"So Pirelli," Malone continued, "What I wanna talk to you about is setting up something so I can get a heads up before any of my spots is hit. Is that doable?"

"Talking about it is no problem, Jamie. But setting something up depends…" Pirelli purposely let his voice trail off."

""Depends on what," Malone asked.

"It depends on who else gotta know about our business. You see, Jamie, things ain't like they used to be, and I don't wanna take anymore more risks than I have to."

Pirelli had heeded his partner's words. If you're gonna play the role of a corrupt cop then you gotta act like a corrupt cop. If you don't act cautious, If you act with impunity like you're not worried about getting caught, it won't be long before somebody smells a rat.

"Tell me about it," Malone agreed. "That fuckin Knapp Commission fucked things up for every body, not only you guys. I used to do business with the Division and the Boro and everybody was happy. I didn't have to worry about a thing and, what's more, they even locked up my competitors. Anyway, that's history. And don't worry about anybody knowing our business," Malone said convincingly, "I tell nobody my business."

"Good. Cause if we can work something out, nobody's to know our business, except maybe Mario."

"No problem there, Pirelli."

"And if you happen to stop by the lounge some evening we have nothing more to say to me. Except, of course, can I buy you a drink, okay?"

Malone smiled, "Sounds good to me, Pirelli. Now that we got that outta the way, can we talk?"

"That depends on how loud you talk, Jamie."

Malone appreciated Pirelli's direct response.

"How about five hundred a month for each spot is that loud enough?"

"What did you say," Pirelli shot back, the palm of his right hand cupping his ear.

Malone laughed in spite of himself. "I said six hundred for each location. Did you hear me now?"

"I tell you what, Jamie. Make it an even two thousand for the three locations and I'll see what I can do," Pirelli said firmly. "And that includes a piece for my man, Mario."

"You got it," Malone said happily.

"Good. Just give me a day or two to see if I can put this thing together. I'm pretty sure I can, but I have to confirm it with a few people first. I'll let Mario know if it's a go. If it is, you give him the addresses of the three locations and a telephone number for me to call with a heads up if any of 'em is gonna be hit. And of course don't forget to include the first month's nut."

"Done," Malone said. "I like your style, Pirelli. If this works out, I'm sure we can do other things together. Meanwhile, I'll wait to hear from Mario," Malone said as he walked out of the office.

Now alone, Pirelli looked under the table and felt what he knew would be there. Taped to the underside of the table where he and Malone had been sitting was a small ten-watt radio transmitter. As Pirelli had suspected, the office had been bugged. The conversation he had with Malone was probably overheard by Mario and probably recorded too. Then for the benefit of those who may be listening, he picked up the phone and placed a call to the Public Morals Division. After six rings, a harried police officer answered the call.

"Public Morals, O'Connor," the voice answered.

"Hiya O'Connor," Pirelli said in a loud clear voice. Is Lieutenant Pastia there? This is a friend of his… "When he gets back, would you ask him to call Pirelli at home?"

… "Yeah, he got the number." … "Thanks O'Connor."

Pirelli returned the phone to its cradle and made his way back to the bar where Mario greeted him with a big smile. He wanted to know how the conversation with Malone had gone. Pirelli repeated the entire conversation that Mario had already overheard.

"Oh, and one thing more," he added. "I included you in on the contract. Is that okay with you?"

"Absolutely," Mario replied.

"Good," Pirelli said.

"Now if I can put this thing together, Malone will give you the first month's nut. You keep three hundred for yourself and put the rest in the breast pocket of my jacket after I hang it up in the back room. There's no need for us to discuss the money or any of the arrangements again unless it's absolutely necessary."

"No problem, Pirelli and thanks for including me in."

"Oh, and one more thing, Mario, you're to keep your mouth shut about our arrangement."

"You got it pal," Mario said gleefully.

The rest of the evening was uneventful. It was almost four in the morning before Pirelli finished up at the lounge and headed home. As soon as he entered his apartment he headed straight for the phone. He was anxious to fill in his partner.

On the second ring, Solly picked up the phone. "Okay Pirelli, this better be good."

"Hey! How did you know it was me, Solly?"

"What other putz do I know that would call me in the middle of the night? What's up?"

"We have to meet tomorrow, Solly."

"And you had to wake me up to tell me that?" Solly grumbled.

"No, but I just wanted to fill you in on some good news."

"Like what," Solly asked curiously.

"Like I just put Malone on the pad. That's what."

"What!"

"You heard me. I put Malone on the pad."

"Hey, that's great kid, looks like we finally got a break."

"A big one, pal. Anyway, I'll fill you in the morning."

"Where?"

"About noon. At Katz's."

"You got it" Solly said happily, already thinking about the Pastrami on club he would order.

CHAPTER FORTY-ONE

P irelli got to the popular lower Eastside kosher deli a little after noon. He found Solly sitting at a corner table in the rear, chewing on an overstuffed pastrami on club, sipping on a bottle of Dr. Brown's diet cream soda.

Pirelli ordered a cup of black coffee and salami on rye. As he waited for order to come Pirelli briefed Solly on the Malone contract.

Solly was elated. The detectives knew that Ardone would hear about the Malone deal and probably approach Pirelli with a contract of his own. Ardone was a heavy earner, a man who would not miss an opportunity to make money.

"By the way, kid, after lunch I'll bring the Chief up to date about your contract with Malone. Then I'll run it by the DA's office just to be on the safe side."

"Run what by?" Pirelli asked curiously.

"The fact that you're gonna be taking monthly payments from Malone. Technically, you'll be committing a crime by taking the money."

"But it's part of an undercover operation."

"Yeah, an operation that only me, you, and the Chief know

about. What if the Chief should grab his chest and turn purple? That'll leave only you and me that know about it."

"What about the Commissioner?"

"Of course the Chief keeps him informed about the investigation but who knows if he gives him every detail."

"Okay Solly, whatever you think."

After lunch, Pirelli headed for his health club for a swim and some steam while Solly headed to police headquarters to brief the Chief on the Malone development.

The Chief was pleased at the way the investigation was finally moving forward. He told Solly that he would alert him if the Public Morals Division planed to execute a warrant on the Eastside of Manhattan. It would be a serious setback for the investigation if one of Malone's banks was raided and Pirelli didn't tip him off in advance.

Before Solly left his office, the Chief called the District Attorney and asked that one of his top assistants be assigned to monitor the illegal payments made to Pirelli.

Later that same afternoon, Solly met with his favorite homicide assistant district attorney to inform him of the Malone contract.

"How you doing, Solly," Warren Buckner said warmly as Solly entered his office.

"Just fine, Warren. And thanks for meeting with me so soon."

"So what's up, Solly? The District Attorney told me he wants me to monitor some kind of an undercover operation you got going. What he didn't tell me is what it has to do with my Bureau."

"To be honest with you, Warren, I don't exactly know where we're going with this thing yet, but it's connected to the McCarthy homicide. Remember, that young cop who was murdered several months ago?"

"I remember it well," Buckner said sympathetically. "And if there's anything I can do to help, consider it done."

"I know that, Warren. Anyway, I hope you don't mind that I asked that you be assigned personally. The last thing I need right now is for some young assistant to be breathing down my neck every step of the way."

Buckner laughed. "I know what you mean, Solly. Why don't you give me a run down on what you have so far and then you can update me as things develop."

"Right now I got an undercover that's playing the role of a corrupt cop. He's trying to get next to some wise guys that may be able to help us with the homicide. He just put a bookmaker associated with the Grimaldi family on the pad. He's supposed to be getting two thousand a month to protect three of his gambling locations on the Eastside."

"Sounds like you're on your way, Solly."

"Yeah, it looks promising. By the way, Warren, I thought I'd voucher the bribe money with you too, if you don't mind, he fewer people in the department who know about this kind of thing, the better."

"I hear you, Solly,"

"I knew you'd understand, Warren. I'll contact you as soon as we get the first month's nut."

"No problem Solly, just be careful."

"Thanks again Warren," Solly said as he headed for the door.

CHAPTER FORTY-TWO

Saturday night was a re-run of the night before. Pirelli arrived at the lounge early. He was anxious to know whether Mario had made contact with Malone. He entered the tiny alcove located at the far end of the bar, removed his tailored sport jacket and replaced it with a freshly pressed bar coat. After placing his own jacket on a padded hanger, he took his position behind the bar and waited for word from Mario. Throughout the long and hectic night, Mario said nothing about having made contact with Malone. Disappointed, Pirelli was tempted to raise the issue with the man but decided against it. 'I hope Malone didn't have a change of heart,' Pirelli thought. 'Or worse, could it be he smelled a rat?'

Closing time neared and Mario turned to his helper.

"Some night, huh Pirelli, you must be out on your feet? Why don't you take off, I'll finish up here."

Disappointed by Mario's silence about the Malone deal he passed on his customary nightcap, retrieved jacket and headed for the exit.

He was instantly refreshed by the cool, early morning breeze. Despite his exhaustion, Pirelli's many hard years on the street came routinely to the fore. His eyes darted everywhere as he walked briskly, continually checking doorways and between parked cars. As he walked through the streets of the city that never sleeps he lit up a thick cigar and puffed away leisurely, still wondering why Mario hadn't mentioned anything about Malone.

When he arrived at his apartment he removed his jacket and draped it over a chair. It was then that he first noticed the envelope in the jacket's left inner breast pocket. He removed the envelope and before opening it, he cried out gleefully. "It's fucking money! I can smell it!"

He quickly tore open the envelope and removed seventeen 100 dollar bills. Then he removed a small yellow piece of paper that contained the telephone numbers and addresses of Malone's banks. He congratulated himself by reaching for the bottle of scotch that was always nearby. After pouring himself a generous drink, he counted the money. As instructed, Mario had taken his share of the two thousand dollars. He rose from his chair and began dancing about the huge room, pausing momentarily to grin at a wall-to-wall bevel-block mirror.

"We're on our way, Solly," he said to the mirror. "Wait until the Chief hears about this."

The next morning, Pirelli called his partner and asked him to come over ASAP. When Solly arrived at Pirelli's apartment Pirelli shared the good news with him. He handed Solly the seventeen hundred dollars for vouchering at the District Attorney's office.

The detectives spent the rest of the morning planning their next move. If their plan worked the way they hoped it would, the wise guys that frequented the Grotto would hear about Pirelli's contract with Malone. When they heard about it, they would ask Pirelli to involve himself in their own illegal schemes.

The detectives reasoned that by having other illegal dealings at the lounge Pirelli would be accepted into the circle of wise guys. Then, over time, he would hear something about either the Cutolo killing or the cop killing, or both.

But what if both Malone and Mario had told no one about the Malone contract? Hadn't they been instructed in no uncertain terms to say nothing about the contract?

Pirelli looked to his partner. "What do you think Solly? You think there's a chance Mario told no one, even Ardone? After all, he followed my instructions to a tee, never said a peep about the pay-off. He just took his share of the cash and put the rest in my jacket."

"That's a possibility I guess. But I doubt it, besides the room was bugged. And you know fuckin well it wasn't Mario that bugged it. No kid, I'm sure Ardone knows about it. It's the rest of the wise guys in the joint that I'm not too sure about."

The detectives sat quietly trying to think of a way to leak the Malone contract.

Solly shouted out. "A staged raid."

"What the fuck are you talking about? A staged raid."

"I'm talking about conducting a phony raid on one of Malone's banks. Then when you tip off Malone about the upcoming raid, there's no way the word won't get out that Malone has an in with Public Morals. And someone in the bar is sure to figure that you're that in."

"Very good, Solly. Who said fat guys can't think about anything but food?"

"Fuck you, Pirelli."

"But how do we set up the raid without telling the Public Morals people too much, after all some of those guys will be asking a lot of questions."

"That's easy, kid, we don't tell Public Morals anything about the raid. All we need is for the Chief to put together a team. He can even go on the raid himself. That way nobody will ask any questions. And when they hit the place find the joint empty, it'll be case closed."

"Sounds good to me, Solly."

"I'll run it by the Chief and see what he sez," Solly continued. "I'll call you as soon as I hear something." The next morning, Solly called Pirelli and told him that the Chief had bought the idea. Later in the day, the two detectives met and mapped out a plan. The raid would be set for a Saturday afternoon. It was the day of the week that a raid on a gambling location almost always took place. After all, the bank would have the week's work and the increased weekend bets on hand.

CHAPTER FORTY-THREE

I t was Friday, and the Blue Grotto Lounge would soon be packed with weekenders as well as Grotto regulars.

Before the crowd arrived Pirelli saw Ardone enter the lounge. Ardone immediately motioned for Mario to join him in the upstairs office.

10 minutes later Mario came down and told Pirelli to go upstairs; Ardone wanted to speak with him.

'Finally', Pirelli mused. 'I get to meet the cocksucker. I just hope I can keep my cool when I talk to him'.

Pirelli entered the office and Ardone greeted him. "So you're the guy that Mario's been telling me about."

"That's me."

"Did Mario tell you who I am?"

"Yeah, he did. The first day I started here."

"And what did he tell you about me?"

"You mean other than you're his boss."

"Yeah."

"He told me you're like a baker, if there's dough around you got your hands in it."

Ardone laughed. "I see you got a sense of humor, Pirelli, not that

Mario would say anything like that about me. Anyway, I hear you're
a very enterprising guy?"

'So he does know about the Malone contract,' Pirelli mused.
"What's that supposed to mean, Frank"

"Listen, Pirelli, I got two things to say to you. One: my friends
call me Cheech and two: my friends don't jerk me off. Ya got it?"

"I got it, Cheech," Pirelli said quickly."

"Now you better get down stairs before the crowd gets here.
We'll talk another time."

Pirelli returned to his place behind the bar an immediately
noticed a woman who occupied the corner stool diagonally across
from his workstation. She was intriguing; clearly different from the
other women that usually sat at the bar unescorted.

Judging her to be in her early thirties, Pirelli appreciated how her
hair fell in long waves cradling a face that was no less than perfection.
Slender yet solidly built, she was clearly the most stunning woman he
had seen in the Grotto to date. Pirelli admired her smartly tailored,
charcoal gray business suit. When she walked to the ladies room her
partially opened jacket revealed an ivory silk blouse that highlighted
full, well-rounded, breasts.

'Good God, she's really something else' Pirelli thought. 'Why
wasn't I working that side of the bar?'

Pirelli shook his head as he attended to the clamor for service that
continued unabated. He chanced another quick glance in her direction
and this time their eyes met. Pirelli then realized that the woman had
been appraising him as well. The woman managed a polite smile.
Pirelli simply nodded and returned to his duties behind the bar.

Some 30 minutes later the woman was still sitting by herself.
Occasionally, she would wave away the cigar and cigarette smoke
that was assaulting her from every direction.

'Nothing I can do for her in that area,' Pirelli thought. 'A bar
served alcohol and alcohol demanded smoke as an accessory.'

After a short break for some much needed relief, Pirelli returned to his workstation. He was disappointed to see Ardone standing alongside the woman. The tall powerfully built man had his hand resting on her shoulder in a more than familiar way. Pirelli had been wondering why so striking a woman, seated alone at the bar throughout the course of the evening, had not been hit upon. Now he had his answer. 'She must be Ardone's main squeeze,' he thought as the couple engaged in quiet conversation. 'I'd better stay away from her.'

A short time later, Ardone's swarthy face broke into a smile for the first time since he had joined the woman. He bent over to plant a quick kiss on her cheek and abruptly left the bar. Eyeing the swift retreat, Pirelli shrugged and turned back to his tasks just in time to see Mario grinning broadly at him.

"So whadda ya think Pirelli," Mario said softly. "She's something else to look at, ain't she?"

Pirelli wearily shook his head. "That she is, Mario. I was wondering why nobody tried to hit on her. Then I saw Ardone show up."

"You mean you never saw them together before tonight?"

"I never saw her at the bar, that's for sure."

"That's probably because they usually meet upstairs in the restaurant, they often dine there."

"Is she his main squeeze?"

"Worse," Mario said. "She's his sister."

"His sister," Pirelli exclaimed, a surprised look cloaking his face.

He turned to the huge bar mirror that enabled him to observe the woman as she calmly sipped her drink. Then he turned back to Mario and said softly, "What's her name?"

"Cassandra,"

"The name fits her like a velvet glove," Pirelli said.

Mario continued to stare steadily at Pirelli while slowly shaking his head.

"How come I got the feeling that you're trying to tell me something, Mario?"

"Ardone is very protective of his sister, if you know what I mean Pirelli. I hope you're wise enough to show your respect."

Appreciating the cynical caution of his friend, Pirelli laughed aloud. "You don't think I would try to hit on her? Do you Mario?"

As he started to walk away, Mario suddenly swung back. "To tell ya the truth, Pirelli, the thought crossed my mind."

"It crossed my mind too," Pirelli said smiling. "But I certainly wouldn't try if I thought it would piss off Ardone."

"Why don't you ask him, he's back," Mario said kiddingly

Ardone rejoined his sister at the bar. After a few minutes he called out across the bar.

"Hey Pirelli, c'mere, I want you to meet somebody."

"Be right there, Cheech," Pirelli said happily, as he finished attending to a thirsty customer.

Pirelli walked over to Ardone and nodded a friendly hello to his sister.

"This is my sister, Cassie."

Pirelli looked at the woman and smiled broadly. "Nice to meet you Cassie, my name's Pirelli."

"Do you have a first name?" the woman said softly.

"It's Anthony. But everyone calls me calls me Pirelli."

"Mind if I call you Anthony?"

"Not at all, Cassie, it'll be my pleasure to have a beautiful woman call me by my first name."

"Enough with the bullshit, Pirelli," Ardone said abruptly. "As you might have noticed, Cassie here likes to sit at the bar alone once in a while. When she does, I want you to keep an eye on her. Most people in here know better than to fuck with her, but just in case some drunk starts to hassle her, I want you to take care of it."

"No problem Cheech. I'll consider that assignment to be an on the job fringe benefit."

"Yeah, well as long as you remember it's a job," Ardone said sternly as he rose from his stool. "Let's go Cassie, it's getting late."

When Ardone and his sister left the lounge, Pirelli thought about the woman. He had an important decision to make. If he could get close to Ardone's sister, then surely he could get close to Ardone.

But he knew it would be risky, very risky. Hadn't Mario made it clear that Ardone was very protective of his sister? How would Ardone react if he was to make advances towards the woman and she complained to her brother? If Ardone didn't like it, if he saw it as a personal insult to him, it could kill the investigation. .

Yet, Pirelli kept thinking about the opportunity to move the investigation forward. It was compelling. "Fuck it," he mumbled.

Pirelli made his decision. He would set aside the risk of offending the woman, or Ardone and make a move on Cassie.

CHAPTER FORTY-FOUR

O n Saturday the raid was set to go. Pirelli had called the contact number a day earlier and alerted Malone of a pending raid.

"Hello", a gravelly male voice answered.

"Lemme talk to Jamie," Pirelli said quickly.

"Who's this," the voice inquired.

"Never mind who it is." Pirelli said, "Just lemme talk to Jamie. Tell him somebody's got a message for him."

"Yeah, well there ain't no Jamie here, ya got the wrong number," the voice replied.

"Wrong number, huh? In that case give him the message anyway. Tell him the good looking skinny guy that drinks a lot said he should expect company at 86th Street, tomorrow at 2 p.m."

Without waiting for a response, Pirelli slammed down the phone. He knew Malone would get the message.

When told of the call, Malone ordered a no-nonsense associate to have a crew work throughout the night to clean out the bank. When the crew was done, the only evidence of an illegal gambling operation that remained were twenty telephone jacks, with no phones attached.

The raid on the policy bank went off exactly as planned. At 2 p.m. the Chief of Detectives and his task force burst into a now empty loft. In order to gain publicity, Solly had alerted a crime reporter friend about the staged raid and when the Chief and his team of detectives departed the loft, they found themselves flanked by two cameras and a veteran newspaper reporter.

Everything had gone off as planned. The Sunday morning editions of the local papers lost no time in making the most from an otherwise ho-hum news day. After reading the news report of the unproductive raid on one of Malone's banks, everyone at the Grotto knew Malone had been warned in advance.

That evening, Pirelli reported for work earlier than usual. When he arrived at the lounge he saw it was especially crowded for a Sunday. He changed his jacket and joined Mario who was attending to a group of wise guys that were gathered at the bar. Pirelli greeted the group with a smile and waited for the inevitable question to be asked. Finally it came.

Ralph Scarpardi, a rugged-looking man with a pocked-marked face and broad shoulders was the first to speak.

"I see where your former boss got egg on his face yesterday, huh Pirelli. I wonder who it was that tipped Malone about the raid," Scapardi said with a big smile.

"What makes you think he got tipped, Scappy," Pirelli asked.

"C'mon Pirelli, don't jerk me off. You know fuckin well somebody dimed him about the raid. Why the fuck do ya think the spot was cleaned out before your guys got there?"

"You got me, Scappy," Pirelli shot back with a telltale smirk on his face. "Why don't you ask him? Then we'll both know."

"You know fuckin well Malone ain't gonna tell me nothin."

"Then I guess we'll never know because it wasn't me, if that's what you're thinking."

"Okay, so it wasn't you. But the least you can do is buy a round of drinks with what you earned," Scarpardi shot back."

"I'll tell you what Scappy, even though I didn't earn a nickel, it'll be my pleasure to buy a round for the boys," Pirelli said smiling as he filled everyone's glass.

Throughout the evening Pirelli was continually peppered with questions about the raid. The raid had been a huge success. Now everyone in the Grotto knew it was Pirelli that had tipped off Malone.

CHAPTER FORTY-FIVE

I t was 2 a.m. and Pirelli was busy wiping down the bar. He looked up, he saw Ardone's sister, the gorgeous Cassie, smiling at him.

"Hello Anthony," she said as she climbed onto a vacant stool.

"Hello, Cassandra."

"Cassie, please." She seemed interesting in chatting.

"Cassie it is. But I'll tell you this, Cassie, either name goes well with an incredibly beautiful woman."

"Very nice, Anthony and a well-deserved compliment I may add," she said smiling. "Do I have time for a night cap?"

"For you, I'll make time, "What'll it be?"

"Can you make a Gin and Sin?"

"Is the Pope Catholic," Pirelli shot back.

"You mean you don't have to look in the Mixing Guide?"

"What's a mixing guide?"

"Okay Anthony, I'm impressed," she said, running a moist tongue over her lips. "Now how about showing me?"

"You got it, lovely lady."

Pirelli went quickly to the task. He quickly visualized the gin, lemon and orange juices, a dash or two of grenadine and powdered sugar. The picture widened to depict vigorous shaking over ice before being strained into a cocktail glass. Finally, he brought his left hand from behind his back and plopped a long-stemmed cherry into the drink. Pirelli slipped a coaster under the chilled cocktail glass and placed the concoction before Cassie.

She stared at Pirelli over the rim of the glass as she took her first sip.

"Well?" Pirelli said fishing.

"Oh my, it's marvelous, Anthony."

"Everything I do for a lady is marvelous."

"Don't be fresh, Anthony, my brother might not like it."

Pirelli hesitated. The thought of angering Ardone once again weighed heavily on Pirelli's mind, not only for his own safety but for the sake of the investigation, too. But his decision having been already made, he continued to press on.

"To be honest with you, Cassie, I'm more concerned about what you might like than what your brother might like. But thanks for the warning. I certainly don't want to have a problem with your brother."

"Don't worry, Anthony. You won't have a problem with him, unless of course you have a problem with me."

The woman smiled, popped a cigarette between her lips and waited. Pirelli pulled out his gold Dunhill and lighted the scented cigarette.

Cassie rolled her tongue over full-formed scarlet painted lips and said, "Thank you for being so attentive, Anthony."

"Does that mean we're friends?"

"We're friends."

"Good. And now that we're friends, can I ask you something?"

"Of course you can, what is it?"

"How do we become better friends," Pirelli grinned.

"For starters, you can make me another one of your delicious drinks."

"If you think I make them delicious here, Cassie, you should taste the way I make them at my apartment."

"Is that an invitation, Anthony?"

"It's an open one, Cassie."

"I'll tell you what then," Cassie said. "Why don't you ask my brother if it's okay for me to accept your invitation? He just walked in the door."

Cassie smiled as her brother and a stunning young woman approached. She wore a tight fitting black silk dress that highlighted a slim, perfectly formed body. The band on her left hand, covered with brilliant diamond baguettes, was overshadowed only by the three-carat engagement ring next to it. She wasn't very tall, only about five-feet five, but the heels she was wearing added a good four inches. She had light brown hair with full curls streaked with patches of blond highlights. Her eyebrows had been shaved off and replaced with soft brown pencil markings. Bluish green eyes were perfectly surrounded by bluish green eye shadow. Many of the Grotto regulars found it difficult to keep their eyes from lusting after her. But they knew better.

Ardone draped his arm about his sister's shoulder and drew back slightly, allowing her to offer her cheek for a brotherly peck.

Then, turning towards Pirelli, he said "So how ya doin Pirelli."

"Not as good as you Cheech," Pirelli replied with a grin as he appraised the beauty holding onto the thug's arm.

"Say hello to Celeste," Ardone gloated. "Her looks are second only to her intellect and charm."

"Beautifully done, Frankie" added Ardone's bride of less than a year. "Instead of becoming a business man, you should've been a politician."

"The gentleman's name is Pirelli," Ardone offered.

Celeste nodded her head and extended her hand to the smiling bartender.

"How do you do Mrs. Ardone," Pirelli said, politely as he could.

"The ladies were just goin to get a bite to eat. Ain't that right girls," Ardone suggested, nodding his head in the direction of the upstairs restaurant.

With the departure of the women, Ardone got down to business. "I learned a great deal about you since the last time we talked, Pirelli. I'm told you're doing just great around here. And I'm not referring to your bartending."

"I'm not sure I know what you're talking about, Cheech."

"It don't matter what you know, it's what I know that counts."

" Ardone's swarthy features evolved into a broad smile. "I know just about everything that goes on around here."

Ardone awaited a reply. But when Pirelli simply shrugged and said nothing, he continued.

"So you have friends in the department."

"I got a few here and there."

"I'm told it's more than a few."

"Look, why don't you tell me where you're going with this, Cheech?"

"Listen Pirelli," … Ardone turned his head in response to Mario tapping his shoulder,

"You got a phone call Cheech."

"What the fuck's wrong with you Mario? Can't you see I'm busy? Tell whoever the fuck it is that I'll call 'em back later."

"But it's your wife Cheech," Mario said apologetically. "She's calling from upstairs."

"I don't care who the fuck it is. Didn't I just tell you I'm busy? Now get the fuck outta here."

Mario retreated without another word.

"Sorry Pirelli. Now where were we?"

"We were talking about friends in my department."

"Right and I'm told you have a valuable commodity for sale."

"Commodity?" Pirelli asked.

"Information, protection, that sort of thing."

Pirelli smiled thinly. "That depends."

"Depends on what?"

"Depends on who the buyer is, what information they want and what they're looking to protect, and more important how much they're looking to spend."

"Fair enough, anyway, I was thinking maybe you and me may be able to do a little business of our own. Interested?"

"I'll let you know when you make a proposal."

"Good. I'll let you know when I have one," Ardone said. "But we'll talk again. We'll talk real soon."

Ardone nodded his goodbye and looked around. "Hey Mario," he called out, "Now go tell my wife to order me a drink. Tell her I'll be up in a minute."

CHAPTER FORTY-SIX

Pirelli and Solly met for a strategy meeting at Pirelli's apartment. After a quick luncheon snack, they spent the next hour discussing the latest developments in the case. The detectives were pleased with their progress to date. Pirelli had gained the confidence of many of the wise guys that frequented the lounge. More importantly, he was speaking directly with the cop-killer. He would now focus his full attention on winning Ardone's confidence and ultimately, get hold of the bullet buried in his shoulder

"Okay Solly, now that we got into Ardone's ear, we gotta figure out a way to get into his shoulder," Pirelli said.

"No shit, kid, the question is how we supposed to do that?"

"Listen Solly, I've been giving this a lotta thought. What we gotta do is figure a way to scare him enough so that he wants to take the bullet out on his own."

"That ain't gonna be easy, pal. And even if you did convince him to have the bullet taken out, how is that gonna help us? We won't know where he'll go to do it and we certainly won't be there when he does."

"Not so fast, Solly. Hear me out. Look, one thing we know for sure is that if Ardone decides to have the bullet removed he can't go to any old doctor. He has to go to one that'll deep six the bullet and not notify the police."

"So what makes you think Ardone don't know a doctor that'll do that?"

"Oh I'm sure he can find a shady doctor that'll do it. But my guess is he's not too anxious to have anybody that knows who he is to remove the bullet, especially a bullet that ties him to two murders. So what we gotta do figure a way for him to come to me for a doctor that don't know who he is."

"How the fuck are you supposed to do that. Don't you think he'll smell a rat if you go to him and tell him you know a doctor that don't know who you are, who'll do the operation, not report it, and deep six the bullet."

"That's not exactly what I had in mind, wise guy."

"Then just what do you have in mind?"

"Remember that upstairs office, the one where I had the sit down with Malone?"

"Yeah, I remember. What about it?"

"Well, we know the room was bugged when I spoke to Malone, and my guess is that it'll be bugged if I ever have another conversation up there. So if I can arrange for me to have a conversation in that office with somebody about a top-notch surgeon who can be trusted, one who won't report an operation to the police, Ardone will certainly hear about it. Then if things go right and he decides to have the operation, he just may come to me for the doctor. I know it's a long fuckin shot, but right now, it's the only shot we got. Anyway, the way I see it, it's worth a try."

"And how are you gonna arrange that?"

"First we borrow an undercover from the Feds; someone who's from out of town so there's no chance of anyone recognizing him. Then we arrange it so he comes to the lounge one night looking for me. I'll tell Mario he's a friend of mine with big money and a big problem and I gotta speak to him in private. Now it's true that Mario might not invite me to use the upstairs office and that'll be the end of that. But you wanna know something large one, I got a feeling he will. He'll wanna hear everything that's going on."

"Sounds like a heavy lift to me, kid."

"I'll grant you it is, but then whatta we got to lose?"

"Nothing I guess,"

"Good! Let's go for it Solly. Run it by the Chief and see what he thinks. Try to sell him on the idea. He's good buddies with the Regional Director of the Bureau and if he asks him to, I'm sure he'll provide us with an undercover to assist us."

"You got it, Pirelli. I'll get right on it."

Solly returned to the squad room where he placed a call to the Chief's office. An hour later the Chief's executive aide returned his call. "He'll see you first thing in the morning, Solly."

CHAPTER FORTY-SEVEN

Solly was at the Chief's office well before 8 a.m. When the Chief arrived he invited Solly in, ordered some coffee, then turned to the First Grader. "So how's it going Solly. How's Pirelli doing out there? You know, I'm getting a lot of heat from the Commissioner."

The Chief listened as Solly laid out Pirelli's plan.

"So what do you think, Chief?"

"I don't know Solly. It sounds like a long shot to me, but then I guess it's worth a try. I'll reach out for the Director later in the day. But remember we're running out of time."

Several days later an undercover agent was assigned to assist Pirelli. The Bureau was glad to help catch a cop killer. Pirelli spent hours with the agent going over an informational conversation he hoped to have with the agent in the lounge's bugged upstairs office.

The undercover, a solid pro, was ready to go and so was Pirelli.

It was a Monday night and the agent appeared at the Grotto in a chauffeured limo. As he entered the lounge, stools began to swivel to permit a careful appraisal of the impressive looking man. He wore a custom-made imported wool suit, a fine Turnbull and Asser

Egyptian cotton shirt with its rolled hand sewn collar enhanced by a boldly striped Zegna silk tie. This outfit and its model stood elegantly in Fratelli Rossetti shoes. The solid gold Rolex President with diamond bezel was not lost on the group. Pausing for a few seconds to allow his eyes time to adjust to the soft lighting, the tall figure walked over to the bar and offered the head bartender a cordial smile.

"Excuse me sir," he said. "I'm looking for Anthony Pirelli. I'm told I might find him here."

"And who are you?" Mario said cautiously.

"My name is Roland Martine. I'm an old friend of his."

Roland Martine was a nom de guerre, invented for him, along with his driver's license and several credit cards, at FBI headquarters. Just in case.

"Hold on a minute, I'll see if he's around."

Mario walked in the back and found Pirelli checking the liquor inventory. He told him there was a man named Martine asking for him.

"Roland Martine?" Pirelli asked.

"I'm not sure, it might be Roland."

"Does he look like money?"

"As a matter of fact, he does."

"That's Roland. Yeah, I know him. We grew up together."

"Do you want to talk to him or should I throw him out."

"Are you kidding, I'll be glad to see him. The guy's worth millions and he probably has a problem and needs my help. Maybe I can earn a few dollars."

A few minutes later Pirelli walked over to the agent and embraced him warmly. Pirelli marveled at the way the agent was able to portray an intense strain in his eyes.

Several minutes later, Pirelli walked over to Mario. "Listen Mario, my friend here has a little problem that he wants to discuss with me in private. We're gonna take a little walk outside. We won't be too long, okay."

"No problem. But if it's privacy you want, why don't you use the second floor office. Nobody will bother you up there. And I'll even send up a couple of drinks."

Pirelli tried to conceal his excitement at being offered the upstairs office. 'So far, so good,' he thought. He was sure the radio transmitter was still in place under the table.

He motioned to the undercover agent and the two men made their way to the second floor office. When they entered, Pirelli headed straight for the table where he and Malone had had their conversation.

"You want something to drink Roland?" he said as the pair settled down. "I'll have something sent up."

"Nothing to drink right now, but thanks for asking."

"Hey! Guys who don't drink can't be trusted, Roland. They taught me that when I was a recruit at the Police Academy," Pirelli joked.

"You'll have to forgive me Pirelli, but I'm not exactly in a joking mood."

"Sorry Roland, I didn't mean to make light of your problem. What's on your mind?"

The agent leaned forward and said, "First let me begin by telling you I'm thinking of putting an organization together for a congressional run."

"Hey, that's great Roland."

"Yeah, I'll be running as a pro-life candidate."

"So what's the problem?"

The agent acted out his part beautifully. He looked carefully about the room for the benefit of anyone who might be looking in on them with a concealed camera.

"It's…it's my daughter," Martine paused, "she got herself pregnant two months ago by a married man."

"Sorry to hear that Roland. How can I help?"

"Listen Pirelli, if what I'm about to ask is a problem for you, just tell me. I'll understand."

"Try me Roland."

"My daughter wants to have an abortion."

"And the guy is putting the squeeze on you, right?"

"Nothing like that, the relationship is over. In fact, he doesn't even know she's pregnant, thank God."

"So why doesn't she just have an abortion? It's legal now, you know. It shouldn't be a problem. Not before the third month."

"The problem is that if she has an abortion, I'm sure it will be leaked when I announce my candidacy. And that, my friend, will put a serious dent in my political future."

Pirelli agreed.

The undercover agent carefully blotted the imaginary glistening beads of perspiration across his brow with a neatly folded handkerchief. "Now if I can somehow arrange to have it done by a physician whose talents are second to none, one who will destroy the medical records after the surgery, then there can be no chance of a leak. As you know Anthony, my old friend, I'm a very wealthy man and money is no object."

Pirelli lit a cigar and stared thoughtfully at Martine. You know Roland it just so happens that I know a doctor that was an old Army buddy of mine. We stayed in touch over the years. Without going into too much detail, let's just say he's a degenerate gambler and is always in need of extra cash. In fact, I hadda help him out one time when he was being squeezed by some loan sharks. So he owes me big time. Anyway, the bottom line is I think I can get him to go along with it. He's a top-notch surgeon who practices way out in Jersey. But I'll tell you right now, Roland, we're talking big bucks."

"That's not a problem. Money is not an issue as long as he's top notch and there are no medical records for me to be concerned about."

"In that case I think I can set it up."

Martine blew out his breath in relief. "I really appreciate this Pirelli. When can you let me know?"

"Give me a week or so. I should be able to talk to him by then. Oh, and one more thing Roland. When I call, be careful what you say over the phone. You understand?"

"I understand perfectly."

Pirelli grinned and climbed to his feet. The two men shook hands and left the office. Pirelli pointed to the glaring Mario and whispered, "See that mean looking face standing behind the bar? The one you saw earlier? Well he's trying to tell one of us to get his ass back to work. You got any idea who he means?"

Martine laughed and embraced Pirelli warmly. "Listen Pirelli, anytime you want out of here I will always have something for you to do. Meanwhile, I'll wait to hear from you," he said, as he turned to the door and eased his way through the growing crowd of patrons.

CHAPTER FORTY-EIGHT

The following night Ardone returned to the Blue Grotto Lounge. He was back from a visit to Vegas. Having had donated a considerable amount of money at a cold craps table, he was looking for an opportunity to recoup some of his losses. He dropped his wife off at home then headed straight for the Grotto. When Mario briefed him about Pirelli's conversation with Martine, a big smile creased his face. He saw it as an opportunity to earn some cash.

Pirelli was off for several days but Ardone couldn't wait. He ordered Mario to get in touch with him. Mario called Pirelli's apartment and left a message that Ardone wanted to speak with him at the lounge at 2 p.m the following day.

Pirelli was at the lounge promptly at 2 p.m. Ardone was waiting for him in the upstairs restaurant. It was closed and afforded the pair the privacy they wanted in the upstairs office. After a few minutes of casual conversation, Ardone quickly got down to business.

"Listen Pirelli," he said abruptly, "I'll get right to the point. It's about time that you and me started to earn a few dollars."

"Sounds good to me, Cheech, whatta got in mind?"

"Well for starters, I think we can make some money off of your friend Martine."

"Martine! How the fuck do you know about Martine's problem?"

"Because I earn my living knowing things, Pirelli, and it just so happens that I know that he is willing to pay big bucks to resolve a problem he has."

"That's bullshit, Ardone. You can't possibly know what Martine's problem is."

"The name's Cheech, Pirelli. We're friends, remember?"

Pirelli feigned anger.

Ardone smiled. "Come on Pirelli. Martine is a wealthy man who has a big problem. A man who needs our help," he said emphatically.

"Whatta mean our help? Listen Cheech, with due respect you can't possibly know what Martine spoke to me about."

"I can't huh? Ardone said smiling. Supposin I told you that I got the upstairs office bugged and that I got your entire conversation with Martine on tape."

"What!" Pirelli shouted out, "That fucking cocksucker Mario. No wonder why he let me use the upstairs office. "That's it, I'm outta this fucking joint. But before I go I'm gonna kick that scumbag's ass."

"Whoa! Hold on Pirelli. Take it easy for Christ sake. Slow down a minute. First of all, Mario has no idea that the upstairs office is bugged," Ardone lied. "In fact nobody knows that I got the office bugged. It just so happens that all the conversations that take place in the office are recorded. I don't discriminate I just keep tabs on everybody. That's how you survive in my world."

"I don't fuckin believe this," Pirelli fumed.

"Take it easy, Pirelli. Listen, this is strictly business so don't take it personal."

Pirelli mustered a phony grumble.

"The way I see it, this could work to our mutual benefit."

"Whatta ya mean, our mutual benefit?"

"Look at it this way Pirelli. This Martine guy is a friend of yours, right?"

"So?"

"So even though he's got plenty of dough, he might feel you gotta go easy on him. If you know what I mean?"

"Keep going."

"If you tell him the doctor you had in mind is in the wind and you had to turn to a third party, like me, to get one. Then you can bang him for twice what you were thinking of banging him for. And to show you what kind a guy I am, since it's your deal, you take sixty percent and I'll take forty. What do you say now?"

Pirelli shook his head. "I say you're some fuckin piece of work Cheech."

Ardone laughed. "I thought you'd see it my way."

Ardone folded his hands like a schoolboy seated at a desk.

"This is only the beginning, Pirelli. We're gonna be doin a lotta things together. And I'm not talking about penny ante shit either."

Ardone got up and smiled. "Anyway, lemme know when you put it in place, and what I gotta do. Mario knows how to reach me."

CHAPTER FORTY-NINE

everal days later, Ardone showed up at the Grotto with his sister in tow. The hour was late and most of the Grotto regulars had gone. Ardone helped Cassie onto a bar stool then turned to Pirelli.

"When you get a chance, Pirelli, gimme a little Grappa and see what Cassandra here wants."

"You got it, Cheech. What'll ya have, Cassie?"

"What else would it be?" she said winking at the smiling detective, "the same as the other night. Please."

Pirelli nodded. 'This one is definitely something else,' he mused.

Pirelli set the drinks on the bar and looked directly into Cassie's eyes. Her smile clearly told him that everything was okay. That it was just a matter of time before they would get together.

"So how are things goin since our last conversation, Pirelli?" Ardone asked. "I presume you've started to work on that thing?"

"I'm on top of it, Cheech. I'm seeing my guy tomorrow.

"Well move it along, will you."

"Listen, I'm looking to move on this as much as you are."

"Great. Just keep me advised. Meanwhile, I've arranged for you to be off this coming Friday. I'm going to a little party at a friend's place and I want ya to come along. I think it's time that you see how the other half lives."

Pirelli leaned on the bar and grinned. "That's great, Cheech. Are we goin alone?"

"Let's put it this way, Pirelli. I'm sure we'll have a better time if we do."

Ardone turned to his sister and apologized. "No offense, Cassie, but it's not the kind of party a lady like you would want to attend."

Cassie simply smiled.

Anyway, I gotta run," Ardone said quickly. "I got some business to take care of. Let's go Cassie, I'll drop you off."

"You go ahead, Frank. I want to finish my drink. I'm sure Anthony will call me a cab."

"Whatever you say, honey. I'll call you tomorrow."

Ardone planted a kiss on his sister's cheek and headed straight for the door.

Cassie sipped her drink slowly as she and Pirelli engaged in small talk. Very quickly, however, the conversation became more personal. Cassie was beginning to feel the effect of the powerful drink and let it be known that she found the slender detective attractive. Suddenly she blurted out, "Are you married, Anthony?"

The slender detective smiled. "No, why do you ask Why do you ask?"

"Because when I fuck, I like to spend the night. You do want to fuck me, don't you, Anthony?"

Pirelli, taken back by the woman's aggressiveness, tried to disguise the shock that masked his face.

Then he began to question his decision about getting involved with her, even if it meant losing the chance of getting closer to her brother.

'I hope this fucking broad is playing with a full deck' he thought.

'What if I do her and she gets pissed at me for some reason. Maybe she's a nymph and I won't be able to satisfy her. If she complains to her brother for whatever reason, it's all over for me and for the investigation, too. On the other hand, if I turn her away now she might really get pissed and go out of her way to hurt me. Well it looks like I gotta make sure she don't get pissed at me, for whatever reason. And that's that.'

"I thought you'd never ask, Cassie," Pirelli said casually.

"Good. Why don't you write down your address for me and I'll meet you at your apartment in an hour. I don't think it would be wise for a lady like me to leave here with a bartender. Now would it," Cassie said with a smile as she took the match book cover that Pirelli handed her. "And be sure to have my drink waiting, please," she said as she headed for the door.

Twenty minutes later Pirelli left the lounge and raced to his apartment. After mixing Cassie's favorite drink, he headed for the bathroom for a quick shower. No sooner had he completed a hasty grooming than the intercom on the kitchen wall crackled.

"A Ms. Cassie is here to visit," the doorman announced as doormen do when they have a secret to keep.

Cassie entered the apartment and after a quick look around, kicking off her shoes, said softly, "You don't mind if I make myself comfortable, do you Anthony?"

"It's a house rule, Cassie" Pirelli said as he walked to the refrigerator to retrieve the woman's drink.

After he poured himself some scotch, he joined his guest who had found her way to the dimly lit living room. She was seated on a plush leather couch with her legs stretched comfortably across a nearby coffee table.

Cassie tasted the drink Pirelli had prepared and said, "My Anthony, you weren't exaggerating. This drink tastes even better than those you made for me at the lounge."

"That's because you're having it in my apartment, Cassie."

"Is that right? And what comes after the drink?"

"Well, I guess that's up to us. Now isn't it, Cassie?"

"It most certainly is. By the way, talking about what comes next, Anthony, how come you never married?"

"Because I never met anyone like you before Cassie," Pirelli said, smiling.

Cassie returned a polite smile. "That's so sweet of you to say Anthony, even if it's bullshit."

"Pirelli laughed at her curt response. Anyway, Cassie, why do you ask?"

"I just wanted to be sure that you didn't marry because you don't know how to satisfy a woman."

"Let me put it this way, Cassie," Pirelli said assuredly. "I've never had any complaints."

"Really! Well let me ask you something then."

"Anything," Pirelli said quickly.

"Have you ever made love to a woman who's accustomed to having multiple orgasms?"

Pirelli swallowed hard. "Yes I have," he replied, his face showing a trace of red."

"And?" the woman asked curiously.

"Like I just said Cassie, I've never had any complaints."

As they continued to sip their drinks, Pirelli hit the button on the nearby remote and the soothing voice of Sarah Vaughn filled the room. Minutes later, he placed his arm over Cassie's shoulder and began massaging the back of her neck.

"I like that" she purred.

"You'd like it even better if we got comfortable," he said quickly.

Cassie jumped to her feet and faced Pirelli squarely. She stared directly into his pale green eyes as she matter-of-factly unbuttoned her silk blouse. Then, unhooking the metal fastener on her tight-fitting slacks she tugged aggressively at the waistband until they fell to the floor. Still staring at Pirelli, she stepped out of the expensive pants and immediately shed her bra, leaving only the sheer blouse and bikini panties on to cover her remarkable body.

Pirelli found the partially clad woman even more exciting than if she had been completely naked.

'God she's beautiful,' he thought. He stood up and removed all his clothing. Then he pulled her close and kissed her deeply, his fingertips playing with her hardened nipples. Pirelli could sense the excitement building within her as his tongue found its way into her ear. Still standing, he began to massage her scalp with one hand while the other worked its way down between her legs. He could feel the telltale wetness as his finger moved gently about her most sensitive area.

Cassie sighed as he lightly massaged her clitoris. The more quickly his finger moved against her the more she sighed. Soon, drowning in unbelievable sensations, her body quivered and she began to move rhythmically against his touch.

"You're making me so hot" Cassie gasped. You'd better stop before I get it."

"I want you to get it," Pirelli whispered passionately.

"Oh God, I love it, she sighed, I love it."

It didn't take long. Moments later, Cassie screamed out, "Oh God."

Pirelli smiled. He could feel her vagina pulsating wildly against his touch. Then bending low, he picked her up and carried her to the waiting bedroom, gently tipping her onto the king-sized bed. The cool of silk sheets pressed against her back and she smiled as her newfound lover straddled her nude body. Pirelli fondled her breasts for a few minutes then began to slide slowly down her limp body, running his tongue across her perfumed stomach. Cassie bent her knees and arched her back like a bow to accommodate him as he continued to explore her firm body. Her legs widened allowing his head to drop below. She writhed with indescribable pleasure when his tongue found her.

"Oh God, what you do to me," she cried, "You're going to make me come again."

Reaching up blindly to massage her breasts, his tongue continued to work feverishly within her while she moved her body against him. Digging her nails deeply into the back of his neck, she screamed out, "Oh God, you're doing it to me again."

Letting out an even bigger sigh than before, she relaxed for a moment, smiling contentedly. The pulsating of her moist vagina told Pirelli that he had truly satisfied her once again.

Suddenly, Cassie pushed him away and climbed on top of the man who had delighted her so. She rubbed her breasts lightly across his chest then began to work her way down his body as he had done to her. She stopped her downward slide for a moment to caress his engorged penis between her breasts. Soon she was running her tongue along the rock hard shaft that was quivering in anticipation. Taking his penis in her mouth, she moved her head up and down ever so slowly in long gentle strokes. She felt the excitement building within him as his body began to move with her. Wanting desperately to satisfy him, she began to bob her head up and down quickly, expectantly.

"No Cassie," Pirelli said, pushing her away abruptly. "I don't want it that way. I want to come in you, with you," he whispered softly.

Straddling her body once more, he again sat upright on bent knees and began to fondle her breasts. Then he bent forward and rubbed his sweating body against her.

Cassie smiled as she held her legs out high and wide about him. She let out a soft moan as he gently entered her, remaining motionless for a moment before beginning to move in and out. Slowly! Patiently!

Cassie tightened her legs around him and said excitedly, "I'm on fire again."

Now swimming in his own sea of passion, Pirelli drove into her, thrusting hard and deep within her. He tried desperately to hold back until she was ready. It didn't take long before Cassie cried out wildly, "Oh God, I'm going to explode."

"Me too," Pirelli cried as he let go, sharing a totally satisfying climax. He remained inside her while they lay motionless, locked in a warm embrace. Moments later the exhausted lovers were lost in a deep sleep.

Four hours later Pirelli was awakened by a soft kiss on his cheek. He opened his eyes and saw that Cassie was already dressed and preparing to leave.

"Gotta run, lover boy, I'll call you."

"What's your hurry, Cassie?" Pirelli asked disappointedly.

"I'm taking a little vacation with a friend of mine tomorrow and I got a lot of things to do."

"Male or female," Pirelli asked curiously

"What do you think?" Cassie said as she headed out the door.

As soon as Cassie left the apartment, Pirelli called Solly and asked him to come over. It was important.

It was noon before a freshly showered Pirelli opened his apartment door and greeted his partner. Solly headed for the kitchen and poured a hot cup of coffee. Then he asked what was so important.

"What's so important is that I fucked Ardone's sister last night," Pirelli said.

"You did what?" Samuels said, a look of utter disbelief masking his face.

"You heard me. I fucked Ardone's sister."

"Schmuck," Solly cried out. "You're supposed to be babysitting her, not banging her. If Ardone finds out about it the investigation could be over. Besides, you got a million broads to play around with."

"Yeah, but this one's special."

"What the fuck's so special about her," Solly said gruffly.

"What's so special is that she's got a pulsating pussy, that's what. And, my friend, they ain't easy to come by."

"What the fuck is a pulsating pussy?"

"Forget it Solly. You'll never experience one."

Solly just shook his head in despair. "I still say you're fuckin crazy."

"Look, Solly," Pirelli said defensively. "I ain't gonna bullshit you and pretend I didn't have a good time with the broad, but my banging her was all business. If everything goes the way I hope it'll go, we'll see each other on a regular basis and I'll be able to get close to Ardone."

"Yeah, well just be careful will you. I'm worried that if he finds out about it he'll take it as a personal insult. And if the crazy prick gets pissed off at you who knows what he'll do?"

"Listen, him getting pissed at me is not what's worrying me right now."

"Really! Well what's worrying you then?"

"What's really worrying me is that she might get pissed off at me and not wanna see me again," Pirelli said laughing.

"It's no use, my good friend. You're fucking crazy. C'mon, let's get some work done."

The detectives spent the next hour discussing their next move. Pirelli would continue seeing Cassie and, with a little luck, the two would begin socializing with Ardone. Pirelli would gain Ardone's confidence and somehow persuade him to have the bullet removed from his shoulder.

Ardone believed that Pirelli had a doctor friend who covered up an abortion on Martine's daughter, a doctor who could be trusted. If everything went as planned, Ardone would ask Pirelli to have his doctor friend remove the bullet from his shoulder. The detectives knew it was a long shot, but it was a shot that Pirelli was determined to make work.

Before Solly left the apartment, Pirelli told him of the upcoming Friday night party with Ardone. Solly expressed concern for his partner's safety. Some of the wise guys at the party might not be too happy about seeing a detective there, even a suspended one.

Pirelli would call his partner as soon as he was safely home from the party. No matter how late the hour.

CHAPTER FIFTY

W hen Friday evening rolled around Pirelli was ready to party with a cop-killer. Heeding his partner's warning, he reached into the top drawer of his dresser and pulled out a leather slapjack, slipping it into his right trouser pocket. Then he tucked his .38 caliber snub nose revolver into his waistband. Just in case. After downing a double shot of Chivas, he was out the door and on his way to meet Ardone at the Blue Grotto Lounge.

When he arrived at the Grotto, Mario immediately poured a double Chivas over ice and set it in front of the fashionably dressed detective. "So you all ready for a big night, Pirelli?" he asked.

"Talking about a big night, lemme ask ya something, Mario. Do ya think me goin to the party with Ardone could cause a problem for him? I mean…"

"Hey" Mario interrupted, "If Cheech ain't worried about you being a problem for him you shouldn't be either. Besides, everybody there will know he brung ya."

Pirelli nodded and gulped down his drink. Mario immediately poured another before moving away to attend to a frantically waving customer. Pirelli sipped his second drink slowly, thinking about what to expect at the party.

Moment's later, Marvin Goldstein, a Grotto regular, joined him. Goldstein was an odd looking man, with a curly mass of thinning reddish gray hair that sprang up in small unruly patches like crabgrass. A mild stammer and a persistent blinking of his deep-set eyes characterized his soft-spoken manner.

Goldstein operated a small clothing store on the Bowery and swore that he ran a legitimate operation, but his numerous cash only deals suggested otherwise. He always seemed to have top quality name brand merchandise for sale, priced much below wholesale.

As he had done with many of the other Grotto regulars, Pirelli had Solly run Goldstein's criminal history. The man was a petty thief who had been arrested many times. But since none of his arrests involved violence or drugs, Pirelli had allowed himself to become very friendly with the man. Actually, he enjoyed talking to him.

"Listen Pirelli," Goldstein whispered conspiratorially. "I've been meaning to talk to ya about something a friend of mine might have goin. You interested?"

"Maybe," Pirelli said, "Lemme hear what it is first"

"First of all, Pirelli, you gotta understand that what I wanna run by you don't involve me."

"So who does it involve?"

"It involves a good friend of mine."

"A good friend of yours, huh, Swags," Pirelli said, referring to the man by his nickname.

"Yeah, a real good friend."

"Is that right? Well in that case, I'll tell you what. You go and tell your real good friend to go fuck himself. Okay?"

"Hey! What's the matter, Pirelli? I thought I could…"

"Well you thought wrong, Swags," Pirelli interrupted, "What kinda bullshit ya giving me? A good friend of yours! Whadda ya take me for a fuckin idiot?"

"No, it ain't that Pirelli, it's just that I don't wanna…"

Goldstein's voice trailed off as he stared at the visibly irritated detective.

"Look Swags. If you wanna run something by me, do it. If I don't like what I hear I'll tell ya and that'll be that. If you don't trust me then we got nothin to talk about."

Goldstein sheepishly agreed and for the next ten minutes spelled out a plan he had to run stolen checks through an art studio he was planning to open under a fictitious name. Goldstein said he had a friend who worked for a big corporation. His friend had access to blank corporate checks and a signature stamp that made them negotiable for up to ten thousand dollars. What Goldstein wanted from Pirelli was advance notice of any complaint made by the corporation of missing or stolen checks and how long he could get by with the scheme.

Pirelli told Goldstein that he could probably get by for a couple of months before the company audit disclosed the loss. As far as a criminal complaint being lodged by the company for the missing checks, he could probably take care of that.

"That's all I'm looking for is a heads up if somebody is on to me," Goldstein said. If I can get by for a couple of months, I'll be in 'Fat City'."

"By the way, Swags, how much is your guys end?"

"He's happy with a thousand a check."

"And you say these checks are good for up to ten large?"

"That's what my guy tells me."

"Good. I'll tell you what, Swags. I'll take thirty percent of what you pass through your account and we got a deal."

"How about I give ya twenty-five."

"Don't jerk me off, Swags. You'd given me thirty-five if I pushed and we both know it. Now do we have a deal or not?"

We got a deal," Goldstein said happily."

"Good. Now the first thing you gotta do before we get started is for you to get me a sample check and the name of the guy that's gettin 'em for you."

"Whadda ya need my guy's name for?"

"Don't start with me, Swags. I gotta know everything. I gotta check him the fuck out, you idiot! I wanna make sure he ain't trying to set you up. Like maybe he's trying to work something off with the feds or some other law enforcement agency."

Pirelli knew that the man's name along with a stolen check would be sufficient evidence to bring future criminal charges against both the man and Goldstein.

"Okay, Pirelli, okay," Goldstein said reluctantly. "I'll give you whatever you need."

Pirelli smiled. "Good. When I check things out, I'll let you know and we'll get started."

Just as Goldstein was winding down his conversation with Pirelli, Ardone walked through the front door of the lounge. He was wearing a Brioni, black chalk-stripped, double-breasted suit with a black Etro cotton dress shirt and matching Zegna tie. A pair of hand-made Santoni shoes completed the ensemble and the two-carat pinky ring he wore sent a clear message to all that Ardone was a man to be respected. When Ardone walked over to Pirelli, Goldstein just nodded to him respectfully and walked to the other end of the bar.

"So what's new, Pirelli?" Ardone said cheerfully.

"What's new is that I got a little package for you, Cheech," Pirelli said, as he handed him a white business size envelop stuffed with eighty crisp one hundred-dollar bills.

"What's this?" Ardone said curiously.

"It's eight large, Cheech, compliments of Roland Martine. If my math's correct, that's thirty-percent of what I got for the deal. That's what we agreed upon, right?"

"Right you are, Pirelli," Ardone said with big smile. "But how come you didn't tell me you had the thing working already."

"I didn't have to. Martine bought your story about me having added expenses. He never said a word about the price."

"When is the thing set for?"

"It's already done."

"No shit! How'd it go?"

"Lemme put it this way, Cheech. The doctor's happy, Martine's happy, his daughter's happy and now we're happy."

Ardone smiled appreciatively. "I just got one question, Pirelli."

"What's that, Cheech?"

"Who's the doctor," Ardone asked, thinking about the incriminating bullet buried in his left shoulder.

Pirelli hesitated. He was tempted to answer the question but decided against it. He wanted to move cautiously. He knew that Ardone would ask the question again.

"Listen Cheech, the Martine deal is history and there's one rule I always follow. I never talk about a done deal. I hope you don't mind."

"Not at all Pirelli, and what's more, I agree with ya a hundred percent."

"Good! Now that we got that outta the way lemme ask you something about the party."

"What is it?"

"Me being a cop ain't gonna be a problem for ya. Is it?"

"Listen, Pirelli, Ardone said abruptly, "All anybody has gotta know about you is that you're with me. And if anyone starts breaking your balls, ya just do what ya gotta do. But just be careful, some of them fuckin guys are crazy. Now let's get goin."

They drove to the party making small talk when Ardone suddenly moved the conversation back to Martine and the doctor.

"Listen Pirelli, how well do ya know this doctor friend of yours?"

"Very well," Pirelli said curtly. "Why?"

"Then lemme ask ya something," Ardone said, thinking about the bullet in his shoulder. "Do you trust him?"

"As much as I trust anyone I guess."

"C'mon Pirelli, you don't have to play fuckin games with me."

"No offense, Cheech, but to be honest with you there's only one guy I trust when I do business."

"Yeah, and who's that?" Ardone asked curiously

"Anthony Pirelli!"

Ardone laughed. "I know what you mean, Pirelli. But to get things done, sometimes you have to trust other people. No?"

"Lemme put it this way, Cheech. You might have to rely on people to get things done. But that don't mean ya gotta trust 'em."

"You wanna know something," the Mafioso said, a smile cracking his face. "Like I told you once before, I get the feeling that you and me are gonna do a lotta things together."

Pirelli returned a smile and just nodded his head in agreement.

CHAPTER FIFTY-ONE

When they arrived at the luxury high rise, Ardone double-parked his late model black Caddy in front of the building and slid out of the driver's seat. The doorman, clad in a full-length red coat with polished brass buttons, rushed to greet him. After shaking Ardone's his hand, the doorman pocketed the twenty-dollar bill that Ardone had stuffed into his palm and immediately parked the car.

When the two men entered the lobby of the Park Avenue apartment building a well-built security guard in civilian clothes, greeted them. Ardone nodded a hello as he and Pirelli walked to the far end of the lobby where an elderly man waited by a private elevator.

"Good evening, Mr. Ardone, the man said politely, "How've you been sir?"

"Fine Walter," Ardone said cordially. "By the way, Walter, is anyone upstairs yet?"

"Actually quite a few people have already arrived, sir. May I take you up?"

"That you may, Walter, that you may," Ardone repeated, as he entered the elevator, followed by Pirelli, for a non-stop trip to the 43rd floor penthouse.

After Ardone thanked the operator with a folded-up twenty-dollar bill, the two men stepped from the elevator and entered a foyer at least twice the size of Pirelli's entire apartment. Pirelli admired the surroundings as they walked across the expanse of fine marble tile and expensively paneled walls. When they reached the apartment door, Ardone seized an imposing brass striker that was mounted on a hand engraved set of double doors. After a single tap, a large, mean looking man, wearing a white dinner jacket, opened the door. Upon seeing Ardone, the man's face split into a wide grin.

"Cheech!" the man said happily, How the fuck ya been? I ain't seen ya since I got out."

"That's because you're too fuckin high class too stop by my joint. Ain't that right Iggy," Ardone said, jokingly.

"Bull shit! I can't wait until I get my parole officer off my fuckin ass so I can start showing my face in the right places again. No offense Cheech, but the cunt thinks the Grotto is a bad joint. Would you believe that shit?"

"Never!" Ardone said laughing. "Buy the way, Iggy, say hello to Pirelli, he's a friend of mine. Spread the word that he's all right, will ya?"

"You got it, Cheech. And any friend of yours is a friend of mine."

"Thanks Iggy. And listen, I'll give you a call next week. We got a little celebrating to do for your home coming."

Ardone turned to Pirelli and said, "Let's go my man, I can use a drink."

The two men headed for the living quarters, momentarily stopping by the library. Pirelli looked into the twenty by thirty-foot room and stared admiringly at the rosewood paneling and matching bookshelves that were fashionable placed about the room.

An oversized glass-topped rosewood desk, a twelve-foot imported plush leather couch and several matching club chairs were pushed off to the side to allow for the temporary placement of a full-size craps table. Ardone smiled at the men crowding around the table. They were screaming feverishly with every roll of the dice while exchanging black and green chips.

"Hey Booty," Ardone yelled out to the stick man controlling the game. "I'll be back in a minute. Save me a hot spot, will ya?"

"You got it, Cheech, I'm sure the boys will love to take some of your dough."

Pirelli followed as Ardone headed for the living quarters. The moment they entered the huge living room the conversation subsided as the many guests began their silent appraisal of the unfamiliar face.

Pirelli turned to Ardone and said softly, "This is some fuckin joint, Cheech. And the scenery ain't that bad either," Pirelli added, admiring several scantily clad young female hostesses that were mingling with the guests.

"Ya see anything you like, Pirelli?" Ardone said referring to the hostesses.

"It would be easier if you asked me if I seen anything I don't like," Pirelli said, eyeing a young beauty that was standing nearby.

"Well in that case, pick one out and I'll set you up later. All these broads are very talented," Ardone said smiling, "very talented."

Pirelli and Ardone made there way to a fifteen foot horse shoe shaped, wet bar that was being serviced by two tough-looking bartenders wearing black shirts with matching black ties. The taller of the two men greeted Ardone. "What's your pleasure, Mr. Ardone," he said respectfully.

"A double scotch over ice for my friend here and I'll have a little Grappa, Albee," Ardone replied as he stuffed a crisp fifty into the man's shirt pocket."

Albee poured a glass of thirty-year old single malt scotch over ice for Pirelli and a snifter of fifty-year old Grappa for his benefactor. While Ardone was busy shaking hands, Pirelli left the bar and walked over to one of the regulars he recognized from the Blue Grotto Lounge.

"Well if it ain't the Grotto's most enterprising bartender," the man said as Pirelli approached him. "What da fuck are you doing here?"

"I thought you invited me, LuLu. At least that's what I told that fuckin monster on the front door," Pirelli said jokingly.

"Yeah sure," the overweight man said. I invited you. I'm lucky I got myself invited. Anyway, say hello to Blah Blah Vilarito and Louie Pip."

"How's it goin, fellas, the name's Pirelli."

"How ya doin Pirelli," Louie Pip said.

After a brief conversation with the small man, Blah Blah Vilarito cornered Pirelli and engaged him in a five-minute non-stop, one-sided conversation. Pirelli was relieved when he heard Ardone cry out from the bar.

"Hey Pirelli, c'mere, I want ya to meet somebody."

Grateful for the call, Pirelli excused himself from the talkative man and walked back to the bar where Ardone was standing with a tall, slim, well-dressed man that could easily pass for the CEO of a Fortune 500 company.

"Trippy, this is the guy I was telling ya about. His name's Pirelli."

Turning to the smiling detective, Ardone said, "Pirelli, this is Joe Tripoli. He's our host"

"And the name's Trippy," the man said quickly.

"Nice to meet you, Trippy," Pirelli said, with due respect.

"The pleasure's all mine. So how do you like my set-up? "What's not too like?"

"Yeah, I know what you mean. Listen Pirelli, any friend of Cheech's here is a friend of mine so enjoy the evening."

"It will be my pleasure, Trippy."

Ardone spent the next thirty minutes introducing Pirelli to the many guests at the party. Everything was going well until they ran into "Fat Tony" Caruso.

When Ardone greeted him, the fat man mumbled a not to friendly hello.

"What's the matter Tony? You got problems on the West Side?"

"Nah, everything's just fine on the West side," Caruso said sarcastically. "Just fine."

"Good to hear you got no problems, Tony."

"Nah! We got no problems. All we got is them fuckin nutty Grillo brothers trying to muscle in on the piers. Then there's them crazy Westies shaking everybody down. And as if that ain't enough, we got the fuckin niggers from uptown starting to run wild all over the fuckin place. And you know somethin else, Cheech?" Caruso added. "Youse guys across town couldn't give a flying fuck about it. But that ain't no problem, Cheech."

"Sorry I asked, Tony," Ardone said. "Anyway we'll sit down next week and talk about it. But for now I want ya to meet a friend of mine. His name's Pirelli."

Caruso stared hard at the slender detective. "Pirelli, huh? Whadda they call him?" Caruso said curtly.

"Everybody calls him Pirelli."

"Is that right? Well supposin I call him shit head like I call all cops."

"Hey, take it easy, Tony, he's a friend of mine. And he ain't a cop no more for your information."

"Yeah? Well he was a fuckin cop when he put my kid brother away for twenty-five years."

"No disrespect, Tony, but your brother put himself away for twenty-five years when he pulled that two-bit stick-up and killed a guy in front of three eye-witnesses."

Caruso just grimaced and said nothing.

"Anyway that's history, Tony. Now knock it the fuck off and let's have a drink. Okay?"

"Okay Cheech, let's have a drink. But as far as I'm concerned you're cop friend here will always be a shit head so keep him the fuck away from me."

Ardone finished his drink and left Caruso standing alone at the bar. He took Pirelli by the arm and led him towards a well-endowed hostess who couldn't have been more than twenty years old. As they walked slowly toward the woman, Pirelli whispered to Ardone. "Listen Cheech, it don't look like that Caruso guy wants me around. Maybe I should get outta here. I don't wanna cause a problem for you."

"Hey! What's a matter, Pirelli, afraid of the fat prick?"

"Yeah, I'm afraid all right. I'm afraid of what I might do if he starts breakin my balls."

Ardone laughed. "I'll tell ya what, Pirelli. If he tries to fuck with ya, you got my okay to do what ya gotta do. He's a fuckin loud mouth and I'd love to see ya put him in his place."

"Okay, Cheech, so long as you say so."

Upon seeing Ardone approach, the young hostess smiled broadly. "How you doing, Mr. Ardone?"

"Better since I seen you, Annie," Ardone said, pinching the woman's cheek softly. "Listen beautiful, I want you to meet a friend of mine, his name's Pirelli. I want you two to get acquainted a little later on. What time's good for you?""

"How's one sound," Mr. Ardone?"

"One's perfect," Ardone said, as he stuffed two crisp one hundred-dollar bills between the woman's almost completely exposed breasts.

"See you later, Pirelli," Annie said to the surprised detective. "It'll be my pleasure to get to know you."

After watching the woman disappear into the crowd, Pirelli turned to Ardone. "What the fuck was that all about, Cheech?"

"I just set you up, that's all. That Annie is the best. First she'll give you a real good massage then she'll suck you so dry that you won't wanna get laid for a week."

Pirelli looked at his watch and frowned.

"What's the matter, Pirelli," Ardone said curiously.

"Couldn't you have made it a little earlier, Cheech?"

"You're hot shit, Pirelli. C'mon let's have a drink, it'll make the time go faster."

The next half-hour was relatively uneventful. Ardone went to the library to shoot craps while Pirelli remained behind talking to the young hostesses that were mingling with the guests. It was when he stopped to talk to one young beauty that Pirelli first noticed Fat Tony whispering to two burly young men that had just arrived at the party. The two men, wearing brightly colored floral sport shirts, glanced over at Pirelli then nodded their heads while Caruso continued whispering to them. Pirelli immediately sensed what was about to happen.

As the two young men started to walk towards him, he reached into his right side trouser pocket and wrapped his hand tightly around the "slap jack" that he had carried with him to the party.

The shorter of the two men positioned himself squarely in front of Pirelli and looked directly into his pale green eyes. "I don't think I know ya pal," the man said menacingly.

Pirelli stared back at the man's gruff looking face, his eyes narrowing suspiciously. "I guess that makes us even friend, cause I don't think I know you either," Pirelli shot back.

"Yeah, well then maybe you better take off. I don't like no strangers around here."

"Hey, what kinda shit is this," Pirelli said curtly. "In case you didn't hear about it, I'm with Ardone."

The taller man who was standing to Pirelli's right jumped into conversation. "Listen cuz, we don't care who ya with. Now my friend here just told you that you ain't welcome here. And he ain't gonna tell ya again."

The man made a curt motion with his thumb in the direction of the foyer and growled, "So why don't you beat it while you can still walk."

"Beat this," Pirelli growled back, cupping his left hand between his legs.

"Why you little sonofabitch!" snarled the big man, as the switchblade that appeared in his hand opened with an ominous click.

The entire room turned to watch the show as Pirelli backed away. "Now take it easy kid. Don't do anything foolish," Pirelli cautioned. "I'm not looking for any trouble. Just put the knife down and we'll talk this thing out. Okay?"

But the young man ignored Pirelli's plea and with the knife held high made a menacing move towards him. Pirelli reacted quickly. He brought his right hand out of his pocket in a wide arc and smashed the slapjack sharply across his would be attacker's nose, breaking it at the bridge line. The crunching sound boomed throughout the room as the young man screamed in agony. Then without hesitating, Pirelli snatched an unopened beer can from a nearby table and brought it down squarely across the skull of the second youth. This time the echoing sound was different. The solid crack of the can of beer across bone sounded like an explosion and the youth sank to the floor unconscious. Aside from the continuing moans from the youth with the shattered nose, a startling silence came over the room.

Then someone let out a yell. Pirelli turned quickly. He saw Caruso reaching for the small automatic pistol that was tucked away in his waistband. But before Caruso could retrieve his weapon, Pirelli's two-inch barrel Chief Special was already pointing at him.

"Go ahead, cocksucker, pull it out and I'll put one right in your fat fuckin gut! Now if ya got any brains you'll stay put."

Upon hearing the commotion, all the men that had been shooting craps came running into the room.

"Take it easy Tony," Ardone screamed out at Caruso as he saw what was happening. "Keep cool for Christ sake. We'll straighten this thing out in the morning."

Caruso cursed loudly at Pirelli as Ardone hustled him out of the crowded room, heading toward the apartment door. Fortunately Caruso remained behind and the two men were able to leave the floor without further confrontation.

When they got back to Ardone's car, Pirelli slid into the passenger seat and silently cursed himself for the pointless way he had handled the entire affair.

'I just blew the whole fucking thing,' Pirelli thought grimly.

Bitterly annoyed with himself, Pirelli was about to apologize to Ardone just as Ardone's face broke out in a big grin.

"That was beautiful, Pirelli. I mean you handled that just fuckin beautiful."

Pirelli was happily surprised by Ardone's unexpected praise. "Really, Cheech. Ya know, to tell you the truth I thought you'd be pissed at me."

"Pissed, for what? Me and that fat fuck Caruso have been at it for months now. The prick sent those two kids over to you as an insult to me. He knows fuckin well that I vouched for you and it was his way of showing his disrespect."

"What's his problem, Cheech?"

"Ah he's got in his head that I fucked him on some thing that we did together a while back. The prick even put a contract out on me a couple of months ago."

"That bad, huh?"

"Yeah, he got some cocksucker in my crew that I trusted to set me up. Luckily I got dimed in advance and was able to avoid a serious problem."

"So what did you do about it?"

"Nothin! The matter was discussed at the top and I was told to drop it. Otherwise the fat prick wouldn't be goin to no parties anymore."

"And what about your friend that tried to set you up?"

"Now that's another story. Let's just say he's not goin to no parties anymore and leave it at that. Anyway, Pirelli, the night worked out good, real good."

"Yeah, but it could've worked out much better, Cheech."

"How's that?"

"Caruso could've sent his goons over after Annie gave me my massage," Pirelli said emphatically.

Ardone laughed heartily. "No problem, kid. It just so happens that I know a lotta Annies."

Ardone stopped the vehicle at a corner phone booth and dialed the number of a private social club not far from where they were parked. After the second ring a female voice with a European accent answered the phone.

"Hello Frenchy, it's me, Ardone. Is Andrea available?… Good. Tell her I'll be there in fifteen minutes. I want her to meet a friend of mine."

CHAPTER FIFTY-TWO

It was almost six in the morning before Pirelli got home from the party. As soon as he entered his apartment he called his partner. Immediately upon recognizing Pirelli's voice, Solly spewed out a string of choice obscenities into the instrument's mouthpiece. "You inconsiderate sonofabitch," he screamed. "Where the fuck you been for Christ sake? You were supposed to call me as soon as you got home."

"I did call you as soon as I got home. Now quit your bitching, I got a lotta things to tell you. But first I'm gonna grab a few hours sleep. I'll meet you in Trimontes at about one. We'll have some lunch while we talk. And don't forget to bring your credit card."

"Fuck you, Pirelli, bring my credit card. I couldn't sleep all night worrying about you and you make fuckin jokes. You gotta be the ... ," Solly continued his tirade for several minutes more before he realized that his partner had already hung up the phone.

It was a little before one when Pirelli arrived at the historic Italian restaurant. Solly hadn't gotten there yet so he found an out-of-the-way corner table, sat down, and ordered an extra dry Vodka martini, straight up, no fruit. As he sipped his drink his thoughts turned to his earlier conversation with Ardone. Now he knew why Ardone murdered Cutolo.

Several minutes later, Solly arrived at the restaurant still grumbling about Pirelli's tardy telephone call.

"Good afternoon to you too, Solly," Pirelli said smiling. "The least you could do is thank me for letting you sleep late."

"You know, Pirelli, this ain't no fuckin joke. You go to a party where half the fucking people in the place are killers and the other half are psychos and you want to know what I was worried about."

"Okay, enough with the bullshit, Solly. We got a lot to discuss so let's order our lunch and get down to business."

Pirelli spent the next twenty minutes briefing his partner on the happenings at the party, including his late morning tryst with Andrea.

Solly began to rant again. "A fuckin broad," he roared. No wonder you were so late."

"All in the line of duty Solly, all in the line of duty."

After Solly settled down, the detectives got down to the business at hand, how to proceed with the investigation. The detectives now knew that Fat Tony Caruso had recruited the late JoJo Cutolo to set up Ardone. Since there was a connection between Caruso and Cutolo, the detectives decided to review the Cutolo file and the police officer's file, again. Maybe they would see something in the files that they had missed before, something that might point them in the right direction. After finishing his dessert, Solly left the restaurant and headed straight for the precinct to collect the files. Pirelli stayed back and ordered a Café Romano with a taste of Sambuca before heading home.

CHAPTER FIFTY-THREE

Two hours later, Solly returned to Pirelli's apartment building carrying the slain officer's and Cutolo's case file. But just as he was about to enter the lobby, he saw the street vendor's orange and blue umbrella. It had been no more than three hours since Solly's lunch at Tramontes consisting of cold antipasto, Veal Francese and a half order of extra al dente Rigatoni al Filetto di Pomodoro that he thickly coated with Parmesan cheese, but the temptation was just too great for him to resist. He edged his enormous body alongside the wagon and quickly placed his order. Then turning his back to the entrance of Pirelli's building, Solly began inhaling frankfurters held in both his hands, somehow managing to balance a can of Pepsi between them.

Solly ate quickly, like a child about to be caught with his hand in the cookie jar. In Solly's case it was the fear of being observed by his partner. Now, wolfing down the frankfurters as fast as he could chew and dreading the appearance of his partner, his eyes darted in every direction. Solly's huge girth and voracious appetite was the butt of good-natured comments throughout the department and Solly always took the ribbing in stride. But when the rebukes came from his partner, it was more than he could handle.

Solly peered nervously up and down the busy street, in his mind's eye he could see Pirelli with his tongue pressed firmly against his cheek, slowly shaking his head while eyeing the frankfurters. Continuing to scan the street Solly turned and poked the vendor's arm. "Gimme one more with everything, pal."

Ten minutes later a sated Solly Samuels knocked on Pirelli's apartment door. He was greeted with a big smirk on his partner's face. When Solly entered the apartment Pirelli asked: "How about a little snack, Solly? You must be hungry after that trip to the precinct and back. I'll order a Sicilian pizza with sausage and pepperoni, well-done, just the way you like it"

Solly viewed his partner suspiciously, the tone in his s voice prompted him to look towards the kitchen window. There he noticed the blinds opened just enough to have allowed Pirelli a clear view of the frankfurter stand.

"So I had a couple of dogs to hold me over till dinner," Solly confessed. "What's the big fuckin deal? You said we had a lot of work to do and who knows what time I'll get home. Besides I see you took care of yourself," he said pointing to the opened quart of Chivas sitting on the kitchen table.

"Okay Solly, I guess we're even," Pirelli said laughing. "Now let's get to work. You go through the cop's file and I'll go through Cutolo's file. Let's see what we can come up with.

Almost forty-five minutes of silence later, Pirelli was still busy reading the Cutolo folder when suddenly Solly shouted. "I got it," sporting a big grin.

"You got what?" Pirelli shot back.

"A plan to get the bullet out of shit head's shoulder, that's what. It's right here in black and white."

"No shit! Lemme see it."

Solly pointed to the medical report prepared by the surgeon who had treated Ardone's bullet wound in the Connecticut hospital.

It stated that the bullet in Ardone's shoulder did not have to be removed unless it started to travel.

"So what's your plan? We go to church and start saying Novenas until the bullet decides to move?"

"No wise guy. We get it to move."

"We get it to move, huh? And that's your plan?"

"That's right, kid. That's my plan."

"And just how are we supposed to get it to move?"

"Here's how," Solly explained, pointing to the report and began to read:

> Although the foreign metallic object lodged in the patients left shoulder presents no immediate danger to the patient's health, it may present a problem for the patient in the future if the object begins to travel, ...

"You just said that Solly," Pirelli interrupted.

"Hold on a minute and listen, will ya. Lemme finish all ready."

> ...therefore the patient should avoid body contact sports that could subject the patient to blunt trauma in or around the posterior of his left shoulder. Such trauma if severe enough could cause the foreign object to break free from the subcutaneous muscle that currently holds it in place and...

"Okay, Solly, I give up," Pirelli interrupted. "Where the fuck are you going with this?"

"I'm goin with blunt trauma, kid. Listen, when I joined Ardone's health club last month to get a look at his shoulder I found out that he plays racket ball regularly."

"So?"

"And you play racket ball too, don't ya."

"Yeah, so?"

"So if you can figure out a way to start playing ball with the scumbag you can give him a shot with your racket right on the back of his left shoulder. Just where the doctor said he should avoid getting hit. If you bang him hard enough maybe the bullet will come loose and start to move."

"C'mon Solly, I can't intentionally hit him with a racket."

"Why the fuck not may I ask?"

"Because it wouldn't be right, Solly."

"Because it wouldn't be right, Solly," Samuels repeated, mimicking his partner. "You gotta be fuckin kiddin, Pirelli. Here's a scumbag who kills two people in cold blood, one of which just so happens to be a young cop and you're telling me it that it wouldn't be right to hit him with a racket? Well lemme tell you something, my friend. If I thought I could get away with it I'd hit the prick with a fuckin sledgehammer never mind a lousy racket. And it wouldn't be on his fuckin back either."

Pirelli just stared at his partner saying nothing.

"C'mon Pirelli, guys get hit with rackets all the fuckin time in that game. Don't they?" I mean who would ever be the wiser, for Christ sake?"

"You know, Solly, I never thought I'd hear myself say this, but lemme figure out how I'm gonna do it."

"Good! And while you're figuring it out, go and buy yourself a heavy racket."

"Okay Solly, but now that I listened to you, how about you listening to what I came up with?"

"Shoot! I'm all ears."

Pirelli pointed out that obviously there had to be other people with Cutolo at the street corner where he met Ardone. He reasoned that if they could find one or more of those people who were with Cutolo, one who saw Cutolo get in the red Buick with Ardone shortly before he was murdered, they might be able to charge Ardone with the murder of Cutolo.

"That's a heavy lift, kid. I mean trying to get a wise guy to cooperate with us."

"Hey, we'll worry about that when the time comes. But first we gotta identify who backing up Cutolo when he got in the car with Ardone."

"That's easier said than done, kid."

"Look Solly, I didn't say it was gonna be easy. But we do have a lotta people on the streets that owe us for past favors, and there are lotta other people out there that would like to put a favor in the bank for the future. So start asking around and maybe we'll catch a break."

"And if we don't?"

"If we don't, then we'll make our own break."

Pirelli suggested that if Solly was unsuccessful in gaining the sought after information from his contacts on the street, he should look at all of the men in Caruso's crew. A check of each man's criminal history would identify those that were on parole and still owed serious jail time. If the detectives could observe one of them violating his parole, it might be the wedge they needed to persuade the violator to cooperate with them.

"I'll tell you what," Solly said, "You figure a way to start playing racket ball with Ardone. Meanwhile, I'll run over to the Organized Crime Bureau the first thing in the morning and see what I can come up with."

"It's a deal, Solly."

"Good. Now go buy that racket, just in case. I'll talk to you in the morning."

After Solly left the apartment Pirelli had several hours to kill before reporting for work. He poured himself a hefty glass of scotch and began returning the many phone calls that were left on his answering machine. As a rule, he would not cut short a conversation unless expecting an important call, so when the operator interrupted, he declined. But the caller was persistent. After the third time an operator interrupted his conversation, he took the call.

"This better be you, Solly, and it better be fucking important," Pirelli said abruptly.

"Who's Solly?" the sensuous voice asked softly.

"Who's this?" Pirelli shot back.

"My, my, Anthony, it hasn't even been a week and you forgot me already. I guess you didn't enjoy our date as much as I did."

"Cassie, what a pleasant surprise, I was hoping you would call."

"Really? You could have called me, you know."

"I would have but you never gave me your number. And I didn't think it would've been wise for me to ask around for it."

Cassie laughed. "You can relax Anthony, it just so happens that I told my brother we're friends. Good friends."

Pirelli's body stiffened for a moment. He hoped that Ardone was not disturbed by his sister's revelation. "And what did he say?" he asked nervously.

"He said if you ever tell anyone in the lounge about our friendship he'll cut your fucking balls off,'" Cassie said laughing.

Pirelli was relieved. "Well in that case, I guess I got nothing to worry about."

"Not as long as we remain on good terms, Anthony. And so far we couldn't be on better terms," she said smiling.

"By the way, Anthony, I know its short notice but are you working tonight?"

"I'm scheduled to. Why do you ask?"

"Because I thought we might have some dinner."

"That would've been nice, Cassie but unfortunately it's not doable. Mario's off tonight and it wouldn't be right for me not to show at the last minute. But I'll be able to get off tomorrow night."

"No can do, darling. I have other plans for tomorrow night. I guess we'll just have to do lunch tomorrow instead."

"Lunch would be great. Where would you like to meet?"

"Why your place of course, after all, we can't chance being seen together in public. Now can we?" Cassie said playfully. "I'll be there around one. Okay?"

"One is fine," Pirelli said happily.

"By the way, Anthony I do want lunch, so surprise me."

"I'll try my best, Cassie. See you at one."

CHAPTER FIFTY-FOUR

P irelli was up early on a gloomy Saturday morning and headed for his health club. Meanwhile, Solly was making his way to Police Headquarters. He parked the squad car in a zone reserved for select department vehicles, then trying to dodge the rain drops, darted straight for the Organized Crime Control Bureau. He requested all of the available intelligence on Fat Tony's crew. For the next several hours, he reviewed the files.

Although dated, the files disclosed that Caruso had a crew of twenty-five associates and ten more wannabees that he called upon when needed. A review of each man's criminal history proved to be fruitful, Solly identified two members of the crew that were on parole and owed substantial jail time.

Joseph "The Gyp" Garafola owed eleven years and William "Crazy Bill" DiAngelo owed ten. Both men were in their early sixties and Solly reasoned that if either of the men could be violated, neither man would be too happy about having to spend his remaining good years in Attica.

Solly left Headquarters and set out to learn what the two parolees were up too. He worked the streets for the remainder of the morning talking to everybody that owed him a favor. He learned that DiAngelo had distanced himself from the crew, but that Garafola was still active in the family. Garafola was his target. If he could violate Garafola, he might have the leverage he needed to win the man's cooperation. He would get started immediately.

CHAPTER FIFTY-FIVE

While Solly was busy gathering intelligence on Garafola, Pirelli was in his apartment preparing for his luncheon date with Ardone's sister.

At precisely 1 p.m. the intercom buzzed. The doorman announced that a Ms. Cassie had come to visit. A few minutes later the woman entered the apartment. She looked stunning; dressed in a tasteful tight fitting coordinated slack set that framed her extraordinary body. After the customary peck on the cheek, he escorted the woman to the couch and turned on the stereo. Hearing the soft music that filled the room, she smiled and asked if they were having lunch, or having a party.

"I thought we'd have both. Pirelli said happily, "That is if you're up to it."

"We'll see, Anthony. But right now I could use a little champagne."

"You got it. But first tell me what your brother said about us?"

Cassie repeated what she had told Pirelli the day before.

Ardone had no problem with their relationship as long as she had no problem with it. Pirelli was ecstatic. Things were proceeding as planned.

Anyway, now that we have that out of the way, Anthony, the answer is yes as far as a party goes."

Pirelli smiled and immediately set off for the champagne.

Cassie sat back on the plush leather couch, kicked off her Gucci stilettos, brought her knees up to her chest and waited for her host to return.

Pirelli came back with a perfectly chilled bottle of pink Crystal buried in a wine bucket full of chopped ice. Cassie nodded her approval as Pirelli eased off the cork and filled two chilled flutes.

"To us, Cassie," he toasted. "If I enjoy this afternoon half as much as I enjoyed the other night, it'll be a marvelous day for me."

"That was nice, Anthony. You're such a sweet bullshit artist."

Their first glass of champagne disappeared, Pirelli re-filled them. Then he walked into the kitchen and returned with a food platter that he had prepared. As they sipped the bubbly and snacked on blintzes smothered with Beluga caviar, cream herring and imported anchovies, Cassie began to feel the soothing effect of the expensive champagne. She stretched out her legs across a glass coffee table, turned to her host, and smiled invitingly.

They continued to snack on the food and sip Champagne when the phone suddenly intruded. "You're not going to answer that, are you?" Cassie asked, her brain now swimming in the sparkling wine.

"Not a chance", Pirelli said, as he disconnected the phone and topped off their Champagne glasses.

"I only ask once, Anthony, and that was the other night. The next move is yours."

Without saying a word, Pirelli reached for her bare feet and began to massage her manicured toes, working his way up and down her calves. Cassie sighed responsively as he pulled her close and began kissing her. His hands fumbled as he pulled her turtleneck sweater over her head and rushed to remove her bra. Then he opened his shirt and pressed his bare chest against her. Moments later, he carried her to the waiting bed and the party began.

They moaned together as he burst into her after satisfying her a third time. Then locked together, motionless, they basked in the warm sun that had worked its way through the partially opened blinds, and dozed.

Twenty minutes later, Cassie jumped up and headed directly for the bathroom.

"What's your hurry, baby? Pirelli asked. "It's still early,"

"Got a lot to do sweetheart, I'll explain everything over a cup of coffee if you don't mind making it."

Later Cassie emerged from the bathroom fully groomed and ready to go.

"So Cassie, What's so urgent that you have to run out so fast?" Pirelli asked as he poured the coffee.

"I'm leaving for Hawaii tomorrow and I got a lot of last minute things to take care of."

"Where are you staying if you don't mind me asking?"

"I'm staying at the Princeville Resort in Kauai."

"Hey, I've been there. That's a beautiful place," Pirelli said nodding his head. "Is it your first time?

"No, I was there last month," Cassie said with a smile. "That's when I met my husband-to-be."

"You're what?" Pirelli was shocked by the startling revelation.

"Oh! Didn't I tell you? I'm getting married next week."

"Getting married? And you only met him last month?"

"It was love at first sight," Cassie said smiling, as she thought about the man's wealth.

"And you met him at the Princeville?"

"Yes, he owns the place."

'Sure,' Pirelli thought glumly. 'Put a man with a lot of money next to a sexy, young gorgeous woman and that'll do it every time.'

"Incidentally, I haven't told my brother yet, so I'd appreciate it if you kept it to yourself for now. My husband and I are going to sail the Islands of Tonga for a few months and I thought I'd call him from his yacht. Anyway, thanks for your hospitality. It was wonderful."

"The pleasure was all mine, Cassie. I'm only sorry that our relationship had to end so soon."

"Oh I don't know about it ending. When I get back to New York, I'm sure we'll have lunch again sometime," Cassie said as she headed for the door.

After Cassie left, Pirelli just shook his head. 'Maybe it's just as well I don't have to get any closer to her' he mused. 'She's fuckin crazy.'

CHAPTER FIFTY-SIX

The next two weeks were time consuming. Solly and his team of detectives were busy surveilling Garafola, observing his every move. Meanwhile Pirelli tended bar at the lounge, waiting for an opportunity to challenge Ardone to a game of racket ball.

The opportunity came early one evening. Ardone had stopped by the lounge for dinner with several members of his crew. Before going upstairs to the restaurant, Ardone approached Pirelli and asked if they could meet the following afternoon. He had a business deal to discuss with him.

"Listen, Cheech," Pirelli replied, "I'm told you play racket ball. How about we play a couple of games in the morning? After I beat your ass we can discuss the deal over lunch?"

"Sounds good to me," Ardone said as he readily accepted Pirelli's bold challenge. "By the way, Pirelli, how many points do I get?"

"Points my ass, let's see how the match goes then we'll talk about who gets what."

The next morning, the two men met at Ardone's health club.

After a quick warm-up, the match got under way. The air-conditioning in the glass-backed court wasn't working too well and both men were sweating profusely. Each had won a close game and both were anxious for the "rubber" to be over so they could jump into a cold shower. They competed fiercely and the winning point did not come easy. When it was finally over, the two men were exhausted.

"Good game, Pirelli," Ardone said, letting out a deep breath. "I was lucky I won the fuckin match."

Pirelli smiled. "Yeah sure, you were lucky. And you wanted points. Anyway, just for being so lucky, I'm buying lunch."

"You got it," Ardone said proudly.

After a refreshing steam bath and cold shower, the two men got dressed and headed for Ardone's favorite restaurant. At the popular West Side steak house, the maitre d' saw Ardone and immediately escorted him to a table reserved for special people. "Is this okay, Mr. Ardone," the man said, pointing to a corner table.

"It'll be a lot better after you send over a bottle of my favorite wine, Tom," Ardone said, as he squeezed a ten-dollar bill into the man's palm.

The wine Steward brought a bottle of vintage Brunello to the table. Ardone tasted the expensive wine and nodded his approval. After lunch was served, Ardone got down to business. He asked Pirelli if he knew any detectives that covered the diamond district.

"Whadda mean by know, Cheech, somebody that I can reach."

"Yeah, you know, somebody that's looking to earn."

"Depends on what the deal is, Cheech. You know things ain't like they used to be. Internal Affairs is everywhere. People are afraid to take chances now."

"This one's easy. It's strictly a larceny with no chance for a problem."

"In that case, I might know somebody. Whadda got?"

"I got this Jew that moves diamonds out of his loft on West 46th

Street. The sonofabitch keeps thousands of dollars worth of stones in his loft at any one time."

"And he wants to pull off a phony burglary, right?" Pirelli blurted out.

"Yeah, how'd ya know?"

"Because I used to catch them when I was in the burglary squad. By the way, Cheech, how big a loss is he looking to score?"

"A hundred large."

"A hundred thousand is a big number, Cheech." With that big a claim the insurance investigators will be taking a hard look at everything."

"Yeah, I know, that's why he needs the case detective to go along with the scam. He's sez he's not worried about the insurance investigators. So whadda think?"

"It depends, Cheech."

"Depends on what?"

"How much our end is," Pirelli said smiling.

"I'll tell him we want fifty percent of the claim. I figure we give your guy fifteen and you and me split the other thirty-five."

"The numbers look good to me, Cheech. But I'll tell you this right now. The Jew has to come up with at least twenty up front before I put anything in place, fifteen thousand for us and five for the case detective."

"Why up front? You don't think for a minute he would try to fuck me, do you?""

"Because if for some reason the insurance company denies the claim, at least we'll have put a few dollars in our pocket."

"Good thinking, Pirelli. More important do you think you can put it together?"

"Maybe, but first ya gotta speak to him and get some more information for me."

"Like what?"

"Like the layout of the guy's loft and the security system he's got. If his system don't lend itself to a break-in, it'll draw too much suspicion. And one more thing, what kinda records does he have to account for the loss."

"You think of everything, don't you Pirelli?"

"Listen Cheech, I didn't survive twenty years in my business by taking unnecessary chances. So you go speak to your guy and after you get the information, we'll see if it can be done. Meanwhile, I'll look around to see who I know in the Burglary Squad."

CHAPTER FIFTY-SEVEN

A fter two weeks, the surveillance of Garafola bore fruit. Solly and his team had caught him violating his parole on three separate occasions; one for associating with a known felon and two for breaking curfew. But were these infractions serious enough to violate the man and send him back to prison for eleven years?

Solly spoke to a parole officer friend who said they were not. Solly needed something more serious and he needed it fast. He knew that a continued surveillance of Garafola would most likely result in observing more serious violations, but how long would it take? Physical surveillance was very time consuming. And even if he could come up with more serious violations, the thug would be entitled to a hearing, and if violated, an appeal. There had to be a quicker way.

The very next day Solly got a big break. He got a tip from a reliable stool that Garafola had a son who attended a prestigious college in Ithaca, and, like many of his classmates, smoked marijuana. But more importantly, the boy was not only a user, but a dealer too, making weekly trips to the East Village to pick up the marijuana for himself and his classmates. Solly was elated. If he could gather enough evidence to arrest the boy, it might give him the leverage he needed to persuade his father to cooperate.

Solly was told the young Garafola was scheduled to pick up some marijuana the very next evening from a street dealer known as "Willie the Weed." Solly got a detailed description of the boy and mapped out a plan. He would have an undercover detective mingle with the crowds that frequented the area and watch Willie as he conducted his business. If the undercover saw young Garafola buying drugs from Willie, he would alert Solly who would be waiting nearby.

The operation went off exactly as planned. At 7 p.m. the next evening, the undercover saw young Garofola buying marijuana from Willie. He signaled Solly that the purchase had been made.

The undercover followed the boy to his auto and again signaled Solly, giving him the car's location. Garafola left the scene followed by Solly. A short time later, the detectives were able to safely stop the young man's car.

Garofola was visibly shaken when he saw Solly squeeze his huge frame out of from the front passenger's side of the unmarked squad car. He was holding his detective shield up high; his right hand rested on the butt of his Colt service revolver.

Garofola nervously cried out. "What's wrong officer?"

"Just keep your hands on the steering wheel where I can see them and everything will be all right," Solly said calmly. The boy complied.

Solly walked over to the driver's side of the car and ordered the young man out. After patting him down for weapons, he searched the car finding a bag of marijuana under the front passenger's seat. Upon seeing the bag in Solly's hand the youth cried out. "Oh no officer, that's not mine. It must have been there when I rented this car. Please officer, you must believe me. This is not my car. I rented it this morning. You can check the rental papers. They're in the glove box."

"I know you rented the car this morning, son," Solly said. "And I also know that you drove down from school to visit 'Willie the Weed'. Now before you say another word, you and I are gonna walk over to that phone booth on the corner. I want you to call your father. Tell him you're about to be arrested for possession of marijuana. Tell him if he wants to talk to me before I process the arrest, he should go to the sixth precinct at 8 p.m. and ask for Detective Samuels. And tell him to come alone. If he brings a lawyer with him, we'll have nothing to talk about."

The young man called his father and repeated Solly's invitation. The senior Garafola suspected that Solly was looking for a bribe to release his son. He immediately headed for the sixth precinct carrying five thousand dollars stuffed in a plain white envelope. When he arrived at the precinct, a uniformed police officer escorted him to the second floor detective squad room.

Upon seeing the senior Garafola enter the room alone, Solly smiled. "How you doing, Joey?" he said cordially. "I'm Detective Samuels and the woman sitting over there with your son is my partner, Detective Davis."

"How ya doin, Samuels, so what's the story with my son?"

"The story is your son is about to be arrested for possession of marijuana."

"Whadda mean possession of marijuana? He told me the grass you found in his car wasn't his."

"I'll tell you what Joey. Before we talk, lemme tell you a couple of things."

Solly detailed the circumstances that led to his son's arrest; how his son was observed buying marijuana from a street dealer, how he was observed carrying it to his car and how the marijuana was found under the front seat of his car.

"So you see Joey, we got a pretty strong case here. Now I wouldn't blame you if you don't believe me, so before I tell you what's on my mind, why don't you go talk to your son and see what he's gotta say."

Garafola walked over to his son. They spoke for several minutes.

"Well did you get your son's side of the story?" Solly asked

"Yeah, I did. He swore to me that he don't know how the grass got in the car."

"Well in that case, Joey, I guess we can't do business. So I suggest you get your son a lawyer and meet me in court in the morning. We got nothing more to talk about."

"Wait a minute, detective, you asked me what my son told me. I didn't say that I believe him. Did I? Off the record I think he's fulla shit. So let's talk. What do I gotta do to get him out from under," Garofola asked, as he reached into his jacket pocket and removed a bulging envelope.

Solly spoke out. "Listen, Joey," he said sternly. So there's no misunderstanding here, this ain't about no bribe. Your boy is under arrest and he's gonna stay under arrest. The only difference is what he's gonna be charged with. So put the envelope back in your pocket before you make matters worse."

"Then what do we gotta talk about?" Garafola said glumly.

"There's a legitimate way to help your son out," Solly said quickly.

"How?"

"Information, Joey. I need information. Information about the Cutolo homicide."

'Whadda ya fuckin crazy, Samuels? I had nothin to do with that."

"I know you had nothing to do with it, Joey."

"Then what is that you want from me?"

"Listen, from what I hear on the street, Cutolo was hit for trying to set-up somebody for Fat Tony Caruso. All you gotta do is tell me who it was that Cutolo was trying to set up before he was hit."

"Listen, you know I wanna help my son. But I'm tellin ya the truth. I don't know nothin about the Cutolo hit."

"I'm not askin you what you know, Joey. I just wanna know what you heard on the street."

"You gotta believe me detective. I didn't hear nothin on the street either."

Solly had to win the man's cooperation and he began to press.

"C'mon, Joey. We're back to square one. If you can't help me that means I can't help your son. But before we call it a day and you walk outta here, lemme tell ya what's in store for Joey Jr. here. First of all, there's over an ounce of grass in that bag. And that means your son is facing a felony. Now I'm not gonna bullshit ya and tell ya he's going to jail, but I'll tell ya this much. If I speak to my friends at the DA's office, he's either gonna plead to a felony or go to trial. And in addition to the forty or so thousand that it'll cost you for a good lawyer to take the case, if he's found guilty after trial, he's gonna have a record. And my friend, with the evidence I got, believe me he ain't getting acquitted. And that ain't all, Joey. Tomorrow you can read all about it in the papers. I can just see the story now:"

HONOR STUDENT AT CORNELL
UNIVERSITY JOINS THE MOB

The son of Joey "The Gyp" Garafola, a reputed soldier in the Grimaldi crime family, was arrested for running a drug business at the Ivy League College where he is majoring in Labor Relations. The younger Garafola was..."

Now do you really want it to go down like that? After all, the kid has never had a problem with the law before as far as I know. At least nothing that resulted in an arrest. So why change that now? C'mon Joey, what I need from you ain't that hard to give up."

"Ain't that hard to give up, huh? Listen Samuels, you know fuckin well that I wanna help my kid. But if it gets out on the street that I spoke to you about the Cutolo thing, I either run or I'm a fuckin dead man. And you know it."

"Maybe so, Joey, but the only way it gets out on the street is if you put it there. Listen, common sense tells ya that I don't want it on the street either. Think about it. Do I want anybody to know I'm looking at the Cutolo homicide? It'll only make my job that much harder."

Solly knew that he was close to winning the man over and continued to press on. "Listen, Joey, we both know your kid ain't no drug dealer. So why make him one. All I want is information. Information I know you got."

"And if I don't got it?"

"Then it's too fucking bad for you, it's too fucking bad for little Joey here, and to be honest with you, Joey, it's to fuckin bad for me, too."

"And if I give you what I heard on the street, what can you do for my kid?"

"Assuming you're truthful, I'll throw away half the grass and make it misdemeanor weight. Then I'll speak to the DA's office on your son's behalf and between me and you, Joey, if I ask 'em too, they'll give the kid an ACD."

"What the fucks an ACD?" Garafola asked curiously.

The legal term is "Adjournment in Contemplation of Dismissal", which means that if the kid don't get in any trouble for the next six months all of the charges against him will be dropped."

"You mean he won't have a record?" Garafola asked enthusiastically.

"That's right. But lemme tell you one thing right now, Joey. Don't try to bullshit me. It just so happens that I know a few things about the case and if what you tell me don't fit with what I know already, the deal's off."

"Listen, I don't wanna insult ya, Samuels, but how can I be sure that after I tell you what I know, you don't fuck me on the deal?"

"I guess you really can't be sure, Joey" Solly said honestly. But then why should I? I'm a homicide detective. Do I give two shits about what I charge your son with. C'mon Joey, there's absolutely no reason for me to fuck you.

"You know something, Samuels, I never thought I"d say this about a cop but I trust you so I'll give what I heard on the street."

"That's all I'm asking for. But like I said, don't bullshit me."

"I swear on my father's grave that I'm leveling with you. This is what's on the street. Cutolo got whacked for trying to set up Frankie Ardone."

"Who the fuck is Frankie Ardone, Solly said slyly."

"He's a capo in the Grimaldi family; involved with clubs and prostitutes. Word is that someone tipped Ardone at the last minute. There were two zips at a location where Cutolo was supposed to meet Ardone. They saw Cutolo get into Ardone's car and take off without going to the meet."

"Who were the two zips?"

"That I don't know. Word is they were imported from Palermo and went home right after the botched hit."

You know something, Joey, I believe you so I'm gonna help your son."

It was almost midnight by the time Solly had finished speaking with Joey "the Gyp" Garafola.

Before the senior Garafola left for home, Solly promised him that young Joey would be just fine. He would keep the boy with him in the precinct all night rather than lodge him in a urine infested jail cell. The boy would be arraigned in court the first thing in the morning. After thanking Solly, Garafola kissed his son on both cheeks and left the precinct.

CHAPTER FIFTY-EIGHT

olly called Pirelli and brought him up to date on the events of the night. Pirelli had just gone to bed and the loud shrill of the phone shocked him out of a sound sleep. As soon as Pirelli answered the call, Solly shouted into mouthpiece; "Quick Pirelli, get up and piss, the worlds on fire."

"I can't fuckin believe you're calling me this early, Solly," Pirelli screamed back at his partner. "You know fuckin well I worked last night."

"Hey, how'd you know it was me, Pirelli?"

"What other fucking putz do I know that has the balls to call me at seven in the morning."

"Fuck you, Pirelli. At least you got a couple of hours. Me, I've been up all night."

"What happened? You had indigestion?"

"Very funny smart ass. It just so happens that I locked up Garafola's kid last night."

"Hey, that's great, Solly. Did you get the old man cooperate?"

"Yeah, I did. As soon as I get the kid arraigned we'll meet at your place and I'll fill you in. And make sure you have the bagels and nova ready."

It was a little before noon before Solly finished up in court. The boy was released without bail pending disposition of the case at a future date. A bleary eyed Solly headed directly to Pirelli's apartment. As soon as he entered the apartment he made his way to the kitchen table to prepare himself a late breakfast.

"C'mon Solly, you can eat later. Lemme hear what happened, for Christ sake. Did Garafola cooperate or not?"

"I told you he did. But I doubt we can act on what he gave me."

"And why not," Pirelli asked.

"Well, according to Garafola, Cutolo had a meet set with Ardone. There were two hit men close by waiting for Ardone to show up in his black Caddy. He sez they saw Cutolo get into a red Buick and never saw Ardone. Word is Cutolo was whacked for tipping off Ardone."

"Well did he tell you who the two men were?"

"Yeah he did. The problem is they were imports straight from Palermo. And after the thing got fucked up, they went back home." "How do you know Garafola was leveling with you?"

"Because he told me everything that fits with what we already know. He told me about the red Buick, the phony license and a lotta other shit. Also," Solly continued, "he gave me Ardone's name. If he wasn't being truthful that's the last thing in the world he would've done. No kid, I say Garafola gave me everything he knows."

"So much for that, huh Solly?"

"Yeah, I guess we got no choice but to go with plan two. Is it in place?"

"Actually it is, Solly. In fact I played racket ball with Ardone several times already. And lucky for us it just so happens that he hogs center court."

"He what?"

"He tries to control center court. Every chance he gets he jumps in front of me and forces me to play from behind him. So all I have to do is wait until he hits a ceiling shot. Then if he jumps in front of me like he probably will I can bang him with the racket."

"What the fuck is a ceiling shot," Solly asked.

"You hit the ball into the ceiling just short of the front wall. Then when the ball comes down it bounces high. When Ardone jumps in front of me after he hits the ceiling shot I'll pretend to be reaching up for the ball but instead I'll whack him with the racket."

"Sounds good to me, kid, when are you gonna give it a try?"

"The first chance I can. Actually, we got another game tomorrow morning. If I get the chance, I'll do it then."

CHAPTER FIFTY-NINE

The next morning Pirelli and Ardone were on the court. They were well into their second game when an opportunity for Pirelli to whack Ardone with his racket presented itself. Ardone had delivered a well-placed ceiling shot and, as expected, jumped in front of Pirelli to gain control of center court. When the ball came down to the playing floor, it bounced high and over Ardone's head. Pirelli was directly in back of Ardone. He pretended to reach up for the ball. He turned his racket, its edge squarely facing Ardone's back, then slammed the racket into Ardone's left shoulder with such force that the hoodlum immediately fell to the floor in excruciating pain. Pirelli quickly went to Ardone's aid, asking if he was okay. Then he apologized.

"Damn, I'm sorry, Cheech. I should never have gone for the ball."

"Don't worry about it. It's my own fault for hogging the fuckin center."

Ardone kept moving his arms over head for a few minutes before deciding that he could no longer continue with the game.

"I think I had enough," Ardone said. "Let's pack it in."

Ardone continued to complain about his shoulder as the two men entered the steam room.

"Maybe you should have it looked at by a doctor, Cheech. I mean you seem to be in a lotta pain,"

"I ain't worried about the pain. I'm worried about the fuckin bullet I got in my shoulder," Ardone blurted out.

Pirelli feigned a look of surprise. "You got a bullet in your shoulder?"

"Yeah, I got shot about ten years ago."

"So how come you never had it taken out?"

"Cause it ain't necessary. My doctor told me that as long as it don't move I should leave it alone."

"And it hasn't moved since you were shot?"

"No."

"So then what's the problem, Cheech?"

"The problem is that my doctor said it could start to move at any time, especially if the area gets banged hard enough. And my friend that was a pretty good shot I just took."

"So why don't you just have the fuckin thing removed once and for all and be done with it, Cheech? That way you won't have to worry about it."

"I really don't wanna go through no operation unless it's absolutely necessary. But since you mentioned it, maybe you should talk to your doctor friend just in case I do wanna get it out."

"Why can't you get your own doctor do it, Cheech?" Pirelli said, trying to disguise his interest in removing the bullet.

"Because just like your friend Martine, I don't want a record kept of the operation. And I don't want anybody who knows me to know that I got a bullet in my shoulder. So let's just leave it at that."

Pirelli ended his inquiry; "Whatever you say, Cheech."

"Good. Now listen, maybe I should have your doctor friend take a look at my shoulder, just in case. Then if he says it needs to come out, maybe I'll have him do it."

Pirelli hesitated. He had to be careful. He did not want to appear anxious about the removal of the incriminating bullet.

"Listen, Cheech," he said cautiously, I'd rather you just went to your own doctor first. Just to take a look. If he says it has to come out, then we'll talk about me setting something up. I'd rather not let my doctor friend know my business unless it's absolutely necessary."

"Okay Pirelli. I'll go talk to my guy first and see what he says."

Pirelli dropped the subject praying that the bullet in Ardone's shoulder would begin to travel.

"By the way, Cheech, did you get a chance to speak to the Jew with the diamonds yet?"

"As a matter of fact, I did. And you were right, Pirelli. He deals in large quantities of diamonds okay, but as far as his records are concerned, forget about it. They're all fugazy. If you looked at his books you'd think the prick was starving."

"That's what I figured. And that could be a big problem, Cheech. If he can't show where he bought the shit, the insurance company is sure to give him a hard time with a claim that big. He's gotta have records."

"Hey that's his problem, ain't it?"

"Yeah, it is and I want it to stay that way. So tell him we got a deal if he comes up front with the twenty large. Then he can worry about the insurance claim. Otherwise tell him to go shit in his hat."

Ardone laughed. "You're a pisser, Pirelli. But you're right we'll get the up-front money first."

Ardone kept massaging each his shoulder trying to ease the pain.

"Listen Cheech, you sure you don't want me to take you to a hospital or something?"

"Nah, I'll be all right."

"Then in that case, I'm gonna get out of here. I'm working tonight and I got a few things to do before I go in. By the way, Cheech, are you stopping by the lounge tonight?"

"No. As a matter of fact I'm goin to Vegas with my wife for a few days."

"Have a good trip, Cheech. Call me as soon as you get back and lemme know how you're shoulder is."

"You got it", Ardone said.

Pirelli left the health club and went straight home. As soon as he entered his apartment, he telephoned Solly at the squad room and left a message for him to call. Thirty minutes later, Solly returned his call.

"That's what I said, Solly. I banged him real good. … Not now, putz, well talk in person in the morning. Get over here about eleven. And if you want bagels, bring 'em."

CHAPTER SIXTY

The following morning Solly arrived at Pirelli's apartment shortly after 10 a.m. carrying a large brown paper bag containing a dozen assorted bagels, a container of cream cheese and a half pound of Eastern Nova Scotia salmon.

Seeing the large bag, Pirelli just smiled and shook his head. "Hey! Didn't you bring any bagels for me, Solly?"

"Very funny wise guy. What's the matter, didn't you ever hear of a freezer? I'm tired of havin to schlep bagels every time I come here."

"Yeah, you're right Solly. I'll freeze whatever's left over when you're done eating. I'm sure I can make room for two or three bagels."

"Is that right?" Solly shot back. "Well if you got rid of half the fucking Vodka you got in your freezer you'd have enough room for two or three dozen bagels. Now, we gonna get down to business or what?"

"Business it is, Solly," Pirelli said as he poured the coffee.

After preparing their breakfast, the two detectives sat down for a serious conversation.

"Okay kid, now tell me all about it," Solly said as he bit into the first of two bagels he prepared for himself.

"Let me put it this way Solly. If that bullet in Ardone's shoulder is ever going to move from a shot in the back, consider it done. I hit him so fucking hard it's a wonder my racket didn't break."

"What did he say?"

"Well as you can imagine he wasn't too happy, but he really didn't say much. The prick knows he hogs center court and blamed himself for jumping in front of me. Then he really shocked the shit out of me."

"Why? What did he say?"

"He told me about the bullet in his shoulder. Of course he said he was shot about ten years ago. But he did say there's a bullet in him and that he has to have it looked at every now and then to make sure it hasn't moved."

"Did you get a chance to suggest that he see our doctor?"

"I didn't have to, Solly. He suggested it."

"No shit, kid. You mean we hit a home run."

"Not just yet. I told him to have his own doctor check it out first."

"You did what?"

"You heard me, Solly. I told him to go to his own doctor first to see if the bullet moved. Then I told him if it moved I would talk to my doctor friend."

"Schmuck, what did you say that for? What if the bullet don't move?"

"Then I guess we'll have to figure out something else."

"I don't fucking believe you, Pirelli. He wants to go to our doctor and you tell him to see his own doctor first. Whatever made you to do such an idiotic thing?"

"Idiotic huh! Listen to me Solly, what if I take him to our doctor and the bullet hasn't moved. What do we do then?"

"Putz! The doctor tells him that it moved and that it has to come out."

"The doctor tells him it moved, huh? And what if he goes to another doctor for a second opinion, then what?"

Solly said nothing.

"I'll tell you what, Solly. He'll think our doctor is an idiot and he'll never go back to him. No, we have to pray that the fucking bullet moves. Then he'll come running to me. Anyway we'll know soon. He's going to Vegas with his wife for a couple of days. He said he'd call me as soon as he gets back.".

CHAPTER SIXTY-ONE

everal days passed with Ardone still in Vegas. Pirelli reported
for a night's work, waiting for the gangster's return.

It was an otherwise uneventful evening until Pirelli heard a
familiar voice boom out from across the large bar area. "Hey Pirelli,
c'mere, I want ya to say hello to somebody."

Pirelli looked up and saw Cheech and his wife standing by the
stairs leading to the second floor restaurant. He immediately walked
from behind the bar and joined the couple.

"Hi Celeste, nice to see you again," he said minding his
manners.

After a cordial exchange, Celeste turned to her husband and
dutifully excused herself. "I'll see you upstairs, Frankie," she said.
"Try not to be too long please. I'm starving."

"Order a cocktail and some appetizers, honey. I'll be up in a
few minutes."

Ardone took Pirelli's arm and walked him over to one of the
empty booths that lined the far wall of the bar area.

"So Pirelli, what's new?" Ardone asked, as he slid into the
booth.

"You tell me. When you didn't come around, I was starting to get worried. I mean about the bullet in your shoulder."

"Why? I told you I was going to Vegas with my wife and wouldn't be back for a few days. Don't you remember?"

"Yeah, that's right, Cheech. But you were supposed to call me as soon as you got back."

"I just got back."

"Anyway Cheech, how's your shoulder?"

"Well, the sonofabitch is still sore. But other than that it seems to be okay."

"That's great, Cheech. I was really worried there for a while."

"To be honest, Pirelli, so was I. At least until I saw my own doctor and he told that the bullet hadn't moved at all. And after I went for a second opinion and got the same answer, I felt a hundred percent better."

"So what's the prognosis, Cheech?"

"Both doctors said that if the bullet don't move in the next week or two, it probably won't. So I'll just have to wait and see.

"When do you have to go see them again?"

"I don't. If the bullet starts to move, my doctor said I'll know it right away."

"How's that, Cheech?"

"Because he said the area will get red and start to swell."

"Really! So whadda you do then?"

"Then Pirelli, we go see your doctor and have the fuckin thing removed once and for all."

"How fast would it have to come out, Cheech? After all, it might take a while to set the thing up."

"Immediately! The fuckin thing is near my heart and if it moves in that direction…" Ardone's voice trailed off as he considered the possibility.

"Hey that sounds serious, Cheech."

"It is. So just in case you'd better go see your guy and put things in place. You think you can handle that?"

"I can try, Cheech. But he may be a little hesitant. After all, we're talking about removing a bullet.

"So what's the big deal? I thought you said he's a top notch surgeon."

"Removing the bullet is not the problem, Cheech. Not reporting it to the police could be."

"Tell him we'll make it worth his while. But set it up. I can't afford to get caught short with this fuckin thing."

"How much are you willing to go for, Cheech?"

"Whatever it takes, I don't give a fuck what the number is. Just set it up."

"I'll see what I can do."

"Yeah! And while you're seeing what you can do if he gives you any shit remind the cocksucker about the abortion he covered up. I ain't taking no for an answer."

"You got it, Cheech."

"Good, now that we got that out of the way, let's get back to the thing with the diamonds."

"Sure, Cheech, but first lemme ask you something."

"What is it?"

"Does your guy know who I am?"

"Whadda ya fuckin crazy, Pirelli, I tell nobody my business."

"Good. Let's keep it that way. Because to tell ya the truth, I'm starting to smell a rat."

"Whatta ya getting paranoid."

"Listen, Cheech. You can call it paranoid if you want to but I call it being careful. Lemme tell ya something, Cheech. I always get a little suspicious when somebody pushes hard to do something. Especially when he's gotta come up front with twenty large. I mean he doesn't seem concerned after you told him about the problem he could have with the insurance claim. Could it be that he's trying to set you up? Like maybe he's working something off with the Feds. I'm sure they'd like to get their hands on you, no."

"You know, Pirelli, I never thought about that possibility."

"Yeah, well maybe you oughta start thinking about it, Cheech. You know there are a lotta people out there that would like to hang something on you, and I ain't lookin to be an added bonus if they do. So before we sit down with this guy I'd like to check him out."

Pirelli used this ruse to identify the potential defendant. He had to be sure that he had the diamond merchant's correct pedigree and address when he would be arrested at a later date.

"You convinced me Pirelli. I'll get the information you need. Meanwhile you make sure you talk to your doctor friend about standing by for the operation. Just as a precaution.

"You got it, Cheech."

"Good, I'll call you in a couple of days. You can lemme know what he sez then. Now lemme go upstairs before my wife thinks I died."

CHAPTER SIXTY-TWO

A day later, Ardone told Mario he wanted to meet with Pirelli ASAP. Since Pirelli was not scheduled to work that night, Mario called him at home. A meeting was set for 2 p.m. the following afternoon.

Pirelli immediately called Solly. The detectives had a decision to make. Should Pirelli wear a wire and record his upcoming meeting with Ardone? They speculated that Ardone would ask about the operation. They knew that if Ardone decided to have the operation they would have the burden of proving that Ardone consented to Pirelli taking possession of the incriminating bullet. And what better proof would there be than to have Ardone's consent on tape. It was decided Pirelli would record the conversation.

The next morning, Solly was at Pirelli's apartment before 10 a.m. After eating a cheese Danish and two bagels smothered with cream cheese, Solly was ready to go. "You know, kid, we have to be absolutely sure that there's no chance of Ardone finding the body recorder I'm gonna put on you."

"Why should he be looking for a recorder on me? He never looked for one before."

"I'm not talking about him looking for it; I'm talking about him accidentally finding it. You know like if he puts his arm around you or maybe brushes up against you."

"I thought they have those small recorders that fit in a pack of cigarettes."

"They do. But the problem with those little pieces of shit is that they run hot and cold. Sometimes you get a good recording and sometimes you don't. No kid, we gotta go with something that sure to give us a good, clear, recording. The equipment will be bigger, but then we won't have to worry about the quality of the recording."

"What do you have in mind, Solly?"

"Well the last time I was at Technical Services, they showed me a new piece of equipment called a Nagra. It's a state of the art recorder."

"How big is it, Solly?"

"It's about three inches wide and maybe five inches long. I think it's about a half inch thick."

"*Minchia*," Pirelli blurted out, using the Italian slang for surprise. "No wonder you said Ardone might accidentally find it."

"Not to worry, kid. It comes with an external mike that has a four-foot long cord attached to it. That means I can put the recorder somewhere on your body where he won't accidentally brush up against it. Then I can run the mike to your chest so it can pick up the conversation."

Pirelli was not happy, he thought it over a while, then grumbled. "Let's go for it."

"Good. I'll run over to Tech Services and sign one out. Meanwhile you start thinking about the conversation you're gonna have with your buddy Cheech."

Two hours later Solly returned to the apartment carrying a Redweld organizer that contained a Nagra. After showing Pirelli the recorder the two detectives rehearsed the conversation Pirelli planned to have with Ardone, then, Solly "wired" him up.

"Okay kid, Solly said, now that we got that outta the way lemme see what all them broads you got see in you."

"What the fuck you talking about, Solly?"

"I'm talking about you dropping your pants kid. The recorder is going between your legs."

"Between my legs?"

"Yep," Solly shot back. "This way Ardone will never accidentally brush up against it, unless of course he goes down there once in a while."

"Very funny, Solly. Very fucking funny. Anyway let's get this show on the road."

It took ten minutes for Solly to secure the recorder on his partner's body. He carefully taped the device to the inside of Pirelli's right thigh just below his groin. By the time Solly was done, he was certain that the recorder would never come loose. Then he taped the microphone wire up along Pirelli's body and taped the microphone to the center of his chest. Barring any unforeseen mishaps, Ardone would not find the recorder and the detectives would capture a clear, intelligible recording of the entire conversation.

Pirelli stared intently as Solly reached for a small ten-watt transmitter. "Now what the fuck is that, he asked.

"It's a radio transmitter. I got a receiver in the squad car. If the thing works right, I'll be able to overhear your conversation with Ardone. God forbid something goes wrong and he finds the recorder on you, I'll crash through the fuckin door in a minute."

"For Christ sake, Solly, stop worrying will you. He's not going to find the recorder."

"I know that, but just in case something unexpected happens."

"Yeah, like somebody drops a fucking drink on me and I get electrocuted from all the shit you're putting on me."

The image made Solly chuckle. "Putz! You can't get electrocuted. The worse that can happen if somebody spills a drink on you and it hits the transmitter is that your sex drive will slow down a little. And that my skinny friend wouldn't be such a bad thing for you as far as I'm concerned."

"Up yours, Solly. Now finish up here so we can get this thing done. I got a hot broad coming by before I go to work tonight."

Pirelli got dressed. Solly carefully inspected him to be sure that none of the equipment showed through his clothing.

"How's the machine feel kid?" Solly asked.

"It feels fine, but how the fuck am I supposed to get at the thing to turn it on?"

"Not to worry, the recorder runs for at least three hours. I'll turn it on just before we leave the apartment and I'll shut it off when we get back. You won't have to do a thing."

"Whatever you say, Solly, whatever you say."

It was almost 1:15 p.m. and everything was in place. Solly activated the recorder and as an added precaution, taped the on/off switch in the on position to insure that it would not accidentally disconnect. Then he recited the standard prologue into the microphone taped to Pirelli's chest.

> Today is Tuesday, November six, 1973. The time is approximately one thirty-five in the afternoon. This is Detective Solomon Samuels of the Manhattan South Homicide Division. I have just activated Nagra Recorder number 20022438 that I have secured on the person of Detective Anthony Pirelli. Detective Pirelli plans to record a conversation that he anticipates having with one Frank Ardone at the Blue Grotto Lounge. At this time we are going to proceed to the Blue Grotto Lounge. This recorder will remain running until otherwise indicated.

To avoid recording any conversation during their short ride to the lounge, Samuels and Pirelli remained silent. When they arrived at their destination, Pirelli left the vehicle and headed directly for the Blue Grotto while Samuels remained in the battered squad car where he would monitor the conversation.

Just before Pirelli entered the lounge, he buried his head into his chest and mumbled into the microphone. "The time is approximately 2 p.m.. I'm about to enter the Blue Grotto."

When Pirelli entered the empty lounge, he saw Ardone seated at a booth reading the sports sections of the *New York Post*. He was nursing a snifter of brandy. Pirelli joined him and signaled to Mario for a drink. The two men sat for a while, engaged in idle conversation. Finally Ardone turned to the business at hand.

"So what's the story with your doctor friend, Pirelli," Ardone asked.

"The story is that I got good news and I got bad news for you, Cheech."

"Is that right? In that case, give me the bad news first, cause if I can't deal with the fuckin bad news, then the good news don't mean shit. Now does it?"

"Relax Cheech, the good news is that the doc will do it."

"Then what the fuck is the bad news?"

"The bad news is that he's gotta keep a record of the operation."

"He's gotta keep a record of the operation?" Ardone repeated. Whatta ya fucking crazy?"

"Listen Cheech, this is a major operation. It's gotta be done in a hospital. You're gonna need general anesthesia and everything. There's gonna be too many people involved to shit can the whole operation. You're even gonna have to sign consent forms. But of course the deal is my guy won't report the removal of the bullet to the police like he supposed to."

"Big fucking deal. He won't report it. There's still gonna be a file kept with the bullet in it. Ain't there? What if somebody finds out about the operation and grabs hold of the file? Then what?"

"That won't be a problem, Cheech."

"Yeah. And why's that?"

"Because the bullet that's going in the file ain't gonna be the one that comes outta your shoulder. That's coming to me. That's if you give the doc the okay."

"Of course he's got the fuckin okay. But I still don't see why…"

"Listen, Cheech," Pirelli interrupted. The doc wants to cover all bases. This way, on the outside chance somebody does inquire about the operation everything will look kosher. Right down to the bullet in the file. Of course, like I said, it won't be the bullet that he takes outta you. It'll be the one that I give him."

"And he had no problem with all of this?"

"Not at all. Of course the twenty large he wants in his pocket solved all your problems," Pirelli said confidently.

"Didn't he wanna know why you wanna make a switch?"

"Of course."

"And what did ya tell him?"

"I told him that you're a gun nut with a big gun collection. I told him that one night you were showing your wife a new gun that you had just bought and she accidentally shot you with it. You knew you'd lose your license if it came out that you failed to safeguard your weapon so when you went to the hospital you gave the police some bullshit story that you were hit by a stray bullet while you and your wife were walking through a park. The local police did an investigation. Of course they came up empty handed. The police suspected that you were fulla shit but couldn't prove it. Then I told him that you're concerned that if by some outside chance the police ever got hold of the bullet from your shoulder they might be able to somehow tie it to your gun. Then you'd not only lose your gun permit but you'd be in deep shit too for filing a phony police report.

Anyway, he bought the story hook, line and sinker. All he needs is a couple of days notice to set things up."

"You're unbelievable, Pirelli. You know, maybe I should go ahead with this fuckin operation even if the bullet in my shoulder don't move?"

"Personally I think you should, Cheech, but then again it's not my shoulder that's gonna be cut open," Pirelli said cautiously. "Anyway, whatta ya wanna do?"

"Lemme sleep on it. I'm going to Vegas for a few days with the old lady. I'll let you know what I wanna do when I we back."

"No problem Cheech, whatever ya say."

By the way, Pirelli, here's all that information you wanted on the Jew."

"Great Cheech. I'll have my partner run a check on the guy right away. I tell you what I came up with when you get back from Vegas. Meanwhile I gotta run home for a while to do a few things before the joint opens. See you in a couple of days."

Pirelli left the lounge and returned to the squad car where Solly eagerly awaited his return. As soon as Pirelli opened the car door, he saw Solly with his finger pressed against his lips to remind him that the recorder was still running. Ten minutes later they were back in Pirelli's apartment. Solly spoke into the microphone again.

"This is detective Samuels. The time is approximately two forty-five p.m. End of recording."

As soon as Solly turned the recorder off, he congratulated his partner. "You did great, kid. From what I was able to hear you got everything we need. Now as soon as I get the equipment off you and make sure the tape rolled, I'll pour us a drink to celebrate."

"You go ahead and have a drink, Solly." Pirelli said humorously. "Me, I'd rather have one of those Danishes you didn't eat this morning."

"Fuck you, Pirelli. Just for the wise crack I'm having a double scotch. And a Danish too," he added.

After the removal of the adhesive tape from Pirelli's body, Solly retrieved the recording equipment. The recorder worked well and the detectives were certain they had captured the entire conversation.

After toasting each other, Solly headed back to the Bureau of Technical Services to duplicate the tape. Pirelli would spend the next several days preparing a transcript of the recorded conversation for future use in court, if needed.

Pirelli took a quick shower and relaxed before returning to the Grotto for a night's work. As soon as he entered the lounge, Mario greeted him. "So how did it go, Pirelli?" the sly bartender asked.

"How did what go, Mario?"

"The thing ya got goin with Ardone."

"What makes you think I got a thing going with Ardone?"

"Because he told me you did," Mario lied.

"He told you, huh?"

"Yeah, he tells me everything."

"Good, then in that case you can ask him how it went," Pirelli said rudely as he walked behind the bar.

Mario didn't ask again.

CHAPTER SIXTY-THREE

I t had been two days since Ardone returned from Las Vegas. He still hadn't contacted Pirelli. The detectives were rapidly despairing that Ardone decided not to have the operation. For the first time since they started their investigation the detectives were at a critical point. If the bullet didn't move, they knew it was just a matter of time before the Chief would end the undercover investigation. Pirelli was frustrated, yet determined to get the incriminating bullet from Ardone's shoulder at any cost.

The detectives were correct. Several days later Solly was called to the Chief's office. After briefing the Chief on the status of the investigation, the Chief just shook his head, sharing the detectives' despair.

"Tell me Solly," Cochran said glumly, "How long has Pirelli been out there?"

"It's been a little over five months, Chief."

"You know Solly, maybe its time we gave some thought about wrapping this thing up. Especially since you guys appear to be at a dead end. At least with respect to getting the bullet out of Ardone's shoulder," Cochran added.

"Yeah, I know what you mean, Chief. But before we do, I'd

like Pirelli to try one more thing to convince Ardone to have the operation, even if the bullet doesn't move."

"What do you have in mind?"

"I'll tell him to give Ardone some bullshit story that the doctor he knows is leaving the country for a teaching job in Italy. And if he wants the operation he's gotta move fast. So if we can just leave Pirelli in place for the next few weeks, maybe we'll get lucky."

"Sounds reasonable to me," Cochran said, nodding his head. "I guess we can leave Pirelli in place a little longer, but only for a couple of more weeks. Meanwhile start putting everything together that we have on Ardone and those other mutts. We have to have them indicted and in custody before Pirelli surfaces."

After leaving the Chief's office, Solly drove directly to Pirelli's apartment. When Pirelli opened the door he saw the glum look on his partner's face that said the Chief was ready to close the undercover operation.

"So how much more time we got, Solly?" Pirelli asked.

"He gave us another month, no more. I told him that you were going to tell Ardone that your doctor friend is quitting his practice and leaving the country and that if he wanted the operation he has to move fast."

"Good thinking, large one. And you want to know something, Solly, it might just work. After all, Ardone's thinks the bullet is liable to move at anytime. And our doctor leaving the country may just scare him enough to convince him to have the operation. Anyway, Ardone will show up at the lounge one of these nights. When he does, well know for sure."

Pirelli was right. When he reported for work that evening, Mario told him that Ardone was going to stop by the lounge and wanted to talk to him. The night dragged on as Pirelli waited anxiously for Ardone to appear.

CHAPTER SIXTY-FOUR

When Ardone entered the lounge, he was accompanied by a striking young woman, whose name was not Celeste. She was wearing a tight fitting, well above the knee, dress of creamy gray silk, a pale blue cashmere jacket and matching stockings that accentuated high cheekbones, full lips and assertive chin. Three of her fingers and right thumb glittered with expensive rings. A sparkling diamond bangle bracelet adorned her left wrist. She knew that bright colors and flashy jewelry made her appear like the tart she was and she smiled as the couple walked pass the several wise guys in the lounge that chanced to look at her, their eyeballs awash in lust.

Ardone and the stunning woman walked over to the bar and were immediately greeted by the smiling detective.

"So what's new, Cheech?" Pirelli said cheerfully.

Before answering, Ardone turned to the woman beside him and said coldly.

"Why don't you go powder your nose, honey? I'll meet you upstairs in a little while."

The young lady just smiled and without saying a word then headed for the upstairs restaurant.

Pirelli complimented Ardone on his choice of women. "I thought your wife was beautiful, Cheech, but that one is something else. You must have something real special going for you."

"Yeah, I got something special goin for me, especially when it comes time to pay her fuckin rent or buy her a new wardrobe."

Pirelli forced a smile. "Anyway Cheech, how you feeling?"

"I'm still feeling fine."

"Listen Cheech, I'm glad you're feeling fine", he lied, "because my doctor friend is moving to Italy. He' gonna teach there. I guess he's looking to fuck all the young female students over there."

"Very funny, Pirelli."

"No, I'm serious, Cheech. He's giving up his practice and moving to Bologna. They got a big medical school there."

"Then I guess I gotta make my decision soon."

"Looks that way, Cheech."

"Let's see." Ardone said, nodding his head. It's been almost three weeks since you banged me with the racket and right now at least, I'm feeling okay. And from what the doctors told me the odds are that if it don't move soon, it probably won't. So maybe I won't have the operation."

"That's your call, Cheech. But maybe you should think about it some more. While you still got the chance, that is. You know once my guy is gone I ain't got nobody else."

"You got a point there, Pirelli. Lemme give it some more thought. But to tell you the truth I ain't exactly thrilled about going under the knife. So if it don't move in the next month, I think I'll say fuck it."

"Whatever you say, Cheech," Pirelli said, trying hard to disguise his disappointment.

"But just make sure your doctor friend is ready while he's still here, just in case it does move before he goes."

Moving on, Ardone asked Pirelli if he had checked out the diamond merchant yet.

"As a matter of fact I did. And by the way, Cheech, his real name is Rosenberg. Where did you get Friedman from?"

"That's the name he gave me, the lying cocksucker," Ardone said angrily."

"Don't take it personal, Cheech, a lotta them use the name Friedman. Anyway it ain't important because he looks legit. So after he comes up front with the cash, we'll sit down and we'll tell him how to report the burglary."

"Good. Cause I'm supposed to meet him tomorrow. I'll call you if I get the up-front money. If I do, we'll celebrate."

"Sounds good to me, Cheech, I'll wait to hear from you."

Pirelli grimaced as he watched Ardone head for the upstairs restaurant. He was certain that Ardone would not have the operation unless the bullet in his shoulder started to move. Time was Pirelli's worst enemy now. He had to come up with a plan and he had to come up with it soon.

CHAPTER SIXTY-FIVE

Pirelli finished up at the lounge and decided to walk the twenty-two blocks to his apartment. It was a clear night and he knew that the brisk November air would help him to think. As he strode slowly up First Avenue, the thought of the cold-blooded killing of Police Officer McCarthy going unsolved kept haunting him.

"Think you dumb fuck," Pirelli mumbled to himself. "You gotta get that bullet out of the sonofabitch no matter what it takes."

He walked several more blocks when suddenly it hit him. But he was troubled by the untoward idea. "You must be fucking crazy," he said to the clear sky. "You can't do that. There's gotta be another way. You'll be breaking the law." But there was no other way, and he knew it.

He walked several more blocks pondering over the idea. Over and over he was haunted by images of Ardone's arrogant face laughing at the world, giving everyone the finger with a catch-me-if-you–can smirk on his face.

Visions of a cop killer walking freely through the vestibule of the Blue Grotto Lounge where a young cop once laid mortally wounded was simply too much for him to bear.

As he continued to walk, he thought of the promise he had made to the murdered officer's parents. Suddenly he shouted aloud. "Fuck it. I'm gonna do it."

Pirelli had made his decision and there was no turning back.

The next morning he would pay a visit to New York University's medical library.

CHAPTER SIXTY-SIX

P irelli was up before the sun. He dragged himself out of bed determined to get an early start. After a cold shower, a light breakfast restored his energy. He prepared a to do list and headed straight for the library. Some five hours and four cups of black coffee later, a bleary-eyed Pirelli returned home. His visit to the school's library had paid off; he had accomplished everything he had set out to do and had collected all of the information he needed. All that remained was for him to buy a few items and figure out a way to be alone with Ardone.

A few minutes later, after listening to the second message on his answering machine, he clenched his fist in victory, flailing wildly at the air above him, convinced that divine providence had interceded on his behalf.

"Pirelli, it's Ardone," the caller had said. "Listen, would you believe the Jew came up with the twenty large? He wants to go ahead with the burglary. So start putting it together, pal. Meanwhile you and me are goin to party tonight. I already told Mario you weren't comin in. I'll see you at my place at around 10 p.m. My old lady is away for a couple of days and I got a special treat in store for you."

A euphoric Pirelli played the message over and over. His chance to be alone with Ardone was just handed to him by the cop killer himself. He wasn't thrilled about the thought of having to party with the likes of this scum, but he was prepared to do anything to implement his plan, no matter how distasteful it might be. He quickly prepared a list of the items he needed to buy and headed out the door.

When Pirelli returned to his apartment, he poured a double scotch over ice. He spent the next several hours sipping drinks and carefully going over his plan. Certain that he had every detail in place he got dressed and headed for the party.

CHAPTER SIXTY-SEVEN

A little after 10 p.m., Pirelli knocked on Ardone's door. He was greeted by a woman wearing nothing more than black bikini panties.

"Hello, Pirelli. Remember me?" the young beauty said smiling.

"How could I not remember you, Annie?"

"Well after all the excitement we had at the party last month, I thought you might have forgotten me."

"Actually you're the only thing I didn't forget. I keep thinking of the massage that that fat fuck Caruso made me miss."

Annie laughed. "Well in that case, I'll just have to make it up to you. Now won't I?" Annie said as she took his hand and ushered him towards the living room.

When he entered the large room Pirelli saw a bare-chested Ardone comfortably spread out on a plush leather recliner, wearing a knee-length white sarong. He was smoking a joint and admiring the two well-endowed women lying nude on the plush wall-to-wall carpeting. The younger of the two was holding an eight-inch latex dilido while she fondled her playmate.

"Just in time, Pirelli," Ardone yelled out "Say hello to Lori and

Paula," he said pointing to the women. "They're just getting ready to put on a show for me."

Pirelli forced a smile and plopped himself down on a nearby couch. After pouring two glasses of Dom Perignon, Annie joined him and the show began. The two women on the rug engaged in sexual play that would make most pornographic videos seem like a Walt Disney movie.

Ten minutes later, Annie reached between Pirelli's legs and began to rub his thighs. Feeling a rock hard penis, she took his hand and escorted him to a den that had a padded table in the center of the room. Without saying a word, she undressed the slender detective and handed him a knee-length sarong similar to the one Ardone was wearing.

"Maybe you'll want to cover yourself with this, Pirelli. After all, I wouldn't want you to be embarrassed," she said as she walked back into the living room to top off their champagne. When she returned Pirelli was stretched out on the table with the sarong lying across his middle. Without saying another word, she removed the sarong, bent over, and cupped her mouth around his penis. When the job was finished Pirelli lay exhausted. When he tried to get up from the table Annie pushed him down.

"Hey, where you going?" she said. "We're just getting started. Maybe now you'll be able to enjoy the massage you missed at the party."

After almost thirty minutes of rubbing and tugging and another orgasm, Annie was done. And so was Pirelli.

"How about we join the party now?" Annie asked, as she turned toward the door, "Unless of course you want another massage?"

"Not just yet honey, but if you give me a couple of weeks to recuperate, I'd love one," Pirelli joked.

After she left the room, Pirelli shook his head in despair, thinking about the young prostitute. What a way to start out in life. Then he turned his thoughts to the business at hand. He put on the sarong and walked over to the chair where Annie had placed his sport jacket. Making sure he was not seen, he reached into the pocket of the jacket and removed a small plastic vial of white powder, transferring it into the side pocket of his sarong. Now ready to move forward with his plan, he strode into the living room. Ardone was lying on the rug with Lori and Paula all over him.

"Come and join the party, Pirelli," Ardone called out.

"Not yet, Cheech, I need a breather right now," he said as he smiled at Annie, grateful that he had an excuse not to join in any activity that included Ardone.

Time passed quickly and everyone at the party was loose. Ardone and Annie were busy dancing to early Sinatra hits, Lori was in the bathroom freshening up and Paula and Pirelli were cozy on the living room couch. It was then that Pirelli decided to make his move. He stood up and announced that he would make a fresh round of drinks. As he walked casually to the bar, he retrieved the small vial from his sarong pocket, carefully concealing it in his right palm. As he poured the drinks, he managed to empty the contents of the vial into Ardone's glass. Then he carried the drinks to the living room. The group joined him and everyone toasted to a great evening.

Soon Ardone began to feel the effect of the doctored drink. Suddenly, he stood up and abruptly announced that the party was over. "Okay girls, that's it," he mumbled. "Get your things together. You knocked the shit out of me and I ain't got nothin left." In a few minutes the prostitutes were dressed and out the door.

Ardone turned to Pirelli. "Christ," he said, slurring his words. "That last drink really did it for me. Do me a favor will ya? Let yourself out when you're ready, I'm gonna pack it in."

"You got it. Thanks for a great evening, Cheech."

As Ardone struggled to get to his feet, he fell forward and banged his head against the coffee table. Pirelli caught him just as he was about to fall again. He managed to drag him into the bedroom. After undressing him, Pirelli placed the thug on the bed then went to the den to retrieve the other item he had brought with him. When he returned to the bedroom Ardone was out cold and Pirelli finished what he had set out to do. Several minutes later he let out a deep breath and bid his host farewell.

"Goodnight cocksucker," he said smiling. "Enjoy your fucking bed. You won't be sleeping in it much longer."

Pirelli headed home certain that his plan was in place.

CHAPTER SIXTY-EIGHT

I t was nine hours later when Pirelli received the call he hoped
would come.

"Speak, it's your dime," Pirelli said as he picked up the phone.

"Pirelli," the voice said. "It's me, Ardone."

"How you doin, Cheech?"

"Shitty," Ardone mumbled. "What the fuck happened to me
last night?"

"Two things, Cheech, one, we had a fucking blast. I mean those
broads were something else. And two, you really tied one on, pal. I
mean you were bad."

"Tell me about it. I woke up this morning with a vicious fuckin
hangover, a bump on my head and a sore shoulder."

"I'm not surprised, Cheech."

"Why? What the fuck happened?"

"Well, after you threw the broads out, you told me you were
packing it in and that I should let myself out. Then you walked
into your bedroom. Next thing I know, I heard you take a fucking
header. I mean you musta gone down real hard from the sound of
it. Don't you remember?"

"No. The last thing I remember is when I threw the broads left. After that I don't remember a fuckin thing."

"Well I'll tell you one thing, Cheech. It's a good thing that you were so drunk, because if you were sober when you took that header you probably would have wound up in the fuckin hospital."

"Yeah, well I still might."

"Whadda mean, Cheech?"

"Because I when I fell I must've hit my shoulder. It feels sore as hell and it's all red too. In fact, I think it's even starting to swell."

"No shit, Cheech? Maybe you should have it checked it out by your doctor."

"Fuck checking it out with my doctor. If it don't get better by tomorrow morning, I'll call ya. And I'll have the fucking thing taken out once and for all by your guy. So call him and tell him to be ready to go, just in case."

"Whatever you say, Cheech, whatever you say."

"Good. Meanwhile, I'm gonna go over to my club now for some steam. I'll talk to ya later."

"Okay Cheech. If I'm not here when you call just leave a message and I'll get right back to you."

Pirelli hung up the phone then quickly re-dialed it."

"Manhattan South, PAA Rogers," the police aid answered.

"Connect me to the Squad, will you please Rogers."

"Hey! How's it going, Pirelli?" the Aide said, recognizing his voice.

"Not bad, Rogers. And thanks for asking."

"Hold on a minute, I'll put you right through."

After the fourth ring the transfer was picked up.

"Homicide, PAA Maris. May I help you?"

"Hi Shirley, its Pirelli.

"Pirelli! How the hell you doing?"

"I'm doing fine, Shirley, just fine."

"I sure miss you around here, lover boy."

"Yeah, I miss you too," Pirelli said. By the way Shirley, is the large one around?"

"Sorry Pirelli, she said, "He stepped out for a bite to eat.

"Did he happen to say where he was going?"

"I think he said he was going to Trimontes."

"Do me a favor and reach out for him, will you gorgeous? I need to talk to him right away and with his appetite lunch could be an all day affair."

Maris laughed. "It's a good thing you guys are so close. You sure know how to break 'em on him. By the way, what number should I give him when he calls?"

"Give him my home number. And keep it for yourself, too. Just in case you're bored some evening and wanna stop by for a drink."

"Can I bring my husband?" Maris said laughing.

"Of course you can, Shirley. But if you do, you'll probably still be bored," Pirelli shot back.

"You'll never change, Anthony," Maris said as she hung up the phone and beeped Solly.

Pirelli answered the phone after its second ring.

"What's up, kid?" Solly asked.

"Where are you, Solly?"

"I'm in Trimontes."

"Without me?"

"No! You're here too," Solly said.

"Whatta doin there?"

"I had a craving for a stuffed artichoke. Do you mind?"

"Not at all, Anyway, I got some good news."

"Lemme hear it, kid. My artichoke should be coming out soon. I hope."

"You mean you didn't eat yet?"

"No. I just got here and the place is jammed. They just took my order a couple of minutes ago."

"In that case, Solly, I got some bad news, too."

"C'mon Pirelli, stop jerking me around, What's up?"

"Well, the good news is that I just got a call from Ardone. He wants to go ahead with the operation."

"No shit!" Solly yelled out. "That's great, kid. So what's the bad news."

"The bad news is we got a million things to do and you gotta get your fat ass over here right away."

"Can't I eat my artichoke first," Solly pleaded.

"Hey! Fuck your artichoke Solly. Now get the fuck over here right away," Pirelli screamed as he slammed down the phone.

Thirty minutes later, Solly waddled into Pirelli's apartment still grumbling about the artichoke, But upon seeing his jubilant partner he quickly forgot about his lost lunch.

"We did it, Solly. We fuckin did it," Pirelli screamed happily. "Ardone called me. He sez his shoulder's acting up and if it don't get better by tomorrow he wants the operation. Can you believe it?"

"I'll believe it more when he sez his shoulder ain't no better and he's on the operating table. You know he can always change his mind."

"That's true, Solly, but I got a good feeling that ain't gonna happen, a very good feeling," Pirelli said slyly.

"I hope you're right, kid."

"I know I'm right. I'm telling you, Solly, we finally got that lucky break you always keep hoping for."

"Yeah, it sure looks that way. But can you imagine that if after all of this we get the bullet outta him and it's too deformed to prove it was fired from the cop's gun."

"Bite your tongue, Solly. Don't even think that way. Anyway,

I made a list of everything we gotta to do in case he wants the operation, so let's get hopping."

Before the day was over, the detectives had everything in place. If all went as planned the police surgeon would remove the bullet from Ardone's shoulder and hand it to Pirelli. All that was left to do was to wait for Ardone's go ahead call. Pirelli would wait by the phone until it came.

CHAPTER SIXTY-NINE

The next morning Pirelli rolled out of bed early. After a three-mile jog, he showered, settled down with a newspaper and waited for Ardone's call.

Two cups of black coffee later Pirelli's confidence began to wane. It was close to 11 a.m. and still no call. "Where the fuck is he?" he mumbled to the living room wall. "It hadda work. There's no way it couldn't work. Could it be he decided to go with his own doctor?"

Pirelli waited. When the phone rang he raced to answer it.

"So what's the story, did he call yet?"

"Oh fuck Solly. I though it was Ardone. No he didn't call. If he called I woulda called you, wouldn't I?" Pirelli snapped.

"So whadda think happened, kid?"

"Who the fuck knows! Maybe he went to his own doctor."

"Un-fuckin-believable," Solly said. "Imagine if after all we've been through, he went to his own doctor. Whadda we gotta do with this cocksucker, throw him off a fucking roof."

"Don't talk like that, Solly."

"Don't talk like that, huh. Well lemme tell ya something, kid. If the prick went to his own doctor and the bullet's gone, the first chance I get I'm gonna flake him with a gun. With his sheet he'll do serious time for a gun conviction."

"I don't wanna hear that kind of talk, Solly."

"Okay then, you didn't hear anything. But just for the record consider what you didn't hear," Solly said as he slammed down the phone.

An hour later the phone rang again. This time it was Ardone.

"… that's what I said," he said sullenly. "Do what you gotta do but set the fucking thing up for tomorrow morning. My shoulder ain't getting no better. In fact it's getting worse and I ain't taking no chances on the fuckin bullet moving."

"You got it, Cheech. I'll get right on it."

"Good. Pick me in front of my building at 8 a.m."

"I'll be there. You can count on me, Cheech."

Pirelli was ecstatic. He immediately called Solly to share the good news. Then he called the Surgeon and told him it was a go. Next, he called on his old friend Chivas and settled down for a long, relaxing afternoon.

CHAPTER SEVENTY

P irelli was parked in front of Ardone's building well before 8
a.m. Ten minutes later he was greeted by the sullen wise guy.

"Good morning," Ardone mumbled, placing an overnight bag
on the back seat of Pirelli's car.

"How ya doin, Cheech" Pirelli said cheerfully.

"So ya wanna know how I'm doin, huh. Well lemme ask you
something, Pirelli. How the fuck would you be doin if somebody
was about to cut open your fuckin shoulder?"

"Yeah, I know what you mean, Cheech."

"How long is this fuckin thing gonna take anyway?"

"I don't know. We'll know when we talk to the doc. But not to
worry, he said the operation's a piece of cake. When he goes over
everything with you, I'm sure you'll feel a lot better."

"By the way, Cheech, your name's Marino and you're from
Chicago. Not that anybody is gonna ask you anything. All you gotta
do is sign a few papers and that's it. Listen, Cheech, I had to vouch
for the hospital bill, so make sure you don't hit the fuckin boards on
me," Pirelli wise-cracked.

"Very funny, Pirelli," Ardone shot back.

It was noon when Ardone was wheeled into the operating room.

The procedure took less than two hours, and Pirelli had his bullet in an evidence container, signed and sealed by the police surgeon. He was ecstatic. The bullet was barely deformed. He was certain that a comparison with a bullet fired from the slain officer's gun, would match.

Pirelli grabbed some coffee and went to Ardone's room to wait. When a still groggy Ardone was brought down from the recovery room, he opened his eyes and saw Pirelli's smiling face.

"So how ya feeling Cheech," Pirelli said, pretending to care.

"Shitty. And it's fuckin freezing in here" the cop killer grumbled. "Get me a fuckin blanket for Christ sake. What the fuck is wrong with me," he bitched, experiencing a bout of dry heaves.

"Nothing, it's just the anesthesia wearing off," Pirelli said assuredly. "The doctor said you might be a little nauseous but otherwise everything went well. He said you'll be outta here in a few days."

"Never mind when I'm getting outta here, did you get the fuckin bullet?"

"Of course I got the bullet, its right here," Pirelli said. Showing him a replacement bullet freshly coated with traces of bloodied animal tissue. "I'll dump it as soon as I get outta here."

"Never mind you dumping it," Ardone said sternly. "Just gimme the fuckin thing,"

"Where you gonna put it?"

"The fuckin thing ain't leaving my hand until I'm walking across the Brooklyn Bridge."

"Whatever you say, Cheech, anyway, do you need anything before I get outta here?"

"Nah, just give my old lady a call and tell her where I am. She should be home by now."

"You got it, Cheech, I'll talk to you later."

Pirelli left the hospital and shot over to his apartment to meet his waiting partner.

"Well the deed is done, large one," Pirelli shouted out as he breezed through the door and showed his partner the evidence container. "We did it, pal, we got the cocksucker."

"The ballistics people will have no problem matching this bullet with one fired from the cop's gun. No doubt about it," Pirelli said confidently.

Solly immediately called the Chief of Detectives; the investigation was over; the detectives had their man.

CHAPTER SEVENTY-ONE

P irelli spent the next several days at the District Attorney's Office preparing for his Grand Jury appearance.

The Jury voted to indict Ardone on two counts of Murder and several other charges.

The following day, Solly and Pirelli were at the Chief's office mapping out a plan to arrest all of the wise guys caught up in Pirelli's undercover web, simultaneously. Once it became public that Pirelli was an undercover operative some of the defendants would surely flee.

Similar arrangements were made to execute search warrants at Malone's gambling locations at the same time the arrests were made.

Pirelli suggested they invite Ardone to the Chief's office before anyone was arrested.

"Let's play with his head a little before we lock the bastard up, Chief. You know, we let him think we're bluffing. Then we bang him real hard with the murder charge," Pirelli said smiling. "The dirt bag deserves it."

The Chief returned Pirelli's smile. "He deserves that and

more. But what makes you think you can get him to come in voluntarily?"

"Solly will get him to come in, right Solly?"

Solly smiled broadly, "A piece a cake, Chief"

"I don't know, Solly. Getting a wise guy to come in voluntarily isn't going to be easy, but give it a try."

The plan was in place. Solly would try to bring Ardone to the Chiefs office. If successful, the order would go out to arrest the others.

CHAPTER SEVENTY-TWO

*

The next morning, Solly was parked in front of Ardone's apartment building waiting for him to appear. When he spotted the gangster, he slid out of the squad car and called to him.

"Hey, how you doing, Ardone," Solly said with a friendly smile. "We never met but I'm Detective Samuels."

"I know who you are Samuels, I seen you in my rear view mirror a few times," Ardone said humorously.

"Not me, I'm beyond that shit. Anyway, can I talk to you for a minute?"

"Sure you can talk to me, but that don't mean I'm gonna talk to you. Unless of course it's about a reservation at my restaurant that you wanna talk about."

"Actually it's the Chief that wants to talk to you. He asked me to escort you to his office."

"You got a warrant?"

"No. No warrant."

"Then I ain't going."

"C'mon Frankie, he just wants to have a friendly chat with ya, that's all. If it was anything more that I would've got a warrant. You know that."

"What does he wanna talk to me about?" Ardone asked curiously.

"He didn't say."

"Then like I said, I ain't goin. And furthermore I ain't got nothin more to say to you either."

"C'mon Frankie, what's the downside?"

"The downside is I got things to do, so I'll see you around. By the way, stop by my joint anytime. You got an open invitation on me."

"Wait a minute Frankie," Solly blurted out. "Then how about doing me a big favor?"

"Like what?"

"Like making me look good with the Chief and coming in with me. You know the game, Frankie. You don't have to say nothing if you don't wanna. All you gotta do is just listen. If I go back empty handed the Chief will be pissed at me. And if the Chief gets pissed at me, I'm gonna get pissed at you. And when I get pissed, I start breaking their balls, especially in joints like the Blue Grotto where they got whores working."

Ardone laughed and shook his head. "Okay, okay, I got the message, Samuels. It'll be my pleasure to make you look good, so long as we know the ground rules. I ain't doin nothin but listening to what he's gotta say and I ain't saying nothin."

"It's a deal, Frankie," Solly said with a big smile.

When Solly and Ardone arrived at the Chief's office, Ardone was greeted by the Chief. "Hello Ardone, how are you? I'm Chief Cochran."

"I know who you are, Cochran," Ardone said. "Your people have been chasing me around for years."

"That they have, Ardone that they have."

"Okay then," Ardone said boldly, "Now that we got that outta the way how about telling me what ya wanna talk to me about, so I can be on my way."

"It's about the murder of a young cop."

"Hey wait a minute, Cochran? I don't know nothin about no cop killing."

"Maybe you do and maybe you don't. But I think you do, Ardone. And if I'm right I'm going to personally see to it that you get life now that all the bleeding hearts around here did away with the chair."

"Really?"

"Really!"

"And who's the cop that I'm supposed to have killed?"

"The young police officer who put the bullet in your left shoulder, that's who," Cochran said confidently.

"You're bluffin, Cochran. You ain't got shit on me and we both know it. First of all, I never had no bullet in my shoulder."

"That's not what the head nurse at Manhattan General told me last week," Cochran lied. "You see Ardone, it just so happens that she's my daughter-in-law and when she noticed that the surgeon who operated on you failed to report the removal of a bullet to the police, she thought it was strange. So she gave me a call. And after I sent one of my detectives to the hospital to check it out, bells went off and here we are."

Ardone just smiled and said nothing, believing the bullet that had been removed from his shoulder was now lying on the bottom of the East River.

Cochran pressed on. "By the way, Ardone, I hope you didn't pay the doctor too much to cover up the operation, because if you did, you didn't get your money's worth. You see he left the bullet in your medical file. And guess who has it now," Cochran said smiling.

"Look Cochran, so I had a bullet taken outta me. So what? That don't make me no cop-killer."

"You're right about that, Ardone, it don't. But if the bullet that was removed from your shoulder was fired from the murdered cop's gun, that does."

"If that's what you're counting on, Cochran, forget it because the bullet they took outta me didn't come from no cop's gun. And that's that."

"Well we'll know in a few minutes if it did or if it didn't. And if it didn't," Cochran said firmly, "I'll apologize to you and wait to catch you another time. Anyway we'll know soon. It just so happens that one of my detectives is on the way back from Ballistics with the bullet as we speak. So let's just wait and see what he's got to say when he gets here."

"Good. And when you do, you'll know you got the wrong guy," Ardone said boldly.

Ardone was seated confidently in a straight-backed wooden chair when he saw a familiar face enter the room. The tanned good-looking detective was holding an evidence container in his right hand, pinched between his thumb and forefinger.

"It matches, Chief. Perfectly! The Ballistics people said it was fired from the cop's gun. There's no doubt about it."

Ardone was stunned. The sight of Pirelli standing there with the evidence container in his hand took a few seconds to set in. Then, he realized what had happened. He jumped to his feet and screamed wildly. "You fucking cocksucker Pirelli, you set me up. You set me up."

Two burly detectives ran into the office and restrained the hysterical man.

"Whoa, take it easy, Cheech," Pirelli shouted back. "Remember how I started to scream when I found out that you taped my conversation with Martine. Remember? You told me not to take it personal, that it was only business. Well all I got to say to you, fuck face, is don't take it personal. It was only business."

Ardone was handcuffed and dragged out of the Chief's office to be formally charged with the murders of Police Officer Terrance McCarthy and Joseph Cutolo.

Within minutes the room was full with Cochran's staff. It didn't take long before Pirelli's colleagues at Manhattan South heard the news and joined the crowd. The celebration was underway and soon everyone moved to a large conference room where the Champagne began to flow. It wasn't too long before the press arrived to get their story. Solly and the Chief were happy to accommodate them while Pirelli conveniently got lost in the crowd.

CHAPTER SEVENTY-THREE

A fter an hour of celebrating, Samuels took his partner by the arm. "Let's go kid," he said, "Rae and Mary are expecting us for dinner at six. And if you want to stop by your place to freshen up, we gotta leave right now."

It took the detectives another twenty minutes to make their way out the door. As they drove to Pirelli's apartment, Solly continued to congratulate his partner on the fine job that he had done.

"I could never have done it without you," Pirelli said gratefully. And I mean that, Solly."

"Yeah, kid, we make a good team. Of course we did catch a big break at the end. I mean with the bullet moving and all."

"That's for sure. But do me one favor, will you, Solly?"

"Anything kid. What is it?"

"Don't tell anybody that I whacked Ardone with the racket. Okay?"

"I didn't plan too, but then why the fuck not?"

"I don't know, Solly. It just doesn't sit right with me. I mean me hitting a guy like that."

"Bullshit! The cold-blooded cocksucker murderer deserved that and more."

"Oh, no question about that, Solly. No question at all."

When the detectives finally arrived at Pirelli's apartment, the hero detective glanced at the wall clock and turned to his partner. "I'm gonna grab a quick shower and freshen up a bit, Solly. Maybe you should call home and tell Rae we'll be a few minutes late. Oh yeah, and tell Mary I'm anxious to see her. I have something important to tell her."

"Okay, but don't take too long, kid. Rae made something real special for us."

"I'll just be a few minutes, Solly. After you call home, grab yourself one of those cigars on my desk and make yourself comfortable."

After calling home, Solly took a cigar out of a temperature controlled cedar humidor that sat on Pirelli's desk and began to roll it between his lips. Then he looked for a match in the top drawer of the desk. When he saw it, a sickening feeling overwhelmed him. Solly was devastated. He knew that his partner had a lot of lady friends over at the apartment and if it were just a little grass he saw laying there, it wouldn't have upset him too much. But this! And even if Pirelli wasn't using hard drugs himself, the mere thought that he would allow the use of hard drugs by any of his house guests was simply too much for Solly to bear. He needed an explanation from his partner, and he needed it now.

Minutes later, Pirelli emerged from the shower with an oversized towel wrapped around his naked body, whistling tunelessly. Solly immediately called out to him, praying that he had a plausible explanation for what he had just seen in the desk drawer.

"C'mere kid, I gotta ask you something," Solly said glumly.

"Can't it wait 'til I get dressed for Christ sake?"

"No, kid, it really can't."

The tone of Solly's voice and the distressed look on the heavy man's face did not go unnoticed. 'Surely it was a call to Rae that did it.' Pirelli thought. 'Was there a serious problem at home? Did something happen to one of Solly's kids.'

Pirelli immediately walked over to his partner and fearing the worst asked softly, "What's wrong, Solly?"

Solly looked directly into Pirelli's pale green eyes and said sternly. "This is what's wrong kid."

Upon seeing the hypodermic needle in Solly's right hand, a big grin crossed Pirelli's face. He was relieved that Solly's problem had nothing to do with his call to Rae.

"Hey! Pirelli screamed. "Be careful with that fuckin thing, Solly," "If you stick yourself with it, your hand will get red and begin to swell, and then I'll have to set up an operation for you."

Solly was stunned. It took several seconds for Pirelli's comment to set in. Then it hit him.

"So that's the lucky break we got, huh kid?"

"You got it, tubby. I told you we'd get that cold-blooded fuck one way or the other."

Solly immediately let out a big sigh of relief and reached out to his smiling partner, hugging him tightly. Then he passed his fingers across damp eyes and said proudly: "You wanna know something? When they made you, they threw away the fucking mold. Let's go celebrate, the girl's are waiting."

EPILOGUE

⁓⁓⁓

The 1011 jumbo jet touched down in California's southern most city. San Diego was about to record another beautiful day in paradise. The wind was gentle, the Los Angeles Dodgers had won their ball game and the city's nightlife was preparing to unfold. Further to the south streams of automobiles waited to cross the border into Tijuana where all kinds of drugs would pass between the hands of smiling buyers and cautious sellers.

San Diego, like many other western cities was intriguing. A brilliant sun gave a glitter to the sparkling white beach bordered with a host of palm trees rustling in the wind. Pirelli stared moodily at the blue Pacific Ocean and rugged mountains looming in the distance. As he followed the swelling waves and listened to their ceaseless crashing on the surf, his thoughts turned to Police Officer Terrance McCarthy and the man that took his life. He continued to sulk, thinking about all the miseries he had witnessed throughout his years as a police officer; the violence he encountered on the streets of the city he loved so much and the corruption he knew festered in many city agencies.

He recalled the cynical remark attributed to Huey Long. "Man was conceived in sin and born into absolute corruption." While not a disciple of the late senator from Louisiana, Pirelli nevertheless agreed that many people lied and a fair amount cheated, the only variable being the degree of chicanery. But most troubling for Pirelli was what he saw as an overly permissive society. He was convinced that the decline of family values would be society's ultimate bane.

He was startled by the touch of a soft hand. Pirelli turned and was greeted with a broad smile and a warm kiss on the cheek.

"It's so beautiful here Anthony," Mary said excitedly. I'm so glad I accepted your invitation to come with you."

"And I am too, Mary. More than you know."

"By the way, I'm so glad you really didn't have a problem with your job, Anthony. I was so worried for you."

"And I'm sorry I had to deceive you, Mary, but I had no other choice.

"I understand, Anthony. And I'm glad I didn't know. I would have been worried sick."

"Well it's over now and fortunately everything turned out just fine."

"Anyway sweetheart, enough about police work for now, let's enjoy the few days we have to spend here. What do you say?"

"I say we have that champagne I saw in our suite."

"You got it, beautiful lady," Pirelii said happily.

Fifteen minutes later, the couple was standing on the wrap around terrace of their deluxe suite enjoying a magnificent view of the Pacific Ocean. Mary sat down on a thickly padded lounge chair and waited while Pirelli retreated into the suite's living room. She nodded her approval when Pirelli appeared on the terrace carrying some finger food and a perfectly chilled bottle of pink Crystal. Popping the cork for effect, Pirelli filled two champagne glasses and offered a toast.

"Amore, salud, dinero, y el tiempo para gozarlo," Pirelli said in broken Spanish.

"I don't know what you said, Anthony," Mary said smiling, but it sure sounds romantic to me. Would you translate it for me please?"

"My pleasure, Mary, It means love, health, money and the time to enjoy it."

"That's so romantic, Anthony."

"That it is, Mary, but there's one thing more I'd like to add."

"And what's that, Anthony?"

"Being here with you gives the toast a lot more meaning for me."

"And me too, Anthony," Mary added.

"Anyway, that being said, let's enjoy the sunshine before we have to return to the real world. What do you say?"

"I say let's have our champagne inside. We can enjoy the sunshine later."

The next morning, Pirelli and Mary were getting ready for their planned day trip to Mexico. As they were about to leave the suite the phone rang. It was Solly. Several hours earlier a high profile newspaper reporter had been found shot dead in his automobile and the Chief of Detectives wanted Pirelli back to the City immediately.

"Whatta kidding, Solly," Pirelli yelled into the phone. "I got three more days vacation left."

"Yeah, and I'm supposed to start mine in two days," Solly yelled back. What's that got to do with anything? Now you coming back or do ya want me to tell the Chief I couldn't get in touch with you?"

"Okay, okay, I'm coming back. I'll catch the 11 a.m. outta West Palm. Have someone pick me up at Newark."

THE END